Something So Sweet

Rick Duchalski

DEDICATION

To everyone who urged, nudged, and cheered.

ACKNOWLEDGMENTS

I do not know what the difference is between being patient with someone and putting up with their crap, but I would like to thank my wife for being patient with me.

Thanks also to all the editors, beta readers, and friends who helped refine along the way.

Part One

CHAPTER 1:
Wandering

If you do it right, you can kill a man with a Kleenex. And it's a lot less messy.

Dirty pulled one sheet out of the tissue box on the table and gently rubbed it between her fingers. All she had to do was push it back far enough into his throat.

Sliding across the room, she eased the door closed with little effort. Then Dirty stood for a moment and looked at the curtain. Her body was taut, her mind was ready, but her hands were shaking madly. Yet from that point on there was never a moment, never a single trembling moment when she thought 'I'll never get away with this'.

She moved smoothly through the room, around the curtain and bed so she was standing right next to Josef's head.

Her mother. Her childhood. Her home. Dirty took out the knife. The blade was in her hand, with the handle pointing straight up at her. She put the tissue over the handle, but then stopped.

No, she thought. *If he moves, I'll cut my hand open on the blade.* Her eyes narrowed. *But I can use the handle to keep his mouth open.*

She draped the tissue over two fingers like a little ghosty puppet, then wrapped it more like a ball or a marshmallow. Dirty eased his jaw open slightly, which was a little awkward for all of the bandages. She rested the plastic handle between his teeth, and readied her fingers.

And as she leaned over Josef's face, she had one final thought:

Fuck.

You.

***

October, 1997. Eight months earlier.

The only thing worse than listening to an asshole, is listening to an asshole who's right, she thought. The old man had been nattering at Dirty from across the aisle since Sudbury, and the bus was only just now coming into Barrie.

"Lemme guess…" he slurred, "he was too good for ya. Kicked ya out."

Just keep your head down, Dirty reminded herself.

"Ya don't look like much, and you could stand to wash off them tattoos." His breathing was labored and she could smell the stale cigarette stench from where she was sitting. "You ain't shit, and you never will be." He paused, and then added "Just like the rest of us." For some reason this last bit made him cackle and sputter, but Dirty kept her head down, clutching the backpack in her lap. Another hour or so and she'd be back in Toronto.

The old man got up to leave when they pulled into Barrie, but before he did, he leaned into Dirty for a final volley.

"What're you, 20? 21? Old enough to friggin' know better.

You can't escape your trailer-trash pedigree, doll. Once you get what you *are*, once you understand that, it's all you need to know. And you…" he straightened up now, "you look like you're meant to be walked on." The old man chuckled and lurched towards the front of the bus, using the seats for support.

***

Dirty stepped off the bus an hour and a half later, coming back to Toronto from Edmonton after a paltry three months. It was supposed to have been longer. It was supposed to have been forever. She followed Peter there after he took the new job. He had gone out first, and she went out about a month later.

When she first met Peter in Toronto, he had been…sweet. Just by his nature he was sweet and pretty and normal and, oh god, was he normal. But boat shoes? Really?

Well, not all the time, of course. He also had his 3-hole Doc Martens just to spice it up.

Gosh.

And that was about all there was to him. But he had nice hair and soft hands and soft words with pleasant things to say, and could you really blame her for settling in with someone like Peter after she finally got the chance to get away from--

Anyway.

He was nice to her, and in a way that hadn't happened for quite some time. And when they slept together, and she lay there after and she knew, she knew it was thin and not forever and he just didn't fit: didn't fit to her and who she thought she was and wanted to be. Being with him made her feel like she was wearing something that didn't quite do what it was supposed to, like she was trying to make it look like one thing when it was meant for something else. Being with him made her feel like she was wearing boat shoes.

Still, when they were together and he would come and see her, he would smile, really smile, and she was the one doing it to him. Her. And they would kiss and kiss and Dirty would always have to make the first move but that was okay because he was into her.

And after, they would cuddle in bed and share a feeling of completion--not that romantic shit, for god's sake, but the more mundane feeling of having completed a task. But maybe that was good enough. Because they went on like that for some weeks, and it really was good and interesting and good enough. And then one day Peter came over and told her that he got a job in Alberta.

Why the hell was he looking for jobs in Alberta? Was he trying to get away from her? Was he here to break up with her now? Did he think that she would just--

"Why don't you come with me?"

Wait. What?

"I'm serious. We could get a place together out there and we can see what happens." Let's see what happens. Not exactly the height of romantic overtures.

There are lots of reasons people move in together, and if Dirty had been giving someone else advice on a situation like hers, she would have said it was a weak, bad idea. Because you can't move in together when you are dating and just expect things to carry on as they had been, just with closer proximity. She'd have said that if you were thinking about being 'only' roommates, without the dating, then maybe. But that's not what you are, going into this; you're lovers, or partners, or something, and when you move in together you are going to still be that, plus. More than roommates. Less than married. But don't tell me you're not playing house together, because you are. And 'let's see what happens' just doesn't accommodate that simple fact. It's just a silly, avoidant kind of denial. That's what she would have said to someone in her situation. Unfortunately, there hadn't been anyone saying it to her.

Still, they *did* get to see what happened, and what it was was fucking awful. By the third week of her being there, there was a weird running-out-of-things-to-say feeling in the apartment, which neither of them had expected.

The first few days had been so filled with sex and chatter and thrill and expectation, but then it started to feel like an awkward morning after, stilted and unnatural.

By the sixth week they were resenting each other–at least those times when Peter bothered to come home. There were drinks with his co-workers, and sometimes (once) she went along. They all talked about work and weird customers they had that day and what the latest update for the system was and why in god's name does the new guy wear that necklace thing around his neck (and you'll notice he wasn't invited out tonight) and what do you do, um, Dirty? And since she hadn't found a job yet, you can imagine how the end of that conversation went.

But the other times—the times when no one else was around and they were not in public and they were left together, not looking at each other, goaded by the closing-in walls of the apartment they nominally shared—those were the times when fear and anger and simmering resentment settled over her like pollen from one of those flowers that smells like a corpse.

He was the one who had asked her to move out there, to pick up her life (such as it was) and start over completely with him. *With.*

Instead, he'd left her twisting, with no support network, barely any cash, and hardly an effort to ease either of those things. She sometimes spent her days walking in ever-increasing squares around the streets by the apartment, always squares so she wouldn't get lost. Other times, her feet hurt and there were holes in her shoes, so she sat in the apartment and watched videos and cried.

And by two-and-a-half months there, Dirty was finished. So when she started packing up her things in the middle of September, she was a) broke, b) broken, and c) making a break for Toronto.

Now, standing in the scholastic cool of the beginning of October, Dirty tried to figure out where the hell she was going. Her actual decision to leave Edmonton had been so swift that before she got on the bus, she hadn't considered what she was going to do when she arrived back in Toronto. But when the bus started moving Dirty realized she now had some time, and she had thought about it the whole trip, about what she would need when she got here. She needed to get home. Wherever that was.

"Danielle?" Dirty leaned her forehead against the plexi of the pay phone, then realized how gross that was. "Yeah–it's me. No, I–yeah–yeah, no. Not at all. No. I'm here. HERE! In Toronto, Yeah, I–uh-huh. Wow, thank you. Okay. Yep Okay…okay, see you soon!"

CHAPTER 2:
Down

Climbing the stairs to Danielle's second floor apartment, having been there for eleven days now, Dirty could still smell the odors from the street vendors, as well as—smoke? Stale smoke? The veins in her forearm and hand were bulging as she hauled herself upwards by the handrail. Her veins often popped out like that now, with so little left on her. She hadn't been eating much these past few months, and what she did eat was often bracketed by a lot caffeine and nicotine.

As she turned to unlock the apartment door, she gagged at the smell that was coming from under the door of the apartment opposite, the one where that pale, skinny boy lived (the one that was staring at her through the peep-hole). She had smelled it before, for pretty much the whole-week-and-a-half she had been staying there, but today it was stronger, grosser.

The inside of Danielle's apartment bloomed before her, surprisingly spacious, with exposed brick on one wall and a skylight in the kitchen. It had only one bedroom, but the living room was big enough for Dirty to stretch out a little. Laying on the couch with Mr. Pudgy the Elephant, Dirty could hear the sounds of the street through the front window. Every once in a while, Danielle's bird, a green budgie named Fiduciary Commitment, would let out a chirp that was somewhere between a G flat and an F shrill.

"I think the cigarette smell from Fern's apartment is getting worse," said Mr. Pudgy. Actually, it was Danielle who said it, using her patented, nasal, Mr. Pudgy The Stuffed Elephant Voice. Danielle often made up dialogues with Mr. Pudgy, sometimes to make Dirty laugh, sometimes for someone to talk to. Dirty hadn't heard Danielle come in behind her.

Carefully placing her jacket on top of the papers and papers and papers she got from the doctor's office, titled something to the effect of *So You've Finally Fucking Decided to Start Managing Your Depression*$_{tm}$, Danielle placed the pile on the floor by the door.

"Know what's extra creepy?" Danielle said. "Apparently that Fern kid doesn't smoke."

***

"Do you have any idea what this is talking about?" Dirty whispered to her grade 11 desk mate. Danielle just stared at the page.

"Not a clue. But I think I hate T.S. Eliot."

"Fuck. This is supposed to be one of those big important things that everyone reads and it makes them sound smart. How can something be important if we don't know what to do with it?" Dirty harrumphed.

They had known each other since the ninth grade when Dirty moved to the school in second semester. The first time they met, she had sat a few seats over from where Danielle sat, and neither of them had paid the other much attention, initially. Even when someone pulled the fire alarm later that week and the two of them had just happened to be trudging down the stairs together, there wasn't much that had clicked. Although Danielle did laugh when she heard Dirty complain that some asshat was making them go stand out in the rain. She had never heard that word before.

A couple of weeks before the start of grade 10 Dirty had been walking over to a babysitting job in the Junction when she saw Danielle on the porch of a house. Before any awkwardness could kick in, they had both pointed and mouthed "Hey!". It was good. Dirty stopped for a moment and the two spoke for real this time. It wasn't much, but it was enough that when they saw each other at the beginning of school, they made sure to sit next to each other.

Dirty probably had a crush on her then, but who could be really sure--it may not have been more than admiration and friendship and hormones. Still, they became inseparable. The first time either of them had ever gotten high they were together, in 11th grade, with that scraggly 10th grade boy who was trying too hard. He had gotten the weed for them from his brother who apparently always seemed to have some around. They were knit tight, even with that ambivalence towards their friendship from Danielle's parents.

Dirty had an especially tough time getting a read on Danielle's father, who often just seemed to sit around not doing much at all. True, she didn't go over there all that often, but when she did, she barely even got an acknowledgment. Danielle shrugged it off for her.

"He's not really a people person," Danielle said in a way that was uncharacteristically trite. But she also didn't seem to want to talk about it, so Dirty didn't press.

One time Dirty had gone over to bring Danielle a scarf she had made. It was the one with that 70s colour vibe of dark brown, a kind of mustardy yellow (wasn't it called 'harvest gold'?), and some other shit. But it was the first real thing she had ever knit, and she wanted someone to tell her she was awesome.

She stepped lightly up the wooden front steps; their creaking always made her feel like she was intruding. Holding the scarf in one hand, she rapped on the door hard enough that somebody should be able to hear it, but not so loud that someone would think she was being pushy or presumptuous.

Nothing.

Dirty tapped her boot on the porch, not sure what to do next. She turned and vaguely looked up and down the street, more hoping than expecting Danielle to magically be wandering up to the house just then.

But nothing.

She turned again and half-peered in the curtained window. Not to be nosy or anything, it's just that she was excited to give Danielle the scarf. What she saw through the window, though, was not Danielle at all, but her father, his eyes wide and pained and red and exhausted, looking at her but not really seeing her. Not really acknowledging her, anyway. Danielle's father was sitting in a chair not far from the window, looking. And after he had looked, he looked away.

Dirty didn't know what to do since he clearly wasn't going to answer the door, so she balled up the scarf and pushed it into the mailbox. Then she left.

***

"Dirty never really asks you how you're feeling, does she?"

"No, not really." Danielle said, answering Mr. Pudgy in a whisper so they wouldn't wake Dirty. "I mean, being depressed isn't something you can just explain to people who haven't experienced it. Maybe because it doesn't *feel* weird, at the time. It just kind of, *is*."

"Is what?" said Mr. Pudgy. Sniggling up his nose like he was about to sneeze, the elephant rubbed it with his front foot. Danielle thought for a moment.

"Imagine looking at a picture of yourself when you're 7 years old, playing softball. You know it's you, and you can remember *that* you enjoyed it, but you can't remember the feeling of enjoying it, you know? It's like the memory of the feeling has been sealed in a dark box; you know where the memory is, and you know the kind of thing that it is. But for the life of you, you can't see it, you can't remember how it *actually felt*.

For the life of you.

"Mm. But it isn't just a simple memory that can't be gotten a hold of, is it? It's your fucking ability to feel. Anything." said the elephant.

"True that, Pudge." Danielle smiled gently.

"It's your ability to feel, to sense anything around you. Everything is numb. Tastes, pain, touch—all the information that goes into your body that is supposed to help you navigate the world. It's just gone. No. Blunted. Or on hold. Or something." Mr. Pudgy the Elephant seemed sullen now.

"You're right, little one," Danielle said, "but that actually isn't all. It also includes wanting. Wanting to eat or sleep or live or play or bathe or anything. It isn't that I actively want to avoid doing those things. It's just that I don't care whether they happen or not. There is nothing driving me in either direction, towards or away from a thing. I just don't care.

Sorry—I just can't care."

"Which means that all a person can really do is choose, right Danielle?" (Elephant sneeze.)

"Kinda. (And bless you.) But here's the problem: each option seems just as good as any other."

"So?" Mr. Pudgy rolled on his side now, starting to get bored of the conversation.

"So... being down in the pit saps your energy to do or to want to do things. So, when you have to choose to do or not do something, you'll probably lurch toward 'not do'. Not get up, not bathe, not live, not eat, not open the window. But that isn't a function of liking those choices over the other ones. It's just a function of inertia." She paused.

"Are you sad?" asked the elephant.

"Not anymore. When hope is exhausted, so is grief." And then neither the elephant nor Danielle felt like saying any more.

Dirty slept and dreamed and didn't feel Danielle move away off the couch. She slept next to Mr. Pudgy who stared at the ceiling, his pudgy legs dangling.

Danielle, for her part, had gone to the bathroom and washed her face. She took her half-finished cigarette and balanced it on the edge of the sink, ash dripping. Then she removed her clothes (quite elegantly) and curled up with a fresh box of razor blades.

When Dirty awoke, there was something odd about the air, but it wasn't coming from Fern's apartment. She had only been asleep for a couple of hours, but something wasn't quite right. Thinking about it later, she could barely remember moving through the apartment, down the hall past the kitchen, saying Danielle's name softly, hesitantly. She remembered hitting the floor. She would always remember the silence. And she remembered Mr. Pudgy staring at the ceiling, his pudgy legs dangling.

She sat in the hall, face pale and her body pointed away from the bathroom. *Do something.* Crawling across the floor Dirty managed to pull the phone down from the counter onto her lap. 9. 1. 1. Holding the phone to her face she could feel her breath bouncing up off of the plastic.

"911 Do you need fire, police, or ambulance?" Dirty froze.

"um...ambulance?" Her voice was quivering and she felt sick.

"What's your emergency, ma'am?"

"Uh, my friend...she..." There was a long pause.

"Is she injured, ma'am?"

"Yeah. Well, not anymore. Well she is, it's just that..."

"Is anyone there in imminent danger, ma'am?"

"Not anymore. No. I found her...she's in the bathroom..."

"Okay. I need you to stay calm and stay where you are. I've got an ambulance on the way, but I need to confirm your address. Is your friend conscious at all? Can she hear you if you talk to her?" Rolling her head back she stared out through the skylight.

"Nope. Really nope. That's pretty much not going to be a thing." Dirty's hands were shaking madly, but a tiny part of her brain could hear how odd her answers must have seemed.

By the time the operator told her to hang up Dirty could see flashing lights outside the front window.

Running down the narrow stairs she unlocked the doors for the paramedics. They seemed so big. Looking at the shape and size of the staircase, then looking at the stretcher, the first paramedic, the bald one, asked Dirty if there was another way up. There wasn't. Not unless you count the terrifying back staircase that led from the alley up to Danielle's bedroom. But

Dirty wouldn't have even tried that while carrying a pencil case, let alone that giant wheely bed. So they left it in the ambulance and brought large boxes up with them.

The sounds that came from the bathroom then. God. Dirty slouched in the front room near the door, not wanting to listen but hearing anyway. It seemed like they were talking way too loud, too loud to seem normal. Were they doing that so Dirty could hear? So she would feel better? Worse? Were they trying to make her feel guilty? This wasn't her fault for fuck's sake. Didn't they know that?   They were muttering now. To each other? They were awful quiet about it, whatever they were talking about.

"Ma'am?" The one with hair came out of the bathroom, but it sounded like the muttering continued behind him. *Oh. A radio. He's on a radio, the other one.* Dirty stood up straight and tried to look innocent and helpful and sad and maybe some other things.

"Mm-hm?"

"Does...does your friend have anyone that needs to be contacted...? Parentsss...?"

Dirty bobbed her head slowly. "There are some, yeah. I think I have their phone number around here. Is there someone I should give it to so they're called?" The paramedic looked at her, his head slowly tilting to the side. His chin was at about 730 when Dirty figured it out. "Oh! Oh...I'm the...I'm the someone."

Oh. 30 minutes later there were three things in front of Dirty, placed square on the kitchen table. The place was silent; the three of them had gone. So now it was her, staring at the phone, Danielle's address book, and the business card left by the paramedic with no hair.

They ended up using a much smaller stretcher/bed/thing

to get up the stairs, since the big one wouldn't fit. Guess the big one is only important for people who are still...who still need...ugh. They were able to get her down the stairs on the smaller one.

boop. beep. boop. Wait for the ring. Dirty felt like she was going to choke on her breath and her message. She—

"hello? Mrs. Parker? I—it's—hi, it's Dirty. There's...what? No, she's not here right now. Right. Okay. No wait! Don't hang up! She—I--I have to tell you that...she's...at the hospital. Yes. I—I'm not totally sure what it is, but the paramedics took her to St. Mike's. Yes. Well, I don't know! I—right. Yes. I know. I gave them her health card. No, I gave it to them! No, I don't have it. Right. It's there. With her. Yes. You are? Okay. I--" but Mrs. Parker had already hung up.

Dirty hadn't meant to lie to her like that. It was her daughter for chrissakes. It's just that she didn't know how to say what she saw, what she knew, how to tell her that her daughter was already....

Dirty looked again at the three things on the table in front of her. God, she didn't want to do this. She felt like she would split open if she had to tell another person what happened. Or lie to someone else about what happened. But she definitely didn't want to call the number on the card. The one from the company that specializes in "crime scene clean-up". She should probably just give it to the landlord. So, she tried another name in the book. The next name said 'Rachel'.

Four days later, a day after the funeral, Dirty stood in the apartment with Danielle's parents. They had been so cold to her. *I mean, of course they're cold. Who the fuck wouldn't be?* But the whole time Dirty wondered if they hated her for lying like that on the phone, when she first called them. By the time they got to the hospital it was probably pretty damn clear what Dirty *hadn't* said.

As Dirty waited in the living room, pretending to pack and re-pack her things, she wasn't sure what was going to happen next, or how to ask. She didn't have a place to go, but this wasn't her place to begin with. Danielle's parents looked hollowed out, exhausted. Her father, who never seemed to say much of anything, didn't say much of anything. Her mother, though, used sharp and vicious movements, placing and moving and replacing things around the apartment. It said enough for both of them. Every clack of a plate or a picture frame, or the sound of a book thrust into a box felt like a stab aimed right at Dirty. They had almost finished collecting their daughter's things.

"Well, I..." Dirty began.

"Yes, um, thank you for your help, young, um, lady." Danielle's mother's mouth was as dry as her words. "But if you could leave us now..." Oh, Dirty thought. That was easy enough, I guess. Dirty blinked, then realized she hadn't moved. Rocking her body into motion, Dirty hoisted her pack onto her back, lowered her head a little, and headed for the door. She wanted to say something, something like a condolence, but nothing came, and suddenly the door was closed behind her. She stood for a moment, and it was a time when she should have been wondering where the hell she was going to go. Instead though, she was returning the gaze of the boy across the hall, the one who was beckoning her inside.

CHAPTER 3:
Seeing

It was the smell that hit Dirty first: the staggering, choking stench of cigarettes that seeped out of every pore of Fern's apartment. The stale air clung to her desperately, and as she struggled to change her breathing, a second realization hit her: Fern didn't smoke. At least, that was what Danielle had said. She blinked, and could feel the yellow, lurching up her nose and down onto the back of her tongue. She watched Fern, who seemed to have his own kind of dirt unrelated to the cigarettes, and she thought she was beginning to understand...sort of.

The jars all had lids on them, you see, but that didn't stop the smell. There was an almost cartoonish cloud over half of the apartment, the half with (most of) the jars in it. It got onto you, into you. It gripped and hung. It reminded Dirty of all that time she spent in high school, smoking up in that revolting apartment of that guy who she would end up dating for some ungodly reason. Not Peter, but before him. In that place, you got used to the smell quickly, like a monkey cage. But an hour or so after leaving you'd find yourself dragging your fingers over your arm, wondering why it felt a little slippery, sticky, gooey. Pushing and scrubbing in the shower, the smell would come back to you again when you reach for your clothes, this body odor of a terrible lover. And later with yourself and your sweat, it seeps out of your pores like a drug or a dirty saviour.

Fern's hands rested uncomfortably on his hips, and every so often one hand would dart from his hip to his belly, then touch his lips and back again to his hip. Over and over, less like a punctuation and more like an intrusion.

Although his tics were distracting, Dirty's attention was drawn back to the rows and rows of jars lining the shelves, counters and part of the floor.

"Sit down, hey? Sit down..." He spoke quickly and nervously, touching his belly and lips between "hey" and the second "sit down". They sat at the table, which was empty save for the lone, gleaming ashtray, spotless. "Th-thanks for (belly, lips) coming over, Dirty. Thanks." Dirty smiled semi-politely, but couldn't figure out how he knew her name.

It was difficult to tell if Fern was naturally lanky or just scrawny as fuck because of his diet. His hair had probably been washed sometime last week, maybe, and it hung about his face in dark, semi-loose curls. Reaching behind him to the freezer door, he pulled out a pack of cigarettes which he carefully placed on the table. Around the apartment the jars looked on like yellowing gargoyles, leaking.

"I thought you didn't smoke, Fern..." Dirty attempted a casualness that didn't quite pass.

"I-I don't (belly, lips) ...but would you like one? Would you?" He fumbled with the pack, then produced a box of matches from the cutlery drawer. Dirty slid one out of the pack, but didn't light it right away.

"Well, what about..." she motioned to the rows and rows of jars filled with cigarette butts.

"Oh!" Fern said, leaping to his feet and careening to the far end of the room. He plucked a jar at random and brought it back to the table where he placed it squarely between them. "Wh-what (belly, lips) do you see?" he asked. Dirty stared for a moment, then shook her head blankly.

"Look!" Fern insisted, pulling out a butt and laying it beside the jar. It was black and flat on the burnt end, and the filter was slightly chewed.

Interested but uncomfortable, Dirty lit her own cigarette—something Fern watched with a wet, deliberate interest. The instant burnt-smell start of it was refreshing to Dirty's nose, as her body shifted with the tickle in her lungs.

"Tell me," she said flatly.

"W-well (belly, lips), if you look, the person—person chewed on the filter; not gnashing, but not gentle either (belly, lips). And when they put it out, they pushed on the heater, but didn't crush it. That-that means (belly, lips) that they were thinking about something very hard, very complex. But they di--dn't find the answer, so they were still really thinky when they put it out-out. If they had been happy, they would have crushed it, like winning–like this!" Fern suddenly jumped up and pulled a jar from the top of the fridge. Peering inside the new jar, Dirty saw that all of the cigarette ends had been smushed, flattened or obliterated. Looking back at the first jar, she realized that they were all alike in their way too. Drawing deeply on her own and letting the smoke drip from her lips, she looked around and realized Fern had filled and itemized all of the jars according to the treatment the cigarettes had received at the mouths and hands of their owners.

"They all-all say something (belly, lips)–and I can tell you where they came from, too–Bay-Bay Street brokers here!" A jar was swept onto the table. "Down and outers–maybe Regent

Park—here!"

Fern was whipping around the apartment now, muttering "they tell you—they don't know it but they tell you..." before finally landing back in his chair, staring at the ashtray. "You put them together and keep them together and hold them together and connect and connect and connect the dots." Fern was gripping his knees tightly and lurching forward and back, his chin jutting out to kiss the air with each forward motion. "If you look, you can know and you can know so much, so much...."

Dirty was ready to forget the whole thing, to leave right then. But two things made her wait: The first was that, as she looked more carefully at Fern, she realized how frail, how small, pale, and pathetic he was. He might be batshit crazy, but he didn't actually seem dangerous. And even if he did get out of line, she was pretty sure she could take him.

The second thing was a jar on the kitchen counter. It sat by itself, and had a silly gold star on it, the kind you might get on a spelling test in grade school.

"Fern..." she said carefully, "what's that one?"

"They're dead. They're all dead. They died. They're dead." Muttering over and over, Fern slid over to the counter, pulled the jar up to his chest, then turned to the table, setting the container in front of Dirty. Her throat went dry.

Fern carefully, even lovingly, opened the jar and pulled out three cigarette butts. Every one of them had an almost flawless look to the filter. One was slightly oval, from lip pressure Dirty guessed, but otherwise all three had a kind of unmolested quality. And in the jar, there were more, some with lipstick bruising, some not. Dirty placed her palm gently on the table and took a deep, steadying breath.

"What do you mean, 'they all died', Fern?"

"Ahhhmmmm..." he bleated; his rocking slowed. "Right in the middle of it, right in the middle, down they went, down they went. Just as they were smoking. This one!" and here he grabbed one from the jar, "this guy was really overweight, standing outside a building on Ossington. Heart attack. Dropped to the sidewalk. Cigarette rolled away...." Fern reached in again and grabbed three more. It looked almost as if he was pulling them at random, but no. Each grab from his database was deliberate, and he knew exactly what he was doing.

"I got these three on the same day! A brick off a building, right in the head! Knife attack! I don't know about the last one. She just dropped."

"You were there for all of them?" Dirty asked, trying to mask feeling revolted and hollowed-out in her gut.

"Sometimes!" he chirped, starting to get wound again. "Cuz they happen all over but they can all come together! They can come together and be together and--"

And suddenly he was up again.

"You can put these ones--" grabbing a jar from the wall "-- with these ones--" he raced over to place it next to one on the floor by the couch. "And you can do that because they all were smoked in the afternoon! But you don't have to! Cuz you can put it over here instead!" But as Fern worked and changed and mixed and matched jars and smokers and times and intentions, the taut, bony fingers on his right hand started picking at scabs and skin, first on the back of his neck and then down on his right side where his love handles would have been if he had had any fat on him. And the faster he moved around the room, the more he picked, and soon trickles of blood and flesh were smeared over his shirt and hand, his breathing labored, his voice gnarled and hoarse.

"Have another one," Fern said quickly, having come back to his chair at the table, although fully half of his body was teetering over the side, his eyes bulging. He didn't seem to care that Dirty hadn't finished her first.

"I'm fine with this one, thanks," she breathed, half-standing and not taking her eyes off of him.

"I noticed-noticed you the other day when the ambulance came to Danielle's apartment. When the ambulance came. Came to get her..." Fern was shaking a little as he talked, and his hands had stopped darting around his body.

Dirty's cigarette was smoldering, the ash long and dangling, un-flicked and awaiting her next move.

"Fern, I have to go," she near-whimpered, her voice rising.

"Have another one..." his voice was fading a little, his eyes glazed.

All of a sudden it was as if there was a shrill keening in Dirty's head, screeching at her to go. Fern wasn't even looking at her anymore, lost somewhere. Dirty pulled her bag to her chest and carved a semi circle to the door, not saying another word to the boy at the table.

CHAPTER 4:
An island in a sea of monsters

Leaving Fern's apartment, Dirty stepped out into the market and turned south. She had managed to slip an extra one out of the pack when Fern was darting around the room, and now she placed it between her lips as she walked. While she was packing, back in the apartment, she had been considering her options. That Rachel woman, for one, had offered to put her up if she needed it, although Dirty knew the offer was more polite than anything else. There were shelters, which she wasn't willing to do (again). And there was Alan. It had been awhile since they had spoken, and lord knew they hadn't left on the best of terms, but it was October, and things were starting to get chilly.

Her head was starting to swirl. Here she was again, alone and unanchored and so unbelievably sad. She felt locked out, like the world was happening to her, and happening completely without regard for her. Her senses were becoming muted, her body felt hollow and this wasn't right at all. This just wasn't how it should be at all.

So as she made her way across Queen Street towards

Parkdale, Dirty let her feet carry her to the place she knew she didn't want to go. She wasn't sure how Alan would receive her; in the waning months of their relationship they had barely touched, let alone... but he would probably make a pass at her now.

Alan wasn't the smartest guy Dirty had ever met. But the problem was, he wasn't the nicest either. Why Dirty had hooked up with him in the first place was a mystery to most, though she *had* been in high school, and a guy with his own apartment can be pretty tempting. Dirty had met him through his scraggly-looking little brother because she was looking to score some weed. She could no longer remember if she had had sex with him that day because she was attracted to him or because she was bored. Either way, Danielle had never approved. Danielle had referred to him as an asshat.

Dirty and Alan had dated, but she had left him a year-and-a-half ago, so why she was ringing his apartment now was going to be beyond him. But she buzzed the apartment, and he buzzed her up. Yup. He was still there. Hell, he probably still had that same stupid ponytail.

***

So, she stayed. It was a roof over her head, anyway. And while staying there, several things happened over the following weeks: there was a murder outside the apartment (unconnected to either her or Alan, but sobering nonetheless); Alan 'came into' some money after putting his best friend in the hospital; and Dirty had made friends with a rat named Pickles.

It was actually Alan's rat, but since both of them (she and the rat) had been spending so much time on the couch, it seemed silly not to introduce themselves.

It had surprised her the first time Pickles had stowed away when she had gone out to skulk around town. She thought the bulge in her coat was a pack of cigarettes, so when she reached in to find it had grown fur, she stopped in the middle of the street. There was Pickles, blinking back at her hopefully.

"Where the fuck's the rat?" Alan drooled when she got home.

"Here," she said flatly, "he decided to stow away in my coat when I left."

"Bullshhitt," he continued, "ya fuckin' took him ya fuck..." *He certainly shows the flexibility of the language when he's stoned like this*, she thought. She motioned to hand Pickles to him, and Alan snatched him away, gave him a token three pats, dropped him on the floor, and went back to the video game. "When are you gonna get a job ya fuckin' free-loader?" he said out of the corner of his mouth. Dirty winced. *The only thing worse than listening to an asshole.*

"Sorry Alan, I..." she wasn't sure if she should let it drop. "Do you need money for rent or smoke n' shit?"

"Naw, you know I got cash, fuck. Loads. You just keep taking my fuckin smokes when I need 'em, fuck." She should've let it drop. Alan leaned over and opened the weed box on the table and pulled out a twenty, flipping it her way. "Get yer own, and leave my fuckin' rat alone."

But some days were better than others. Some days they sat together on the couch, playing video games and smoking weed, not talking much at all. Those were the times Alan seemed most tolerable to Dirty, the most stable. Pickles would keep busy nibbling the carpet fibers, and occasionally Dirty would throw together something they could eat. And for the most part, the apartment was pretty close to how she had remembered it. There were a few (a lot) more pictures of naked women, and someone had finally painted the bathroom for him, but pretty much everything was where it had been. Hell, he even still had that stupid ponytail.

***

Sleeping on the couch in Alan's apartment, Dirty's brain reached back to when she had crawled out of the bus in Toronto just weeks earlier. When she made it to the apartment, Danielle had met her at the front door and hugged her for what felt like forever. Then they swept upstairs and collapsed together on the couch, babbling all the stories that had happened since they'd been apart. "Piece of shit asshat," Danielle would say, every time Peter's name came up–it always made Dirty feel better. It was the first time in months that she was able to relax, the first time since before she left for Edmonton. Later in the evening, when Danielle ran out to get Chinese food, Dirty cried. She bawled until Mr. Pudgy was soaked and snotty, and Dirty's breathing hitched and caught like she was drowning.

By the time Danielle returned Dirty had already cracked open the wine, and could (almost) justify her red eyes. Not that she had to with Danielle. And when she slept that evening, it was like her whole body was letting go, barely stirring for the next 15 hours.

Dirty dreamed of that time, now on another couch, feeling less safe, not in a place where she could sleep as easily because with Alan you could just never be sure.

When she woke, there were three pairs of bleary, irritated eyes on her. The room was filled with blue-green smoke, and Dirty had slept through the first joint, not to mention the troupe oozing through the front door, waiting for Alan's signal to open the weed box. She could see the back of Alan just inside the kitchen, standing with some woman who looked either 45, or 32 with a really bad habit. Just from where he was standing near the stove, Dirty was sure the two of them were doing hot knives.

As for the other three, two were from the bar up the street, and the third was an angel. Well, Martin wasn't actually an angel, but his skin was so bright, his face so young, and his smile so genuine and innocent, Dirty thought he looked like one sitting next to the others. She was glad for her angel then, because the other two didn't seem too keen on making new friends.

"Salut, toé," Martin said brightly, even though it was 4pm. Dirty smiled easily. He looked so fresh-faced and young. She felt grimy, sweaty, gross. Soaking him in with her eyes, he was the cleanest she'd felt in weeks.

Her boy-angel was bleary-eyed too, tilting subtly from side to side in his chair, although he had an eagerness about him as he watched one of the other men roll a fresh one, light it, and breathe deeply.

"Fackin' sheeyit!" the woman lurched out of the kitchen, trying to regain her breath through a coughing attack. Alan was two steps behind, still holding the knives. He looked at Dirty hard, ruefully; she was sitting upright and close to Martin after he moved over onto the couch–maybe too close. She wasn't sure what that meant for Alan. It had become quite clear over the days and weeks that he was not physically attracted to her anymore, so she couldn't decide what kind of claim he wanted to stake now.

Still, Alan came over and sat between them, throwing the burnt, bent knives on the table and grabbing the joint. Martin looked small next to Alan–hell, he was small; not as skinny as

Fern was, but shorter, and the bones in his face were more delicate. The look in his eyes said he was afraid of Alan, and Dirty wondered what it would be like to kiss him.

Dirty watched as it went around the group. She studied their eyes, their hands, their expressions. The room felt…odd. She thought, *it's such a weird experience to share things with complete strangers the way that stoners do. Not the hardcore scene, mind you. But stoners. Even personal space takes on a different dimension when everyone is staring, almost lathering as they wait for the prize. But don't get fooled into thinking that these people are suddenly your friends--things are much more tenuous and everyone knows it, if they think about it. Laughing at thin, bad jokes while passing a joint among strangers just hides the thought everyone has about the group: Just don't break down before I get mine. Because you know it is going to break down at some point. Maybe easily, everyone too baked to care about who is passing out or falling out the door. Maybe really rough, when someone feels like they can finally say fuck you to that other guy cuz now everyone has been smoked up and there isn't anything left to do. Or maybe it isn't even that thought out, and you just feel like punching someone in the throat. Whatever, right?*

It felt like hours before the apartment cleared out again, and Dirty was left almost alone once more. No one had been punched in the throat (this time), probably because Alan had been the one to pass-out. The rest of them left together, with Martin closing the door behind them, glancing and smiling at Dirty in a small, quiet way that she would probably never see on his face again.

She felt grimy and stoned and needed to do something about at least one of those things. Climbing into the shower, she imagined Martin again, naked and sweet, his chest as smooth as his cheeks. She stood there for a while, arms crossed, the water pelting her skin. She smiled at first, but the water was working hard against her face, pulling her mouth down. It was slowly winning over her eyes too, and by the time the hot water wasn't anymore, she was clean, sober, exhausted, and fucking miserable.

She looked at the mold in the grout of the shower and it disgusted her. It hadn't yesterday or the day before. But now she was looking more carefully. Now she was stopping her brain and herself from going on autopilot; watching and breathing and crying more slowly--not slowing down in relaxation, but despair. The grime and the grossness and the ash and the misery. She could look around now and see it for what it was. And it felt brutal. It felt like things were just happening to her, and all she had been doing was waiting for each consecutive punch. And it felt like the world didn't have anything good that it was going to send her way. It felt like things were breaking down before she got hers.

Each day was like trying to walk as softly and quietly as she could through a wild animal enclosure. Each day was about staying small, just trying to avoid being bitten or scratched or mauled or chewed up. And if you spent each day doing that, you didn't have anything left over, left over for yourself. Not even enough for you to bother to stop and cry and scream and notice that there is fucking mold on the grout. There had to be more to this than just surviving. This was her life goddammit, and what the fuck did she have to show for it?

Part Two
November 1997

CHAPTER 5:
Stuck

Henry decided to make the weekend trip from Ottawa to Toronto in the daylight, Friday afternoon, because things just got worse after sundown. This 'highway' was really just a road, and it was a narrow, winding bastard of a two-lane, bulging with 18-wheelers and S.U.V.s. So as Henry's Golf crept up behind the rig, he wondered how long he would have to wait to pass.

There *was* a kind of magic to driving Highway 7 in the fall: at the edge of the road the rock faces stared back, lit up by every conceivable colour of autumn leaf. It was beautiful enough to break your heart, assuming the oncoming traffic didn't kill you first. Although by this time in November, most of the leaves had faded and dropped. The trees becoming skeletal and wet.

Henry did okay, mostly. He liked his job, and liked the house he was renting, and even owned a dog. His love life was kinda fucked up, but he pretty well had a handle on things. Steve had gone on another bender that week, stealing money from Henry and then disappearing; and somehow Henry always took him back, against the advice of Cheryl and everyone else. Steve was the mistake Henry loved making. Repeatedly.

Steve was gorgeous and seductive and alluring; he could ask people to do things and they would all just *want* to do it. He was a slinking Aphrodite in the streets *and* the sheets, but he wasn't quite bright enough to be a master manipulator. He knew well enough that people liked doing things for him, and he occasionally used that knowledge, but only when he stopped long enough to think about it.

It was supposed to be relaxing, this weekend, and Henry figured it *would* be when he got there. But right now, he was tired of looking at the ass-end of this truck. Trying to sneak a peek, Henry eased the car towards the yellow line, trying to see the oncoming traffic. Immediately a horn hit him as two Jeeps whizzed past, nearly ripping off his side view mirror. Henry gagged back into his lane and overcompensated, his tires licking the gravel shoulder. Breathing heavier, he dropped back a little further from the truck in front of him, hoping this would help his eyes reach around.

It was okay, at first, when he and Steve had got together almost two years prior; back when even Rachel liked Steve, and Henry was brand new at his job—when the money was flattering and Henry just wanted to feel good. And pay off his student loan. And fuck a lot. Which he tried to, but was never really able to match the picture in his head of what that was supposed to be like. And soon Henry went one way and Steve went the other, Henry settling down and Steve winding up—the coke, the not-with-Henry-sex, the week-long parties. And more and more, being around Steve just made him feel...sad and disappointed. Possibly in Steve, possibly in himself.

"You need to make Steve a Debbie." Cheryl once said.

"I'm sorry, what?!"

Cheryl smirked. "It's a way of getting over someone. Of getting them out of your head. So, listen up and pay attention, young man. You've had the experience when you go out with someone and it's just a really bad scene, right?"

"Clearly." Henry deadpanned.

"So, let's say his name, as in this case, is 'Steve'. Well, problem is, every 'Steve' you meet after that is spoiled for you, right? I mean, as soon as you're introduced to someone new, but with that name, you've attached all this emotional baggage to him that doesn't (necessarily) belong there. Or worse, you're with a new Steve and all you end up doing is thinking about old, bad Steve." Listening intently, Henry was making those funny little lines on his forehead where his brow furrowed.

"So, what you do is refer to your ex—in fact, *all* of your exes—as 'Debbie,' so the names don't get spoiled for the rest of 'em. Which is particularly important in your case." Henry frowned.

"Wh…y?"

"Think about how many gay men there are named Steve. You would never get laid again!" Henry let out a squeal at this, then slapped his hand over his mouth for fear of sounding weird.

"Problem is," Henry said finally, "what if a person ends up dating someone who's actually named Debbie?"

Cheryl seemed to consider this for a moment, then answered. "How many 'Debbies' do you know? Not 'Deb', or 'Deborah'. Actually 'Debbie?'" Henry paused, his eyes growing wide as he searched his mental roll-a-dex for someone, anyone with that name.

"Son of a bitch–I can't think of any!"

"Well," Cheryl concluded, "I guess we're safe then."

Physically, Cheryl was big. Imposing, to be honest, standing a good 6 inches taller than Henry. And Henry thought she was luxurious; there was a lusciousness found somewhere in the breadth of her hands and her great (big) hair. And they were smoking buddies too, at work. Standing by the office side door, Cheryl would listen to Henry's horrifyingly graphic stories from the weekend, and Henry would listen to her honking laughter.

Dave would be there too, most days, sniffing around their ankles and thinking about how great the car was. Dave, also known as Dave the Smartest Dog in the World, seemed to love coming to work with Henry, probably because he got to chase his ball in and out of the rooms up and down the hall, and because the smell of the carpet in Henry's office always seemed to give him good dreams.

The thing was, when it came to all those sex-romp stories that Henry would tell Cheryl, it was all a lie. Well, almost all of it. In one sense they really did happen. They just didn't exactly involve him. They were things he had seen happen or had heard about from his other friends. Or if they did involve Henry, it was in some adjacent way, with him watching in horror from the corner of a room while something crude or orgiastic happened around him.

On those weekends or even weeknights when he would be at the bar for a drink or three, each time with the hope of maybe picking up or getting picked up, he would watch how easy it was for everyone else to fall in and out of bed with each other. In and out of bed, or the car out back, or the bathrooms, or whatever. And Henry would see these guys being cool and available, and they all made it look so goddamned easy. Henry wanted to be easy, too.

He wanted so badly to be the person he talked about—

ballsy and desirable and courageous with boys. And Henry certainly wasn't a prude; he liked sex and sexy things, and didn't even have a big problem with people using drugs and such (which showed up a lot in the clubs anyway). But when he had the chance to start something or even join in, he froze or shrunk or fled. The chattering in his head about him being small or not good enough or that he would do it wrong would get out ahead of his wanting to just do it anyway goddammit, and his mind became a ball of panic and he would turn away or stupidly mutter nothankyou or some other asinine emasculating nonsense. He figured that Cheryl would never really know what was him and what wasn't, so he collected the stories and just changed the names. Or name.

Henry did try, though. And when he and Steve started dating and some of the stories he would tell Cheryl became slightly more legitimately about him, Henry felt a little less like he had been lying before. The weird, exciting, sometimes even dangerous things that Steve got into made Henry feel a bit closer to the casual slut/playboy he thought he wanted to be.

Henry knew that around the next bend was a long stretch of straight, flat road–perfect for passing, if it was clear. Slipping the car back into fourth, he fell back some more, ready to take a run at it. Sure enough, the lane was clear and Henry mushed the gas hard.

With most cars it would have been a satisfying revving, eating road with a sexy roar. In the Golf, though, it was a lurch forward like a gluttonous belch. Past the rear wheels and mid-section of the truck, he inched his way up. And the road was clear, or had been, until someone turned onto it from a side road, and suddenly Henry had company coming at him.

The rig wasn't slowing to let him in, and the Golf was no sports car, so this was going to be close. The other vehicle was

ts lights in a frantic move-the-fuck-over way,
where to go. He pushed down hard, shoulder
the truck driver and, looking over, Henry
saw him, tongue out, grinning like a demon.

By the time Henry yanked his car in front of the rig, he was close enough to the other one to see the driver mouthing words that are generally not shared in polite company. Like 'cunt' and 'arsehole'. Henry shared a few himself, started to put some distance between himself and the truck, and took a long hard pull off of his cigarette, his hand trembling.

He had no idea how many times Cheryl had told him that he should leave Debbie-Steve for good– 'Just move on goddammit,' she would say, pushing the words through the weight of her frustration. They had worked together for so long, Henry and Cheryl, and she watched the whole soap opera week after week. Initially, she thought Steve was a good shit, but somewhere along the way the word "good" just got lost from the description.

And so now, Toronto. A weekend. A break. Henry would get to hang out with Jared and Daniel, and hopefully see some other friends, and just try to find his feet again.

***

"Plans for tomorrow, hon?" Jared had already refilled Henry's wine glass, and both Jared and Daniel had been staring for several seconds before Henry realized they were speaking to him.

"Mm? Mmm. Thought I'd go down and see Rachel. A friend of hers died last month, and I never got a chance to come down and see her about it." Henry furrowed his brow saying it, as he guessed he should.

"Other than that, I thought I'd spend a good chunk of time bothering you fags."

"Good. That was our plan. Meet you back here 6ish?" Although Henry had been paying little attention, he suddenly realized the boys were sitting much closer to each other than before, and were now trying to exit gracefully.

"Sounds good. Why don't you guys head up then. I'll clean up when I finish this smoke." Henry had been right; while the two of them had left the room casually, Henry could hear Jared giggling before they had reached the top of the stairs. Sitting in the candlelight, Henry rubbed his cheek, the bones in his face feeling fuzzy from the weed. Listening carefully, he could hear the crackle of his cigarette each time he took a drag.

***

The next morning was lazy and sun-drenched, Henry laying in the middle of the guest bed listening to the sounds of the house and starting to break a sweat under the weight of the duvet. The room itself was not that big (it was tiny, truth be told), and wasn't great as a private living space like the master bedroom down the hall. Actually, it felt like the room had been designed to be just big enough to frame the bed, and little else. Still, the mottled salmon paint (Daniel) and twisty candle wall sconce (Jared) made it one step closer to cozy, rather than making Henry feel like he was in a closet.

Swinging his feet onto the carpet and bouncing up off the bed (practically vaulting himself into the hall, since the door was so close), Henry stood for a moment feeling his surroundings, eyes narrowing. Stepping stealthily out of the room, Henry moved to verify his suspicion. Standing at the top of the stairs in his underwear, he exclaimed, "That's why I like that boy! He keeps the heat on in his house!"

Although neither Daniel nor Jared were home, Henry imagined that he had been speaking to Daniel in a triumphant, told-you-so manner. Ever since their time together as a couple, there had been a raging battle between Henry and Daniel about the appropriate, comfortable temperature for a home. While Henry preferred something close to 23 degrees, he maintained that Daniel would have been happier had the measurement been in Fahrenheit.

Standing there now, Henry realized that Jared had a) come from Henry's school of thought on the matter, and (more importantly) b) somehow managed to win over the ice-queen. In any event, it was already 11:30, and Henry needed to call Rachel.

That afternoon Henry and Rachel stood outside a café on College Street; Rachel's chin was jutted out as she blew smoke straight up over her head. They had just finished lunch and, following their tradition, stood in silence until the first cigarette was finished. It wasn't a race, so much as an arbitrary time line. It was a little too cold for them to eat outside, but slipping out for a smoke was manageable.

"So how have you been holding up, really...?" Henry asked somewhat stiltedly after they had gone back inside. Rachel sat for a moment, looking at her grease-riddled plate.

"It's been a rough month, hon," she sighed. "After Danielle...died, I took some time off. I hadn't really seen her in three or four months, but when I heard..."

"about what happened to her..." Henry tried to finish her sentence.

"about what she did to herself," Rachel corrected, more sternly than she had intended. Silence. As Henry opened his mouth, unsure what he was going to say, the waiter returned.

"Some dessert, my lovelies?"

"No, I'm good." Rachel waved her hand.

"I think…do you have any lemon meringue pie?" Henry asked sheepishly.

"Interesting choice…. Did you know that 'lemon' is the sexiest word in the English language," the waiter asked with a faux-innocence. Rachel's eyebrows raised. He was staring right at Henry when he said it.

"In order to get to the word, you have to start with the first letter, obviously. To do that, you have to gently use the very tip of your tongue, teasing it out. For the next letter," he continued, "you've gotta back off, pulling it back in your mouth, making a space big enough just behind your teeth, your tongue leaving it alone for now. For the third letter, though, you've gotta hold it gently between your lips, giving it a little vibration, but not too much or your lips will press too hard and you'll have to do too much work to let go again."

Henry's face burned hot; looking at the waiter, then at the table, nowhere felt safe.

"And for the finale" he continued, "you need a little flick from your diaphragm, almost a grunt, 'uhn'. Contrary to the appearance of the word, the end has a pelvic-thrusting 'uh' sound, rather than the ecstasy sound of 'awh', which is still good, by the way. L-E-M-O-N looks like it should be pronounced lem-awhn, but we actually say_it lem-uhn. Uhhhhn. Then you finish it off with the tip of your tongue on the top of your mouth, again with a little, tiny, vibration." Pause. "I'll be back with your pie." Rachel was giggling madly as the waiter sauntered off.

"That felt dirty," Henry squeaked. Raising his mug in front of his face, though, he silently mouthed 'lemon'.

"So, how's Seeger?" he asked, after the embarrassment had

subsided.

"Small and wily." She smiled.

Seeger was Rachel's new kitten, and at only 19 weeks his hunting skills were honed to the point where he had successfully brought down a large spider, a tennis ball, and a particularly intimidating piece of pizza crust–each carried in and displayed proudly on the kitchen floor just for her.

Henry wanted to tell Rachel about how he had been feeling, in the car and at Daniel's—about his life, or some shit. He felt stupid just thinking about saying it out loud.

"And how's Dave the Smartest Dog in the World?" she asked.

"Really good," he said. "Had to leave him with Cheryl, though, cuz Jared's really allergic. He likes the new guy at work though..."

"Jared does?" Rachel cocked her head to the side.

"No, twit, Dave." Henry twisted his mouth in mock spite. "The new guy's name is Andre. Well, sort of new. Two months, and stick-straight. Got a girlfriend even. No chance." Henry paused. "But an ass that could launch a thousand ships..."

"I dunno about *no* chance." Rachel batted her eyes. "I bet you could do some damage. You've got Dave doing the groundwork for you anyway..."

"No, no, no," Henry shook his head frantically, "nooo workplace sex. No friggin' way."

"Coward," she cooed.

CHAPTER 6:
Except for the fish

The rest of the weekend for Henry was uneventful, as was the drive home on Sunday night. Uneventful, except for the fish. On Saturday night Daniel and Jared decided to take Henry to a club in the hope that he might get laid. Of course, Henry knew what they were up to, but decided to go along with it anyway. What his friends neglected to tell him was that it was a special night at this particular club. Special, because Brad Fish was going to be performing there.

Brad Fish, also known as Bradley the Fish, Bradley and the Fish, or sometimes Brad the Fisher of Men, was a legend when it came to live sex shows on the Toronto circuit. His show usually involved various kinds of food, often seafood, used as part of increasingly creative insertion techniques.

When they got to the Omni that evening the place was leaking testosterone out onto the sidewalk. White muscle shirts, camouflage muscle shirts, button-down polo shirts (really?), blouses, leather pants, bicycle shorts, short shorts, construction boots, high heels, boat shoes, thigh-high boots.

Standing in line with Daniel and Jared and everyone else,

Henry felt like a shrimp; at five foot five he kinda was, and when it came to getting hit on at clubs, his size often meant he was either fetishized or ignored.

There were always creeps and bears who wanted to take him home in ways that seemed one drink away from kidnapping. And the athletic, elegant boys *he* was interested in almost never gave him the time of day. Security barely gave him a look—looked over top of him, actually. But Henry didn't mind, most of the time, and carefully folded his jacket before giving it to the coat-check girl. Or guy. Or Alfred.

Walking around a glass cubed wall with Daniel and Jared close behind, Henry hesitated at the opening, a bit overwhelmed by the enormity of it. Feeling a push from behind, Henry half-stumbled into the room, suddenly standing in the middle of a bare patch of floor, feeling naked.

The push was accidental--Jared had goosed Daniel and caught him by surprise. He jumped forward, running into Henry. There were a half-dozen glances at him, as if to say 'who's the missus trying to make a grand entrance?'

Straightening himself, Henry strode to the bar with Daniel and Jared close behind. Much later, Henry would reflect on whether it was a good idea to drink that many vodka sodas in a row. Either way, he was loosening up.

Forty-five minutes later, the dance floor was packed. Grinding, sweaty, lusty. Even Henry was letting it rip. He turned around and watched an absolutely gorgeous piece slide and shake across the floor. Not towards Henry, but kinda near him. So, Henry decided to go for it. His hands sweating, his left hand balled while his right dangled, he was going to reach over and grab some meat. His shoulders shifting back and forth, Henry couldn't take his eyes off the prize. And just as the guy was close and Henry was reaching out, he veered and

.Henry...totally missed. He barely got some side-thigh, and the guy didn't even notice. He stood there feeling like he had shown up in a costume to a costume party that wasn't.

Then came the surge. It would be tough to say exactly where it started, but at some point, the three of them were being shoved with the rest of the crowd down towards the back of the club to gather around the stage. The swell of bodies lurched towards the risers, black curtains pulled back, with nothing but a wooden box and a stripper pole on the platform.

Henry stood close to the middle of the pack—not too far back but still tough for a smaller man to get a good view.

"Ladies, ladies" boomed a voice over the loudspeaker. "This is the moment at least some of you have been waiting for! Put your meaty paws together for the one and only...Braaad Fishhhhhhhh!" The lights went out. And then a single spotlight shone on the stage, illuminating the most chiseled torso Henry had ever almost seen. Peeking between shoulders, Henry watched Brad writhe and gyrate to some god-awful stripper music, intermittently drowned out by screeching cat-calls from the crowd.

Brad's routine started with a lot of teasing and self-rubbing, leaving very little to the imagination since he was only wearing a neon green G-string. But then things got...weird. And it started with an octopus.

Because Henry couldn't see that well, he wasn't exactly sure that Brad was doing all the things that Brad was actually doing. All that Henry could see was that Brad was pulling up what appeared to be a fairly dead octopus from the box, parading it around the stage for a bit. And for some unfathomable reason, the room was going fucking wild. Brad strutted and gyrated back and forth across the little stage, swinging his hips to music that wasn't much more than heavy bass and the sound of lasers going pewpewpew.

When Brad was finished with the octopus, the room hooting and squealing, Henry convinced himself that he really did want a closer look. Confidently drunk, he pivoted and nudged his way past shoulders and elbows, almost making it to the front. And suddenly Brad was staring right at him.

"You!" A trickle of sweat slid down Henry's spine right to his ass crack. "You," Brad said again, pointing. "I need you to be my magician's assistant. Get your sweet ass up here." In a breath Henry was being pushed, grabbed, and then lifted onto the stage, feeling awkward and exposed and decidedly less drunk.

Writhing toward Henry, Brad oozed his hands over Henry's chest, slowly walking him backwards to the pole. Henry couldn't see much because of the spotlight, but he was pretty sure he could see Daniel in the crowd covering his mouth with both hands in horror, shock, and glee.

The pole against Henry's back now, Brad was turning and working his bare ass against him. *Where do I put my hands?!* Henry panic-thought. Which is when Brad slowly turned around and took Henry's hands in his. Sliding Henry's palms over Brad's chest, Brad then reached out into the darkness beyond Henry's sight. Unseen, someone handed Bradley a bottle, which he opened, pouring something into Henry's hands. *Is this oil? Is it lube?!* Whatever it was (it was lube), Brad was guiding Henry's hands, Henry smearing the stuff over Brad's chest and arms.

"Wait here," Brad said, and he glided into the darkness for a moment. Left onstage, alone and on display, Henry was terrified and awkward and paralyzed. He could feel eyes all over him, even if he couldn't see them that well. And then

Brad reappeared, handing Henry a large implement, a dildo that looked like a realistic fish. Yes, it was oversized and theatrical and goofy, but it made for a great show. Henry could only stand there motionless, holding it like an army private's first time holding a rifle. Brad started to stroll away again, but all of a sudden, he turned and came running back at Henry, shouting, "ARE YOU READY?!"

Henry was so startled that he flinched. And squeezed. His hands were slippery from the lube, and when he clenched like that the dildo fish shot out of his hands with astounding speed, jabbing Brad Fish right in the eye. Brad reeled backward, clutching his face while Henry stepped forward, a reflex of concern. Stepping into a pool of lube that had collected on the floor in front of him, Henry slipped forward, headlong into Brad, knocking both off of the stage. Landing on top of Brad Fish, Henry heard Brad's arm break, which pretty much ended the show for everyone.

***

By the time Henry hit Ottawa on Sunday evening, he was on his last cigarette and wondering what he should wear to work tomorrow. Salty crystals of snow whistled across his windshield; too small and light to fall to earth, they were being pushed there by the swelling winter wind. Autumn had finally buggered off, and the new season was hate-fucking the city. Highway 417 snaked into Ottawa, and as the lights of the buildings were obscured by the sandblast, Henry's car scurried home under the cover of white night.

"What're you wearing?" Henry purred into the phone in his house as Cheryl answered. Giggling madly, she played along.

"I've been waiting for you," she cooed. "All I've got on is a feather boa and a smile."

"You walk around your house in a feather boa?"

"Well, it's laundry day. How was your trip, baby-cakes?"

"Mmm," Henry sighed. "Fairly relaxing. Some good, some not so good."

"Hmm. That sounds a little fishy. Wanna talk about it?" she asked.

"No, no I do not. Okay if I pick Dave up tomorrow? I think I'm just going to chill out the rest of the night."

"Sure," she said. "I'll bring him to the office in the morning."

Hanging up the phone, Henry sat in the living room staring out the window, watching as the snow began to pile higher and higher. He started thinking about Steve again, wondering if he would call.

Henry flicked on the radio. The CBC was re-broadcasting some weird spoken word/conceptual art bullshit from what sounded like someone's basement. Then he remembered a talking-to Cheryl had given him about 6 months before. It hurt then, and maybe because of that Henry had rejected it at the time. It shoved itself back into his head now.

She had asked him why he kept going back to Steve over and over again. "Each time is like a car-crash, and you're the one who gets hurt. Every time. So why keep going back to the same intersection, man? Do you actually get something out of it?" He considered it again now and wondered

Do I? What does it mean when you hang on desperately to someone else?

"Why don't you just take a break from him, just to see? Go do something you've always wanted to do, something you're excited or passionate about," she'd said at the time.

Maybe you do it because letting go of him means not having him to

distract you, and so you have to face your own bullshit? If you make him the thing you're passionate about (or…pretend he's the thing you're passionate about?) then maybe you don't have to face the not knowing of what you really want? I mean, what if you don't know what that is? Having to look at that place where you really don't know if you are going to be okay, not sure of what it is that should be driving you forward. Sad and alone and hoping for distraction because the thing that is waiting for you in your head, when you stop and listen, is the sound of indecision, the sound of what do I believe in? Those quiet, frightening times when you ache and cower from not knowing what it is you are supposed to mean, what it is you are supposed to do.

How do other people do this? How do they just…decide? Because it's not a matter of picking just anything; there's supposed to be something that grabs you by the nuts, a vision that's clear and visceral and unequivocal. And not feeling anything, you start to wonder what the fuck is wrong with you and what the hell do you do now? Just pick something anyway? And it hurts. The not knowing hurts.

But if there is someone there you can focus on, throw yourself at, crawl inside of, consume and let consume you, then maybe you don't have to think so much about that other stuff.

And maybe that other person will help; maybe he will secure you long enough that you can look around and find the thing that ties to your chest and pulls you forward. But maybe that other person is just giving you cover for hiding your eyes. And maybe giving you a little bit of protection and distraction from that place where the floor falls out means that you'll put up with all sorts of shit. All. sorts. of shit.

"Fuck off, CBC" Henry muttered, and flicked off the radio.

CHAPTER 7:
A thin, icy crust

"Chicken salad, huh?"

"Mmhm," Cheryl burbled. Henry crinkled his nose as Cheryl sat on the sofa in his office, munching away. As it happened, she did quite enjoy chicken salad sandwiches, but she also knew that Henry got kind of antsy about the smell of it in his office. She did it on purpose. For added effect she was even chewing with her mouth slightly open, the food making a sploiky sploiky sound.

"But seriously though," Cheryl said after she had swallowed, "who names their kid 'Scooter'?" Cheryl was talking about Rachel's boyfriend, since Henry had just finished giving her an abridged version of that weekend, sans poisson. Cheryl had met Rachel once or twice before, but had only heard tell of Scooter through stories.

"It was his utenym," Henry said. Cheryl bunched her forehead up into a wrinkly mess. Henry clarified. "You know how when someone is going to have a baby and before the kid is even born they give it a goofy name, like, just something to call it until they can figure out what its actual name is going to be? Like 'Cletus the fetus' or some fucking thing?" Cheryl nodded, chewing again. "So that's a uterus-name, or a utenym. Anyway, Scooter's utenym was apparently Scooter, and somehow it just stuck as a nickname. I can't even remember what his real name is anymore. I think I knew at one point...."

Henry was stabbing his tomato salad. It bored him. He was thinking about finding something to do that wasn't boring. He didn't know what that was yet, but whatever it was going to be, it needed to have the quality of being un-boring. "Want to go get a beer?"

"Honey, lunch is almost over. We'd never make it back in time." Cheryl had a somber, too-bad tone in her voice. They sat quietly and finished lunch, then went to have a smoke.

"What do you want to do with the rest of your life, Cher?"

Cheryl smiled. "When I've got the money, I'm going to move north to a place near where I grew up. I'll buy a bit of land and start a donkey sanctuary." Henry almost choked.

"A what?!"

"I know. I said a 'donkey sanctuary'. It's silly, I know."

"No! No, not that. It's just that I've never heard of a donkey sanctuary before. Is it really a thing?"

"Yup. There are only a few in North America, but yeah, they're a thing. I like small towns, and there is something deeply satisfying about animal care for me. And there is something extra exciting about it, since there are so few sanctuaries around. It means that I would be needed." The last sentence hit Henry in the chest.

***

Kachink.

Henry was circling his spoon in his cup, sitting near the window of his most tolerated coffee shop. Where he was sitting today it got chilly every time the door opened. It may have been Sunday.

The counter at the front was an odd, hammered-out copper colour; for all he knew, it was actually copper. But it was smooth and cool to the touch, and there was something about the sense experience with it that often made Henry feel calmer, or brighter, or better. On top of the espresso machine was a giant gold eagle, hideous. Aesthetically it didn't fit with the rest of the place, and so it just kind of popped up from the machine and glared at you. But the part Henry liked the most was the sound of the milk being frothed and steamed. It sounded like the gold eagle was squawking in rage, and then being slowly drowned. You just knew it when you heard it.

"SOY MILK. SOYY MILLKK. Understand? Comprende?" The woman at the counter was getting increasingly aggressive and condescending to the girl behind the counter.

"Sorry about that..." she offered weakly.

"Really. I find that hard to believe. You know why? Basic English. Isn't it weird how the word 'milk' is just one word, but 'soy milk' is two? How is it that a person with even the most basic grasp of the language could miss the fact that what I asked for in my latte involved two words and not one? Do I look like I drink something that comes from a cow?" As if to demonstrate, the woman stood back and waved her hand across her body like a gameshow hostess. "Is this what businesses can expect from employees who only deserve minimum wage? Are you going to pick up your sad little tip jar after work and count all your shiny quarters? Why. Is. This. So.

Difficult?" The girl behind the counter was steeling herself against it, gripping it tight and tensing her shoulders.

Henry felt sick. There was no way somebody should be able to get away with this. He wanted to step in. His stomach was tight, his throat had dried, and both of his hands gripped to fists. His lips dried as well, pressed tight together either to brace him for moving in or to stop him from saying something too far over the line. And he knew he should say something, do something. But he just sat. He just sat.

"Here's what we're going to do," the woman continued. "You're going to make me another one, and you're going to give it to me for free. And while you're doing that, I'm going to call your manager on the phone and explain the kind of shit service people can expect from this place. From you." But just then she looked at her watch. "Oh, for fuck sakes! Look what you did. Now I'm going to be late for my goddamned book club!" Picking up the original offending drink, she tipped it straight into the garbage and then let the empty paper cup skitter across the smooth copper counter. Without saying another word, she picked up her scarf and bag and plowed out through the door.

The girl behind the counter bowed her head now, fighting back tears. Henry felt...guilty. He should have stepped in, or spoken sharply from across the room, or stood up for her somehow. But now, the moment was over.

Henry didn't know what else he could do, so he picked up his things and went over to give her an extra tip with whatever was in his pocket. It was a few shiny quarters. He smiled weakly, impotently, and then he left.

Trudging along the sidewalk towards nowhere in particular, maybe the market, maybe the mall, Henry tried to brush off what had happened, as well as what hadn't happened. He felt shaken, nervous, jacked-up, even though nothing had happened to him. But the thought of what he could have done kept replaying in his head. Not the guilty part about what he didn't do but should have, but a looping movie about what it would have been like to step in and speak sharp words and do the right thing.

Henry realized he was walking more quickly than he needed to, so he consciously slowed his pace and his breathing with it. Where was he going again?

He thought a bit more about his conversation with Cheryl, about her plans, and about how it was about doing more than whatever they were doing now. It was something bigger, and interesting, and it had a kind of moral quality to it, he guessed. Or that it was something that could be believed in? And maybe that part makes the choice seem somehow less...arbitrary? Animal care. Yeah, that's something he could do. Or maybe something like it. Something.

In the final week of November, the city bent, twisted and convulsed with the extending and retracting claws of winter. The first snow had fallen, then melted almost completely away, but there was no turning back. What were left were the occasional respites from the bite, the days when Henry and Dave could walk down by the sunken, muddied (but flowing) canal, clomping around feeling invigorated rather than oppressed. Quietly though, those days became fewer, and by the time December took its first steps, that same flowing canal had been slowed by a thin, icy crust.

Part Three
December 1997

CHAPTER 8:
A stranger, again

Pulling the door closed behind her, Dirty stepped out into the street and was not even close to being dressed warm enough. But as she made her way across Queen Street and then north on Roncesvalles, she was more focused on the three things she shouldn't have had, but did. The first was Pickles the rat. And though he had hidden in her jacket many times before, this time she had put him there on purpose. The second was the wooden weed box that had been sitting on Alan's table. She hadn't really wanted to take it, but she knew she could use the fifty or sixty bucks that was usually inside to get a head start. The third thing she shouldn't have had was the pulsating, bleeding gash on the top of her head where the ashtray had hit her.

November had been bad. None of her job prospects had come through. Dirty hadn't made any friends apart from the gruesome lot that trundled through with Alan on any given day. Martin had been by a couple of times, which had been nice, but Dirty thought he had started to lose his shimmer. And Alan, well, had somehow gotten worse. The yelling started on an almost nightly basis–this guy had pissed him off, that guy had ripped him off–and there was the shoving, too. Through most of the month he hadn't actually hit her, but if you had asked Dirty, it didn't really matter.

Pulling the straps on her pack tighter, she reached into her jacket to make sure Pickles wasn't being crushed. The upside to the chilly weather was that it had helped to stop the bleeding. She felt a mess, and once again she found herself on the move, without any idea where she was going.

She had been walking for forty minutes already but for the last five or so the wind had become punishing. There was an almost spray to the air, wet but not quite rain, but when it hit your face it *hurt*. Dirty pushed on for a few minutes more, the mini-storm daring her to keep up with it. And then she finally felt like she could stop, like he wasn't coming after her, like she was far enough away. For now.

Pulling her body into a coffee shop on a corner she half-fell into a chair, well back from the window. She ordered coffee and closed her eyes, her hand lightly brushing the cut on her forehead.

"Fuckin' bitch!" Alan had screamed, yanking Dirty out of a dead sleep. "Get off my fucking couch!" Dirty scrambled to move just as he kicked over the coffee table. It seemed that, as Dirty had slowly pieced together, someone had managed to leave a couple of bags of pills that were being brought to Alan on a bench in the bar up the street. Too intimidated to make up an excuse, whoever it was had ran back to his own apartment and called Alan on his cell phone. Then he locked the door, no doubt. Dirty threw some questions at Alan, to distract him from throwing things back, but he was starting to spiral.

"I'll kill him! He's gonna pay, hard!" Dirty wasn't sure what 'paying hard' looked like, because that's just a stupid sounding construction, but she decided not to egg him on. He picked up the garbage can and threw it. Then he threw a chair.

Scooping her things quickly into her bag, Dirty wasn't planning on leaving, but simply trying to be as inconspicuous as possible. Blow-outs like this had happened a couple of times, and each time Dirty squished herself into a corner of the room until it blew over. This time though, as she turned to step next to the 'book' case (which, of course, was full of porn), Alan let fly with the little glass ashtray, the pointy one.

She would never be sure if he was aiming at her directly, but it worked out that way, and the pain was instant. She had hit the floor with a thud, and could have sworn she saw, just for an instant, a flicker of hesitation (regret? shock?) on his face. But then his phone rang again, and whether he needed to or he was using it as an excuse, he was gone.

Dirty touched her forehead once more now, feeling the ridges where the scab would form but was now just made of dry(ing) blood. The pretty woman behind the counter had brought her coffee, and Dirty leaned forward to let the steam tickle her nose. Slowly undoing her jacket, she felt the rat-sized bulge in her pocket, making sure he was there. Then she wrapped her hands around the mug, the blood in her fingers reaching for warmth.

Thinking about the moments just after Alan left the apartment, she sort of remembered moving her pack over to the couch, the bag barfing her clothes out of the top. She pushed them down and then stopped, eyeing the box on the table. 'You have to go now,' her brain pushed, and she knew she would need money if she was going to get far enough. So, she grabbed it and forced it down into the bag. Whatever Alan had left in there would probably get her a few warm meals, anyway.

Dirty's head was tilted forward drowsily, and the warm air of the café had defrosted her skin, which caused a fresh rivulet of blood to creep down her face. Dirty hadn't been the first to notice though, as the coffee lady suddenly reappeared, kneeling quietly beside her.

"You got dinged," she cooed, placing a damp towel on Dirty's forehead. It was gentle and pleasing, and made Dirty want to cry.

September. It had been September when she had gotten back to town—she had arrived at Danielle's apartment, the way they had held each other then. And that same night, falling asleep in each other's arms, exhausted from the joy of seeing one another. And the week after, when Danielle had shaved (most of) Dirty's head in the bathroom—the way Danielle's hand had cradled the back of her skull. Danielle had been the last person to hold her, and it had been September.

Her head swimming, fighting back tears of exhaustion, Dirty moved her hand to steady herself. She half-tipped the mug, the dark liquid snaking its way across the table and onto Dirty's leg.

"Marina," the woman said as she moved to stop the spill, although Dirty was hardly paying attention.

Leaning forward and looking into Dirty's face, she tried again.

"My name's Marina. What's yours?" Smiling weakly, Dirty told her. Surprisingly, Dirty's name didn't seem to faze Marina.

"That's Ruben," she said, motioning to the young man watching intently from behind the counter. Breathing deeply (for the first time in what seemed like hours), Dirty straightened her back and tried to take in her surroundings.

"Sorry," Dirty began. "I've just had a really tough day."

"Damn," Marina said, smiling, "and it's only 10:30."

"Mar..." Ruben called. As she walked over to him, Dirty rubbed the spot on her head where the cloth had left its baptismal coolness.

Marina swept back to Dirty's side, holding out her empty hand. "C'mon," she coaxed. "Ruben's apartment is upstairs. I'll let you in and you can crash for awhile." Blinking her disbelief, Dirty had to be helped to her feet before she realized what was required of her. Slinging her pack on, she traced Marina's steps out the back door and up the cold-stung metal fire-escape, leading to the second floor.

"You really don't have to..."

"But my friend, all strangers and castaways come in the name of Zeus!" Marina said with a comedic flourish.

Inside, damp heat burbled and hissed from the old steam radiators, filling the tiny bachelor space with a stifling tropical moisture. Her tongue hanging out in mockery of the overpowering warmth, Marina led Dirty to the couch, Dirty's legs giving out just before she touched down, landing her with a satisfying frumpf.

"I have a friend...," Dirty said, motioning to her pocket as fatigue cradled her mind and body. She took Pickles in her hand, not sure what to do. Looking up, she saw Marina frowning–not in displeasure, but to show her mind in problem-solving mode. Suddenly, her clouded brow broke over her easy blue eyes, a light of satisfaction in her face. "Ruben had a bird–died last month. We've still got the cage, though." Before Dirty could react, Marina had scooped up Pickles and was chauffeuring him to the hanging birdcage in the bathroom. By the time she returned, Dirty was half-sitting, half-lying on the couch (which was also the bed, had they the energy to pull it out), the warm hands of sleep leading her to unconsciousness. By the time Marina let herself out, Dirty's breathing was already deep and slow.

***

Twelve years old. The age Dirty had been when she had gone to live with her grandmother. It was seven in the evening, and Dirty was sitting on the floor of Ruben's apartment, telling the story and smoking deeply.

Dirty's father had died when she was five, leaving a good amount of money for Dirty, as well as for her mother to start a business. Financial advice, or some damn thing, Dirty recalled. But somehow, slowly, her stepfather Josef had crept in like fog or treachery. Even the money that was rightfully hers had found its way into the books of the business, and under his fingers she would never see it again.

"You sneaky piece of shit. I know what you did and I'm going to make you pay. In pain. Do you really think you can disrespect me like that and get away with it?" Josef was leaning down, whispering to a 10-year-old Dirty.

Dirty looked down at her shoes, looked away scared, but in her mind, she was thinking "you can hit me, but you're still a piece of human garbage. And nothing is going to change that." She was just careful not to say it. Dirty's mother walked in the room then, and Dirty and Josef both straightened up, acting like nothing was going on.

Josef hadn't married Dirty's mother yet, but he sure as hell was making himself comfortable. He...he...*ruled*, y'know? Every time he was in the house it felt like everyone was just waiting. Waiting to be told. Waiting to be moved. Waiting to be given shit about something.

"He never actually laid a hand on me, but..." Ruben and

Marina both held their breath, not wanting an interruption to spoil the possibility that Dirty would finish her sentence and the story. "The constant threats and demeaning words and the...the grinding me down, y'know? It just got too much...." She trailed off.

"Of course it did!" Marina exclaimed finally. "You were fucking 10 years old!" Dirty nodded sagely.

"Yeah...two more years of that before I came to live with my grandmother in Toronto. And I've never been back. Even after my mother died. He phoned me to say that if I even set foot in that city, he would..."

"You mean, after the funeral?" Ruben asked gently.

"No, I mean *for* the funeral." Dirty said flatly. Marina and Ruben stared, ajaw.

"He stopped you from going...to your own mother's funeral." Marina was squinting, trying to imagine it.

"So." Dirty said with harrumphed finality. "That's why I can't go back."

Starting to feel overwhelmed by the attention, Dirty tried to change the subject. "So...," she veered, "what about you two?"

***

Curled in the sleeping bag they had lent her, Dirty carefully listened to the 4 AM city. Lying on the floor, she could hear the hushed drone of the cars through the window pane, mixed with the gentle-timed breathing of Ruben and Marina lying in the bed. Safe, for now. But it never does last, does it?

CHAPTER 9
Clever

Morning fluttered into the apartment like the second reel of a film. Dirty awoke to the soundtrack of the thick steam heat and the backdrop of the clumsy white gobs of snow falling outside the window.

The snow wasn't staying, though; the temperature had risen during the night, and the chubby snow-tears were dissolving in black wetness as soon as they hit the road. Standing at the window, she looked down on the bobbing umbrellas.

Ruben and Marina had already left by the time Dirty was out of the shower, so she stood in the middle of the apartment lighting a cigarette and semi-naked, deciding what to do next.

Forty-five minutes later she was standing in the cold, but Dirty was sweating. She hadn't meant to take as much as she had, of course, but it wasn't like she could go back, either. Waiting for the streetcar, she scanned the street both to see what was around, and from a good bit of paranoia. Polish bakeries, Polish delis, Polish coffee shops, a Vietnamese vegetable and convenience store, Polish travel and video, and Alan running towards her.

Except it wasn't Alan, unless he had become a woman in her mid-forties in an expensive jogging suit. Dirty shook her head clear, moving her thumb over the two-dollar coin in her pocket, trying to calm down. Fifty or sixty bucks, that's all he ever had in there. How was she supposed to know there was way more in there than usual?

Breathing deeply, she touched the bulging plastic baggie that was now in her pocket. She couldn't risk going back there, to return it that is. Even if her intentions were honest, Alan would still rip her to pieces. And besides, having this much created a few more options for her. Turning her eyes back to the road, Dirty realized the streetcar was already waiting for her to board.

"Hi there, how are ya? Bit of a chill out, eh?" Dirty was greeted by a verbal barrage from the driver. "Sure, step on up there ya go only a toonie wherever ya wanna go thanks! Hey, need a transfer? Gotta have one of those my name's Mike by the way" and on and on. Amused, Dirty decided to sit at the front.

"He's like this every day," a woman next to Dirty whispered, reading her smile. "He's hyper or something. Give him a chance, he'll tell you all about it." The woman rolled her eyes. Continuing his monologue, Mike alternated between talking directly to Dirty and announcing the stops over the much-too-loud intercom.

"So, where ya from I like your hair it's pretty cool NEXT STOP WESTMINSTER WWWESTMMINSTERRR IS THE NEXT STOP so anyway I really like this time of year don't you..."

"Oh yeah," Dirty said enthusiastically, though her second syllable was lost in his verbal snowstorm.

"ANYONE FOR BAKED GOODS? THERE GOES A

GREAT BAKERY... I grew up in Toronto eh? Lived here all my life love drivin' this streetcar though they bounce me around to various routes all the time but that lets me see most of the city NEXT STOP DUNDAS WEST SPLIT COFFEE TIME LOBLAWS GAS STATION SMALL BARKING DOG," Dirty was mildly concerned that at some point Mike would get confused and continue his conversation with her while speaking into the intercom, but he seemed to be in perfect control.

"What's your name, anyway?" There was a pause that caught Dirty off guard.

"Uh--Dirty." The woman next to her seemed alarmed.

"Cool!" Mike was off again. "COMING UP DUNDAS WEST STATION HOP ON THE SUBWAY AND HEAD ANYWHERE YOU'D LIKE TO GO got your transfer, Dirty?"

"Sure do."

"Good lass HERE WE ARE FOLKS! WATCH YOUR STEP! KEEP WARM! HOLD HANDS!" Hopping off the streetcar, Dirty smiled brightly and returned Mike's vigorous wave.

"Bye Dirty! Be good!"

"Thanks Mike!" Grinning all the way down the stairs onto the platform, Dirty eased into the subway train and picked a seat in the corner, where she had the widest possible view of the crowd. Riding further into the city, she wondered what a guy like Mike did on his off-time. Ritalin, most likely.

The train started to glide on its way and Dirty sat, rigid and cautious. At each stop more people were getting on than off, the space inside thickening with bodies. The glut of standing passengers now made it impossible for her to see everyone around her. She felt tiny, having to look up just to see the faces immediately around her. Her stomach clenched to a fist as she stood up, not sure where she should be but needing to be somewhere else.

NEXT STOP BATHURST ST. BAATHHHURRSSTT.

The announcement came over the intercom in a barely-audible crackle. It was like listening to someone talking to you through the box at a fast-food drive-thru. While you were standing on the other side of the parking lot. In an electrical storm.

Squeezing through the now tightly-packed crowd, Dirty popped out onto the platform and made her way to street level. As she moved towards the stairs, three young men were walking towards her. The one closest to her wasn't even paying attention, but the other two were staring. Holding her breath as they passed, she stepped up the stairs and through the turnstiles, out the automatic doors and into the cold.

Walking along Bloor street she watched as the midday shoppers zipped across the road, zooming in and out of the big bargain store on the corner. Like them, today she had direction too: She had kept Rachel's number safe all this time, and what she had found this morning gave her the opportunity to ask. She couldn't quite remember where Rachel had said she lived, but being downtown was as good a place to start as any.

"Hi, we're not home right now, but if..." Dirty hung up before the message could finish. Right. People work during the day. Still standing in the booth, Dirty wondered how she was going to negotiate this little hurdle. That, and she really needed a cigarette.

The clatter of the payphone plexi doors in her wake, she strolled a little further down the street, fists pushed down into her pockets. As she crossed Spadina, the smell of the pizza joints reminded her that she hadn't eaten all day, and it was already 1:30.

The bag in the wooden box hadn't contained fifty or sixty dollars like she had expected. Instead, she had found a bundle of twenties, which she later totaled to six hundred and forty dollars. Which is not to say that Alan would have been gracious about it if it *had* only been fifty bucks—it wouldn't have mattered either way. Still, Dirty couldn't help feeling guilty—she hadn't meant for it to be like this.

Sweeping into a convenience store, Dirty bought a chocolate bar and a pack of Vantage 9's, which she felt was a pretty good start, nutritionally-speaking. It was December 15 and the sky was grey, the clouds loaded and ready. The bitter, wet, slush-rain had stopped earlier, but the air drooped around your body, bloated and cold and seeping.

How cheery. A grey Christmas. A big, grey, lonely, shitty, hungry Christmas. Why break with tradition, right? Tossing the candy wrapper in a can, Dirty slid the foil out of the pack and fingered the line of fresh cigarettes. Sliding one up and into her hand, she let it hang off of her moistened lips as she snap-lit a match with her thumb and forefinger. Breathing deeply, she struck out again along the street, heading further downtown.

***

Dirty had finally been able to contact Rachel at about 4:00 PM. It had taken Rachel a moment to make sense of the voice on the phone—not because she didn't recognize the name, but because she wasn't sure of the noun.

"Hi, um, it's Dirty."

"What is?" Confusion on both ends induced a lengthy pause. "Oh!" Rachel finally exclaimed. The two spun off into excited chatter, as if they had done so at least a few times before. It was a familiarity that confused Dirty, but she was grateful for the friendly tone. Soon though, Rachel could sense a shaking in Dirty's voice–as it happened, she wasn't upset, but she was getting cold.

"So, where are you staying?" Rachel had asked.

"Yeah, oh, some people I met recently..." Dirty said tentatively. "It's temporary," she continued, "but okay. Anyway, I was wondering if you have space, I mean, I can pay..." she felt clumsy and stupid.

"Actually," Rachel said, "Scooter and I have a spare room in our basement, and we've been looking for a renter." Rachel and Scooter did in fact have a spare room in the basement, that part wasn't a lie. But having a renter hadn't been a topic that they had discussed with each other. Dirty took a polite moment to 'think' about it, and as the conversation finished, they agreed that she would come to see the place the following evening.

***

Later that evening, back on the floor of the apartment, Dirty and Marina were smoking and talking as Ruben curled another rolling paper closed. Dirty was telling them about her voyage into the city and her conversation with Rachel.

"I connected with her because she used to know my friend Danielle," Dirty explained. The name was out of her face before she realized that she would be opening a wound.

"Who's Danielle?" Marina asked innocently.

Right. "A friend..." Dirty began. "She...we...She died last month. Or 6 weeks ago. About that, anyway." Plonk. Both Ruben and Marina straightened.

"Oh love..." Marina cooed. "You two were close..."

"Like you wouldn't believe." Dirty's smile wavered then brightened with her remembering. "Yeah, we got into all sorts of mischief. We met in high school. One time we were downtown and, oh! you should know that neither of us ever had a lot of money, so sometimes we had to get creative...So this one time we were downtown, and Danielle was particularly broke that day. She was really down about it—embarrassed, you know? Especially because her parents didn't have a lot, either." A radiating glow of recollection poured off of Dirty now.

"So, there we are, wandering around near Tipman park, when I get this idea: We go over to that area where those old guys are always playing chess. At least they used to. Hell, maybe they still do." Marina and Ruben shrugged. They didn't seem to know either.

"I had thirty bucks in my pocket. So, we go over and watch a few of the games. And the whole time I'm watching this one guy, maybe in his forties. And I'm making sure to get some long eye contact with him. But Danielle has no idea what's going on, right?" Dirty noticed that Marina's face was screwed up in puzzlement, not sure what was going on either. Dirty gives her a 'wait for it' hand motion.

"So, I've never played chess before, but I kinda know the rules, right? So, I sit down at a board, but not the board of the guy I've been making eyes with. The board *next* to his. And I say to this other guy, I've got twenty bucks, but I don't really know what I'm doing, so what kind of odds will you give me? And he says to me he'll give me 3 to 1 odds of playing him to a draw *and* he'll take two of his pieces off to start.

"So, I make the first move like I've seen people do before, and pretty soon after..." and here Dirty paused, still pleased that her plan had worked out so well. "I notice that the guy I had been making eyes with at the next board has arranged his pieces just like mine! He's got his head down in a book, pretending like nothing is going on, but he's showing me what to do with each move! It was awesome!" Marina's jaw looked unhinged and Ruben's face was gloriously bright and amazed, in a way that made Dirty feel weirdly warm inside.

"So, I ended up playing to a draw, and we walked away with a wad of cash. I had to explain to Danielle what had happened, cuz she couldn't figure it out. But it was good..." Dirty smiled, satisfied with the memory, and in that tiny moment she forgot that there was only one of them left now. But then it came back.

"There was another time in high school—Danielle and I were hanging out in the arts hall bathroom when this girl comes in..." Dirty trailed off and squinted, searching for a name. "Florida. Florida Merl."

"What an awful name." Marina said.

"Seriously," Dirty agreed. She began again. "So, this girl comes in sobbing and crying and carrying on. We don't really know her, but all of a sudden, she starts talking to us. About all this stuff. Guys teasing the shit out of her, flicking her braids in class, stuffing things in her locker, yelling at her in the halls. A lot of regular high school stuff, but some of it sounded like it was getting worse and worse, you know?"

"So, I'm like, 'I'll tell you what we're going to do: I have this tiny spray that I got from someone, and it's called Clear The Room. It's for practical jokes and stuff, and it smells absolutely rancid. We're gonna put a little on a cotton ball or something and every time we see one of those bastards in the hall, we're gonna sneak up behind and give em a little touch. Just a little. Just enough. It has to be subtle enough to make someone paranoid, and not too strong that it becomes obvious. The key is to make them so freaked out and self-conscious about how they smell that they won't have time to even think about you. Then they'll know what it's like.'"

"But you know," Dirty continued to Ruben and Marina, "she just wouldn't stop crying. She wouldn't stop. Here I am, giving her a solution for god's sake, so what the fuck is the problem?"

"So, then Danielle goes over to her and starts saying stuff to Florida, but I can't really make it out. But pretty soon the kid is crying less, and nodding at her, almost totally chilled out. It was kind of annoying, you know?"

"Because they weren't taking your idea seriously?" Marina asked.

"Yeah! The solution was right there!"

"Dirty." Marina was looking at her in an almost disappointed way. "She didn't want you to solve her problem. She wanted to know that someone could hear what she was going through. And it sounds like that's what Danielle was doing, no?"

Dirty harrumphed. Then she sat quietly for a moment. *How could I have not seen that before Danielle did? I should have gotten there before her.*

"Okay!" Ruben said encouragingly, trying to find something lighter. "Personal secrets game! Marina already knows this, but you don't." Ruben leaned in to Dirty, conspiratorially. "I only have one...kidney." He raised his eyebrow as Dirty gave him a quizzical 'rrreally?' look. "Yep," Ruben said, leaning back in his chair and rubbing his stomach in dramatic fashion. "Was born that way." Dirty nodded and pursed her lips in an *I'm impressed* way.

One thing to know about Ruben is that he grew up in Toronto, living there his whole life, with no real inclination to go anywhere else. His mum lives in the north end of the city, and he sees her every so often. When Ruben was 15 his dad died of liver disease. Probably.

Now, when someone is getting medical care, of course they are supposed to get the same care as everybody else. No favorites. But the fact was that when Ruben's father was alive, he was a total goddamn prick. Less so with his family, but more so with the doctors, and unequivocally with the nurses. Especially that one with that meaty brown mole on her lip.

Anyways, Ruben always imagined that he would end up doing something interesting, but until he figured out what that was, he was happy to pour coffee and play darts with his friends on Thursday nights and skateboard everywhere until the snow made it impossible.

"Right. Marina's turn!" Dirty said cheerily.

"Okayyy." Marina said pleasantly, placing her clasped hands delicately in her lap. "I have slept with more than 46 people in my life."

Dirty cocked her head to the side, a seemingly important question forming on her lips. But there was silence.

In another moment Marina started to worry that maybe she had said too much, that maybe she had freaked Dirty out or offended her or something.

"So, like, 47?" Dirty asked.

"...sorry?" Marina said, confused.

"More than 46 people. That would be, like, 47?"

"Well, yeah, I guess..."

"No, it's good. I don't mean anything by it. It's just when people give a more than or less than thing, it's usually around a round number. Like 'more than 100'. Could be 103, could be 112, you don't know."

"Mm." Ruben chirped in. "46 does seem pretty specific..."

"Well...I dunno, I just..." Marina wasn't sure what to say. "Maybe I stopped counting after 46, and maybe it's a lot more, but I'm not sure..."

"Did you stop counting?" Ruben asked.

"Well no, but I could have. And then maybe I might say something like 'more than 46'."

"Absolutely," Dirty said. Then there was quiet.

CHAPTER 10
Goofy proportions

"So, tell me again–who's going to be living in our basement?" Scooter was sitting on the edge of the couch across from Rachel with his hands pressed together under his chin, as if he were praying to understand what the hell she was talking about.

"She's a friend–sort of, well–yes–more of a friend of a friend, and..." Rachel's resolve was starting to dissipate; she had wanted to hit him with a "this is how it is" ultimatum, but he was always so damn calm that she couldn't get him to polarize (about anything, actually). Now that she was losing momentum, she knew she had better try something more subtle.

"Please!!" she pleaded.

"Honey..." Scooter said evenly, "I didn't say I was necessarily opposed to it... and we could use the money..." Rachel's lips tightened slightly when he said this, but she stayed silent hoping he would talk himself into it. Finally, after a long pause he said, "but I still want to know more about this person who's going to be sharing our home." That of course was a bit of a sticking point, since Rachel knew so little about Dirty to begin with. But she began with Danielle, who he knew about–and remembered more than she thought he had.

"Two years ago," he ventured, "you told me how you had been feeling when Danielle had started..." he paused for the right words,"–when she changed. Got sick. Whatever. Remember?"

Fuck. Rachel thought. Somehow, even after all this time she felt guilty for pulling away from Danielle. Avoiding her, really. When Danielle had started acting (being) different, she just...if she had to admit it, in a quiet secret place where no one could hear it, she just didn't have time for it.

But not Dirty, Rachel thought. She imagined Dirty was the kind of person who would stick by her friends no matter what. Now *she* needed help, and Rachel could be there.

***

It was December 23rd, and Dirty had been at Rachel's for a week. They settled in well, she and Pickles, together in the basement which was actually quite comfortable. She was starting to warm up to Scooter as well—not that he was off-putting exactly, but he sure was big. She did not, however, feel completely comfortable being in their home at Christmas–she just figured that most couples, given their preference, would do some cozy naked things, with eggnog and shit.

As it turned out, they had plans to go to Scooter's parents' house on the 24th and wouldn't be back until late on the 25th. Rachel had expressed some concern about Dirty being alone on Christmas Eve, but Dirty had told her that in fact, she was going to visit her own mother out in the west end. It was the best she could come up with, anyway.

Sitting on her futon/couch in the basement, she and Pickles

stared off into nowhere, being generally thankful that they were warm. It was snowing again, not that Dirty could tell, though. It had already drifted high enough to cover the little half-windows that were meant to offer at least a pretense of natural light. But sitting in the warm dark, the cloak was comforting, insulating, safe. The crash that came from over her head shook the entire house, pushing Dirty out of her seat as Pickles flew across the room to hide in her shoe.

Rushing up the stairs and into the kitchen, she found Rachel looking ready to fight and Scooter sitting on his ass. Dirty stared wide-eyed, but she didn't have to ask before Rachel read her expression of confusion and shock.

"It's okay, honey, it's okay," she said quickly, realizing how the situation looked. "We were just wrestling."

"Yeah," grunted Scooter from the floor.

"Again," chided Rachel. They narrowed their eyes at one another and then, as if on cue, turned towards Dirty.

"I think you need more snow in your life," cooed Rachel as she zoomed past Dirty to the patio door. Distracted by her movement, Dirty didn't register Scooter move towards her, and she suddenly found herself scooped into his arms like a child.

"Bastards!" she yelled as the three combatants wangled themselves into the yard, ending in a pile in a snow drift with Scooter and Rachel packing tufts of snow on Dirty's head and down her shirt. In the moment, Dirty was terrified, being grabbed like that. It took her brain some time to register that they were *playing*.

An hour later the three sat in the living room, still shivering over mugs of hot chocolate and Bailey's, leaving Dirty to wonder if this was the sort of thing that families did.

Even later, still in the living room, they talked about

families for real. Dirty knew that Rachel and Scooter were going to see Scooter's parents over Christmas, but she wasn't sure about the situation with Rachel's family.

"Marjorie is my mom," Rachel said, putting a little feigned haughtiness on the pronunciation of 'Marjorie'. It seemed to make Scooter shift uncomfortably. "She'll be holidaying in the Bahamas this year. Dad left her 6 or 7 years ago. She can be a piece of work sometimes, but she's still a good sort." Scooter pushed his face deeper into his drink.

Dirty ended up telling them the same story she had told Ruben and Marina, about Josef being a terrible human and how he was the reason she felt like she could never really go back to Ottawa. When she had told the story to Ruben and Marina, the part about her mother's funeral seemed to really set them off. Now, Dirty just omitted that part. Other peoples' emotions were exhausting sometimes. This time, though, she did include the bit about how she had cut herself badly when she was eleven, using a knife to cut through an ice cube because her step-father would only ever drink his scotch with exactly one-and-a-half ice cubes. Not more. Not less.

"You know," Rachel ventured, "I go and visit friends in Ottawa a fair bit. If you ever want to go with me...to have some backup..."

The thought of going back while he was still there gave Dirty a burning coil of revulsion in her stomach. She casually placed a hand over her mouth, as if thinking, but it was really to hide the angry sneer she thought she might let slip if she thought about it any longer.

"Thank you. I--I'm not sure." And Rachel let it drop.

***

Christmas came and went in the house, and Dirty managed as best she could. The 24th and 25th ended up serving a therapeutic purpose, the quiet of the house making her feel like she could claim the space for her own. Having the animals to take care of, the cat and the rat, seemed to help too, and by the time Scooter and Rachel returned, she was started to feel like her old self again. Whatever that was.

"Plans for New Year's, D?" Rachel asked. It was noon on the 26th and the three of them were lolling in the kitchen, reeling from yet another of Scooter's massive brunch fry-ups. Holding the cup to her nose, Dirty was momentarily lost in the hot swirling breath of her coffee. It made her want a cigarette. Bad.

"Oh yeah, I'm heading over the Ruben and Marina's. They're taking me to a house party... somewhere." As Scooter rose to clear the dishes, Rachel nodded at Dirty and pressed two fingers to her lips. They rose silently and slipped out the patio door, Rachel sliding her pack out of the breast pocket of her flannel shirt.

Rachel smoked. Dirty smoked. Scooter did not smoke. That had been his one rule when they moved in together: He didn't mind her smoking, just not in the house. The closest she had gotten to that was Scooter allowing that god-awful over-sized ashtray to remain in the living room (Cuba Libre! it said inside). She couldn't use it, but she liked its goofy proportions.

And while Scooter didn't smoke, he did have that porn thing that nobody knew about. He tried to keep it in check, and kept only a couple of magazines in the car under the seat (rather than in the house). And videos. He kept those in the car, but would sneak one in the house to watch when no one else was home. Sure, a lot of people might think of that particular kind of kink as weird, but he liked the goofy proportions.

At the base of the patio door now, as was becoming custom, sat Seeger-the-Death-Cat, staring patiently at the two women outside. His right paw was placed gently on the glass.

"I think he wants a butt," mused Dirty.

"Mmm, no I think he just wants to come out so he can kill another bird," Rachel said.

"How can something so sweet be so vicious?" Dirty said, shaking her head. The two stood in the cold, staring at the little fur-demon through the glass, both of them now too frozen to think of anything important to say.

∗∗∗

By the 31st, the city was wading in white, and the TTC had had to shut down for a day already. It was up and running again now, and as Dirty pulled her boots on, she knew she had to hurry to catch the next bus. She had finally cut off her last, longish bit of hair in the front (or rather, had asked Rachel to cut it off for her), leaving an inch and a half of chocolate fuzz which she carefully slicked and gelled into little spikes. Scooter and Rachel had already left for their party across town, and Dirty was set to meet Ruben and Marina at Spadina station in 30 minutes. Pulling her flannel jacket around her, she made a quick check of the place to make sure it was locked up. She was ready to have a good time. It was New Years, after all.

"Fuck!" she thought, realizing she had almost forgotten her wallet. Racing down the stairs, she nearly tripped over Pickles, who was picking at the carpet fibers.

"Okay baby, gotta go," she said, leaning close and rubbing his nose. "Be good, k?" And as she swept upstairs, breaking into a dash for the front door, she left the basement door slightly ajar. Streaking down the steps after locking the door, she moved out into the city, leaving Pickles alone in the house. With Seeger.

When Dirty got to the station, she couldn't see them anywhere. Dirty stood for awhile at a bench, then the convenience kiosk, then by the stairs. Nothing. A few minutes later, she spied a young man looking at her, half-smiling. Dirty pulled her jacket tighter and walked the other way, to the other set of stairs. He followed her.

Dirty wound her way back to the kiosk and bought a chocolate bar, hoping the guy would just keep walking and carry on to wherever he had to go. But instead he walked up and stood beside her, his head tilted slightly toward her, glancing sideways from under his baseball cap.

"Hey Dirty, wassup?" Dirty froze, not knowing what to do. The guy started giggling.

"Do I know you?" she said forcefully, hoping to scare him off.

"Maybe…" he said coyly. Then he pulled off his hat and undid his absolutely beautiful hair.

"Marina?!" Dirty squealed. "What the fuck are you—what the fuck? Why—you look—you look amazing!" Marina was laughing harder now.

"Your face. Oh my god if you could have seen your face!" The two hugged, and then Dirty stood back to get another look.

"What is going on?"

"Ruben and I like to do costumes for parties, even when it isn't a costume party. It makes it easier to get in and out of situations if you give yourself permission to act out of character. Ruben is meeting us there—he was too chicken to dress up before we left, so he's getting dolled up there."

"But I don't…"

"You don't have to worry about anything, luv." Marina said, patting her backpack. "I've got everything we need in here. Come on. We got work to do!" Arm in arm they walked back to the platform, laughing the whole way.

Part Four
January 1998

CHAPTER 11:
The 'seduction' of Andre

The spiny fingers of the night before needled Henry's brain as he struggled out of his bed, only to fall back down again, feeling gross and heavy and light-headed. Placing an achy hand over achy eyes to block out the light, all he could manage was a truncated, half-hearted salutation to the next 52 weeks.

"Hap-y-fuck-New-Yerrr," the final syllable accented by a sloppy belch that made him sound like he had a mouthful of oatmeal. As he lay there, Henry probed his memory, trying to piece together what the hell had happened. Cheryl's party. Dina's tequila. Marie-France's wine. My weed. Andre's... Oh god. Bolting upright, panic split the clouds of his hangover like a Grecian thunderbolt. Grabbing the receiver, he dialed Cheryl's number as quickly as his shaking hand would allow. Oh god.

Pickuppickuppickuppickuppickup, he prayed.

"Muh?" Cheryl answered, reaching across the body lying beside her to grab the phone.

"Cheryl? It's Henry," his voice shaking.

"Oh, hi hon, I–oh. Oh. Oh Henry. Oh..."

"No, no. don't say 'Oh Henry.'" He was lying on his back again with his hand over his eyes.

"Oh baby," she continued, a genuine note of embarrassment in her voice.

"What. did. I. do," he breathed. There was a pause as Cheryl tried to break it gently.

"Well," she began, "I think Andre's girlfriend Melissa wants to talk to you. Mmm, correction: I don't think Melissa wants to talk to you ever again."

"Ohgodohgodohgod. She hates me."

"Well baby," she continued, "you blew her boyfriend. At a party. In my bathroom. I'm sorry to say, but she probably hates you." Henry squeezed his hand over his forehead–the hangover had been much easier to deal with than this.

"Now isn't the time for me to yell at you, is it?" Cheryl asked.

"No, but you'd be perfectly entitled to anyway," he sighed.

"Mmm, maybe later. But you've got some work to do. Today is Saturday. We're in the office on Monday. That's you, me *and* Andre. And things are going to be pretty sticky if you don't talk to him before then, if you'll pardon the pun."

"Maybe it'll be a snow day on Monday," he suggested feebly.

"Henry..."

He sighed. "You're right, you're right. Should I call him today?"

"I would suggest tomorrow. Andre's probably got some other things going on today." Considering it, Henry shuddered.

Hanging up the phone, Henry returned to his self-consolation, this time sitting on the edge of the bed. Looking up he saw Dave the Smartest Dog in the World with head on paws, staring accusingly.

"Oh, go lick your balls!" Henry spat.

***

Henry spent the rest of Saturday nursing his hangover and trying to allay the creeping paranoia about just how many people at the party knew what had happened. He had Tylenol for the headache, and orange juice for the dehydration, and a long hot shower for the overall scungey feeling. But there was nothing he could think of to get rid of the looping waves of nausea that came when he thought about making that phone call. Still, those few minutes in the bathroom last night had been pretty fantastic....

Quickly wiping the thought from the corner of his mind, Henry stared out the bay window, watching the soft, white, frozen foam that had been coming down since 5 AM. The street, the lawn, the parked cars, the trees were all covered in a hushing blanket, homogeneous and immobile, the entire streetscape held in silence.

On the other side of the city, Andre sat at his kitchen table, head lowered, as Melissa rummaged in the bedroom and packed the few things she had there.

Good thing you're not living together he could hear his older brother saying–or rather, what he would say if he ever found out, which he wouldn't, godammit. *But he's right*, Andre thought, *if she's leaving me, at least the cut will be quick.* But there were still too many things going on in Andre's head to count.

I can't believe the woman I love is leaving.

I can't believe she won't listen to me.

I can't believe I was...

Not unlike Henry, Andre was not a terribly big guy. But he had a weird, booming voice that didn't match the rest of him, and so it often made people take notice. But now he couldn't even muster a whinge, or any kind of sound to protest Melissa walking out of his life.

His head swirled while he stared into his coffee, and Andre had failed to notice Melissa standing near the door, eyeing him ruefully. Looking up, he found himself caught–no, pinned—under her gaze. Pain. Anger. Disbelief. Betrayal. Utter confusion.

Her eyes welling with tears, she shrugged at him once as if to say *what the hell has all this been to you*? And then she was gone. Stunned and staring into his coffee again, all Andre could mutter was

"Happy fuckin New Year."

Outside, Melissa clomped through the freshly fallen snow to her friend Loretta's waiting car. The crisp air against her face did nothing to cool her temper. She climbed inside and hurled her bag into the backseat with ferocity.

Slowly, the car crept along the unplowed street, making a careful plodding turn onto the unplowed boulevard, finally reaching an unsatisfying 35 km/h. So much for the rueful Hollywood peel-out. As if reading her thoughts, Loretta turned to her friend of eight years and said, "You want satisfying? You should have left him last summer."

***

Sunday came quickly for most, the day before lost in the vagueness of recovery. On the canal, some of the keener ones traced circles in the ice, depending on their skill or clarity of brain. Elsewhere, the heart of the city began to pump normally again, the pulse of the tourists circulating through the few open shops and cafes, plumes of white breath about their mouths.

"So..." Henry began. He had called Andre that morning, and through the curt, awkward exchange they had agreed to talk about...things. By 2:00 that afternoon, they were sitting across from each other in a bagel shop on Dalhousie street.

"So..." Andre agreed, not meeting Henry's eyes. Henry pummeled his brain for a way to crack the tension when Andre spoke again.

"Melissa left me. Yesterday." Still unable (or unwilling) to meet Henry's eyes, Andre fumbled to light a cigarette.

"When did you start smoking?!" Andre didn't answer. He had finally decided that he didn't have time for small talk bullshit.

"I am so sorry," Henry appealed, not knowing what else to say. The corners of Andre's mouth turned down, his brow creasing.

"Yes..." Andre breathed. Henry's back straightened. Sighing, Andre continued low and slow, "I hate you and you make me sick." Henry almost spilled his coffee. He hadn't exactly been expecting warmth and good cheer, but even still, this hurt.

"Look," Andre continued "I'm not stupid enough to believe that I had no role in what happened. But I feel like...." Here he looked down, not searching for the right words, but rather coming to terms with the ones that had come to mind. "I feel like you took advantage of me." Andre stopped; his whole face pinched down hard. "You...you knew I was off my head, and you followed me into the bathroom..." His head was shaking back and forth, somewhere between disbelief and 'no'. "And you just kept saying 'don't worry about it, it's cool, a mouth is just a mouth, a mouth is just a mouth'..." and here Andre took on a seething mimicry.

Henry's mouth was no longer a mouth. It was just a gaping,

silent hole as he began to understand what he had actually done. He pulled his hands back from the table and placed them impotently in his lap. God, his throat was dry. So dry he thought he might not even be able to breathe.

"I... I... just thought..."

Andre arched his hand and placed it squarely on the table. It looked like a spider.

"I didn't come here to hear why you think you did what you did, or what it was you thought you were doing. I don't really care. I came here to tell you that what you did was wrong, and that I see you for what you are." Andre paused. "If I didn't need this job—I mean, *really* need this job, I would pick up and never be in the same place as you ever again. But I do need it. And that just is what it is. So, stay out of my way. Don't talk to me. Don't play chummy co-worker with me. We may have to work together, but I assure you that I am not your friend." And here Andre paused once more, and then rose from his seat and left.

Lighting a cigarette, Henry sat frozen in his chair, staring out the large window overlooking the busy market street. His hand was shaking. *C'mon,* he thought. *It can't really be that serious. He's just... I wasn't trine...Jesus. And besides, they were both super drunk and stoned.* Henry's lips were pursed as he cast his eyes down to the over-bleached table cloth, pollocked with specks of ash and coffee cup rings. He sat and stared and looked at nothing at all for minutes. His cigarette was burning out. He went home.

CHAPTER 12:
Marie-France

That first week of January saw a wrinkled beginning slowly smooth out to an even rhythm; by the end of the third week things seemed pretty well back to routine. Routine, except that along with Cheryl and Henry, Marie-France had now joined the smoking circle. Sometimes Andre was there too, saying nothing. He just smoked and pretended to watch the traffic.

It was Friday and bitter cold, and the cigarette heat that tickled their lungs lasted only seconds before the cold crept back in. Dave wasn't even allowed out today. Henry had decided to keep him tucked inside.

"Marie-France, does this mean that you're officially a smoker?" Cheryl asked playfully. When standing side by side, it looked like the two women were cast not in approximately, but rather precisely the opposite mold. Where Cheryl was broad, Marie-France was tiny. Where Cheryl was loud, even ostentatious, Marie-France was the wallflower. A very bright woman (though in part due to her size she was often referred to as "girl"), Henry found her engaging, once you got her to relax. Marie-France smiled a smile that seemed sheepish (or possibly coy. One could never be quite sure).

She spoke with an accent, but there was something else, too. It wasn't a stutter but a breathy hesitation. The air that carried her voice was pinched off after every second or third word, giving her a halting sound. It was as if certain words were the wrong shape and were getting caught coming through her mouth. "It was the" would become "it was th--e", the final sound sometimes barely escaping with its life.

Most of the group huddled close together for warmth, like a herd against some unseen predator. Unseen, but one they could all feel. As the last cigarette went out, one of them made a quick grab for the door, with the others flooding in behind him. Walking down the hallway, each of them dropped silently from the line into their own offices; first Marie-France, then Dina two doors down. Before Cheryl could get to her own office, though, she felt Henry take her arm and guide her into his. Closing the door behind them, Henry looked at Cheryl guiltily.

"What...?" she asked, narrowing her eyes. Pursing his lips, Henry went over and sat at his desk, hands clasped in front of him neatly.

"He called," he said, just as neatly. Cheryl's chin pointed up just slightly.

"He called..." Henry began again, "and said he wanted to get together. Said he wanted to hang out, talk about things."

"You had sex with Debbie, didn't you!?" Cheryl cursed. Henry looked down like a boy caught in front of a window with some rocks, ready to get them off.

"Damnit Henry..." Cheryl was rubbing her large hands over her face. She paused a moment more, sighed, then said, "Okay, tell me what happened."

"There was a message on my machine on Monday. Nothing

big, just that he had something to ask me, and could I call him back. So I called, not that I had any intention of being nice to him, mind you. But he sounded great, and happy to hear from me, so I went along with it. Anyway, we agreed to get together on Wednesday and…"

"That's why you looked like hell yesterday!!" Cheryl cut in.

"Shut up. Anyway, I went over to his apartment to pick him up and…" Here Henry trailed off, unsure how to proceed.

"And you fucked his brains out as soon as you got there," Cheryl concluded. Again, Henry's guilty, sheepish grin gave all the confirmation she needed.

"Did he ask you for money this time?" Henry didn't respond.

"Henry!!" Cheryl wailed, covering her eyes and forehead in a motion that seemed both religious and exasperated.

"I just…" Henry started, but trailed off again.

The pair sat in his office for most of the afternoon, talking more about Steve, about what Henry should do, and about having sex when sometimes you should just walk away.

"Whatever happened with you and Andre? Did you two…end up talking it out?" Henry froze, but tried not to show his panic. Under the desk his legs were stone, pressed inwards on each other as if to brace him. Above the desk his right hand was splayed, looking like a spider, while his left knuckles were pressed under his jaw in a way that he hoped would pass for casual.

"Didn't…we just didn't…we agreed to let it lie. I apologized for being that drunk and…" he trailed off, looking for a clean summation, the spider flexing. "We agreed to let it lie." Cheryl nodded slowly.

"Yeah, it was a mess. But I'm glad you two figured it out."

***

5:30 came quickly, with Dave the Smartest Dog in the World already prepared to hop back in the car for the quick ride home. Cheryl had made Henry promise that he would keep it in his pants, at least where Debbie-Steve was concerned. At least for the weekend.

As Henry and Dave headed for the car, he noticed Andre had already gone. Pushing out into the cold, Henry saw Marie-France getting into her car across the small lot.

"Big plans for the weekend, hon?" he called.

Marie-France turned, her face bright red, though he couldn't tell if it was the temperature or genuine embarrassment.

"I–I'm going up to de Gatineaus dis wee--kend," she blurted "with someone..." Henry raised his eyebrows theatrically.

"Really...?"

"Mmm...," she replied. "I met 'im at a bar two weeks h'ago and..."

"You were at a bar?!" Henry exclaimed. He was beginning to see her in a whole new light. "Well Miss, just be careful not to sleep in on Monday morning, uh? Bonne fin de semaine."

"J'esp--ère," she smirked. Standing by her car, she watched Henry get into his and drive away.

Henry, sweet Henry, with his delicate wristbones and those wrinkles around his eyes when he smiled at her. She scrunched up her nose a bit to stop some tears. Then she got in her car and left, with the sadness of Oenone.

When she first saw him, Marie-France had had no words. Or, she didn't have *the* words. The right ones, the ones that would match what she was feeling in that exact moment. And the reason she didn't have them just then is that she had never *had* the feeling she was having in that exact moment.

Shock. Visceral desire. Elation? Maybe that, too. Maybe that, because there is a thrill, a non-sexual thrill, when you see something so beautiful and elegant and graceful that you feel volcanic joy. But at the same time, you feel embarrassed, even humiliated, just being in the same existence as its beauty. It almost hurts, but you would kill just to make the feeling stay. Yet Marie France had never had that feeling before. So she never had had to search for the words.

"Hi." Henry had said. He spoke to her first that day, leaning into her office. "I'm Henry." Marie France smiled with a legendary awkwardness. Her expression looked like she had eaten a lemon while politely trying to swallow a frog.

"...Allo..." she finally managed, trying to rise to meet him. He took the cue to come in and shake her hand. But halfway to her feet, she realized her right leg was asleep, and she stumbled over her own desk. Marie France put her wrists down to steady herself, but her right hand bumped her coffee cup, sending liquid pouring across her desk toward Henry.

She clumsily tried to right the cup but, in the process, tipped over the little vase she had brought in, the one with the single flower and full of water. The water went in a different direction from the coffee, heading straight for the little paper bag that contained the raisin and date muffin she had brought in for a snack.

She couldn't look him in the eye, and she just stood there now holding her sad little snack.

"Oh dear." Henry said, quietly but supportively. "Is your muffin soaked?"

The initial meltdown of awkwardness started to dry up after a few excruciating weeks, at least enough that Marie France didn't feel like her face was on fire every time they spoke. By two months in, she could swear that he was a little bit in to her, you know?

Nothing big, but the way he would smile and say hello and check on her to see if she had been invited to lunch with the others; it was thrilling and it started to make her feel bold. She was finally able to even *start* conversations with him!

Marie France was trying not to let her head get out in front of her. They only just met a few months ago. And are workplace romances really such a good idea? It's probably best to start slow. Maybe ask him to dinner? Maybe put her hand on his--

So what's a girl to do when someone like Cheryl ends up saying that thing that she said? The words were hot lead poured into Marie France's heart, getting heavier the longer they stayed there to cool. It wasn't a lot, but the density was the thing.

"He is probably the nicest little gay man I have ever met." Cheryl was standing in the doorway of the breakroom, smiling and still watching the door after Henry had left. She hadn't said it to Marie France directly; Marie France had been behind them the whole time, wrestling with the vending machine. But she heard and swallowed.

Gay. Gay? Gay. She didn't know how to feel. He's gay. Was this better or worse than if he had been seeing some other woman that wasn't her?

Worse.

Because if he's gay then things with Marie France (even silly, fantasy things) become...impossible. Impossible. And if he's gay then when he smiled at her, she'd know it wasn't *that kind* of smile. Ever. And if he's gay then if he ever put his arm around her as they hustled across the street for lunch, she would know that he would never be feeling *that way*. The way she was sure she would feel.

The day she found out and for the rest of that week she went home and cried. The first day or two was because she was in agony. After that it was more like mourning—grieving because she didn't know how to start again with him, to make things normal.

How would she ever be able to start again with him? To be able to look at him and at least pretend that he hadn't stabbed her in the heart. To be able to talk to him and maybe make *something* special happen between them, even if it wasn't The Real Thing. But something. To be able to keep him close, somehow.

***

"I don' know...it seem hexpensive...".

"I know it seems like it. But everything you said you wanted is in there. Big enough that you don't feel like a mouse on the highway, but not so big that you feel like you're driving a boat. Good on gas and safe as hell."

"Mm. Dat's true..." Marie France desperately needed a car, but she had never bought one before. She didn't even know where to start. That part was true. But she realized (hoped?) that maybe there was a way back in to being with Henry. Or near him. A way to start. So, she asked Henry to help her figure out how to buy a car.

And here they were. After looking at 7 different kinds, they were here at the Volvo dealership, at Henry's urging. But Marie France kept quiet. Looking down, staring at the paper with the price breakdown. "I... can't afford it. I mean, I can afford it, but not the down payment. I jus' don' have enough saved up...". Embarrassed, she folded the paper in her lap and looked out the window. "I should jus go for a cheaper one."

"No way," Henry said with finality. "If this is the one you want, we can make it happen. I can loan you the down payment, and you can just pay me back whenever you feel like it." Henry's face was vibrant, hopeful, encouraging. Marie France wanted him to look at her like that forever. Her face burning, she jammed her hands over her eyes.

"Okay. Okay! Let's do it," she said quickly.

She filled out some paperwork, and there was some hand-shaking and confusion over how the money would be moved around, and soon she and Henry were back in his car, driving back through the city.

"Are you totally excited?!" he beamed, taking her hand enthusiastically. Marie-France's heart leapt into her throat as she sat there, trying desperately to return his grip—*but not too strong! It doesn't have to mean that much. It's just excitement over the car. But not so weak that you seem aloof. Or ungrateful. Or something. Oh god.*

'It's wonderful, 'enri. Tank you so much for this. An I promise I will start paying you back right aw-ay."

"Don't even stress, luv. I'm not going anywhere, and there's plenty of time. B'sides," he said with a sly smile, "I know where you work...."

CHAPTER 13
Josef

Working her way out of the city core, Marie-France let out a long sigh at the arrival of the weekend. Lighting another cigarette (still a new vice for her), she coughed once and continued with short, shallow drags. Draping her wrist over the steering wheel of the Volvo and leaning back in a particularly uncharacteristic posture, she felt cool, dangerous, dangereuse.

Luckily, the streets had been kept clear for the past few days so that, despite the cold, they were quite free of ice—at least in the city. What it would be like in the hills was a different matter altogether.

Suddenly she remembered and felt ashamed. She remembered that she had never actually paid Henry back for the time he had loaned her money for the car. Five thousand dollars, for god's sake. For a while she mentioned it every week or so, mostly to let him know that she wouldn't be shirking that responsibility. But also, because each time she brought it up was a chance for them to talk about something that was just theirs, just between them.

Every time he would smile and be generous and would

lower his voice so he could speak privately and sincerely and directly to her. There was a hint of embarrassment in it for her; a mix of humility and gratitude and a smudge of shame that she had needed someone to help her financially. The embarrassment was like a hair shirt, though, reminding her of her yearning and supplicating commitment to her gorgeous god.

It was just that…she had forgotten to bring it up recently. Not that she didn't want his attention any less; it was just that she had legitimately forgotten about bringing it up. It just fell off her radar for some reason. But she was terrified of the thought that Henry might think she was trying to get away with something. The better part of a year had passed since she (they) bought the car, but it was still going to take her a little more time to save up in order to pay him back.

***

The new year brought new possibilities for Marie-France, but that's not to say that she was a changed woman exactly. It's just that she felt like she had been renewed lately, felt that she suddenly had–or realized she had–the ability to try some new and different things. True, she had been pretty well the only one on New Year's to go home alone; that was nothing new. But the freedom the others had exhibited—the abandon had struck her as something thrilling, quick, fresh, beautiful, infectious. Well, perhaps a slightly milder form of that. In any event, a few days after New Year's she had been sitting in a bar by herself, (happily) drinking wine and smoking at a corner table.

That was when she saw someone she knew–or perhaps knew of. They had been introduced previously and had intersected several times, but they were not well-acquainted. Smiling faintly, Marie-France caught the eye of that other woman who was clearly having difficulty figuring out why Marie-France looked so familiar. The other woman began to approach Marie-France, but it was only when she reached the table that she realized that Marie-France worked with Andre, her ex.

Standing there, unsure of what to do next, Melissa just smiled stupidly—a silly, forced half-smile that, in another context, might have been a great cover up for someone experiencing a great deal of physical pain.

"Melissa, righ--t?" Marie-France asked warmly.

"Y-yes," she said, extending her arm stiffly. It had been five days since the New Year's fiasco, and Melissa clearly wasn't really sure how to deal with this.

Marie-France re-introduced herself and, seeming unsure what to do next, Melissa sat down at the table with her. The pair sat together for awhile, making what little small-talk they could. Marie-France knew something had happened on New Year's but had no idea of the gruesome details. She had gone home before it had happened.

From the bar, a man had turned to watch the pair. He was well-dressed and older than either of them. Not old, mind you, but a significant enough number of years to give him a distinguished air.

"Do you know that guy?" Melissa asked quietly. Marie-France, not being terribly well-versed in the subtlety of bar-talk, looked up from the table, directly at the man, and said simply, "Non."

"Don't look at him," Melissa spat, horrified. Confused, Marie-France spun her gaze around the bar as if she were innocently inspecting the decor.

"I-I-I'm sorry," she fumbled, with a delicate emphasis on the second syllable, which made Melissa instantly feel bad for snapping at her.

"I don't know him either; he is kind of handsome, though," Melissa said coyly, trying to smooth out the tablecloth with her hand. Both of the women were single, and in Melissa there was the zeal of the newly relationship-free.

She had come to the bar to meet up with Loretta, who was going to take her on a "man-hunt," as she put it. Melissa wasn't sure she was entirely up for that sort of thing, but Loretta seemed determined; and besides, when Loretta got going, all you could do was hang on for the ride.

Marie-France, on the other hand, was not feeling quite so ambitious, so her shock was palpable when Loretta showed up, coming to the table to announce, "Let's get some cock!"

As Loretta sat down, Marie-France smiled sheepishly, and introduced herself across the smoldering ashtray. The three women sat for about half an hour, with Loretta downing two-and-a-half bloody Caesars in that span. What surprised Marie-France the most, though, was Loretta's pseudo-sexual relationship with each new celery stalk as the drinks kept coming. If nothing else, it had served to renew the interest of the man at the bar.

"Strippers," Loretta said simply, a string of celery remnant dangling unflatteringly from her lip. Marie-France raised her eyebrows, unsure how to proceed, while Melissa smiled darkly.

"BRING ON THE STRRRIPPERS!" she yelled, shocking the entire bar into an abrupt silence. Sliding out from behind the table, Loretta gathered her things and prepared for her next conquest.

"There's a place down the way, back in the market, that we're going to. Wanna come?" Melissa said to Marie-France, who was clearly uncomfortable with the whole scenario.

"Non, tank-you. I-I tink I'll be going 'ome soon anyw--ay." Her response was less than convincing, but enough of a green-light for Loretta to be off and running.

"Ah right—bye, hon!" she said, sweeping out into the sub-zero evening. As Melissa followed her out, Marie-France felt both the physical void left around her, as well as all of the eyes that were still staring in the direction of her table.

Marie-France suddenly felt stupid in her winter boots with the faux-fur trim around the top; looking around the room she realized how much more stylish everyone was. She wanted to pretend to play it cool by concentrating on her drink, but her glass was empty. When she looked up again, she saw the man smiling—slyly—and watching her carefully. Then he waved her over.

She was completely taken aback, unsure of the protocol. Wasn't he supposed to come to her? Buy her a drink? Or were men not supposed to do that anymore? Were women supposed to take the initiative? Feeling awkward in her awful boots, Marie-France stood up and, nervously clutching her empty drink, strode across the floor as if the glass might provide some further use now that its contents had vanished.

The man was grinning now, and she was grinning too, grinning through the almost painful blushing. "Allo," she said. The man grinned but said nothing. Marie-France's smile began to falter and, with still no actual response, her excitement was quickly turning to embarrassment. *Isn't this how it's supposed to work?* she thought. *Why doesn't he say anything?*

"Why don't you sit down?" He said finally, after an excruciating pause. He spoke and her chin lifted slightly, as if her mouth was trying to capture what he said: not the words, but the sound. His voice was dark, and in her ears it crumbled like freshly ground coffee.

She moved quickly to follow his direction, relieved to be spared further social discomfort. They had talked then, for what seemed like hours to her (and it was she who, curiously, did most of the talking, now flourishing in her native French). But then she began to think, *what if this goes further? So, what if it does, though? Wasn't that the point of the evening? Am I drunk? Enough? Oh God, does he hate my boots?*

"Come home with me," he said.

"Where?"

"To Hull."

"How do we get there?"

"I have a car," he said.

"You're pissed."

"We'll take a cab then. Let's go."

Marie-France stood and smiled, and began to collect her things and put on her coat. When she was ready and standing in front of him, he didn't move. He looked at her at first as if admiring her, taking her in. But the more time passed the more it felt like he was testing her, to see how much she could take.

Her body was numb. And just when she thought she had had enough, he finished his drink with exactly one-and-a-half ice cubes in it, got up, and led her out by the arm.

She had seen him a couple of times since that night. And this coming weekend in the hills felt clandestine and maybe a little slutty. The sex had been a bit rough so far, but she was getting used to it, and she preferred it to no attention at all.

CHAPTER 14:
The place that hurts

Henry took another long luxurious pull from his cigarette, holding the phone in the other hand as he listened to Rachel tell him about her houseguest and the calamity of New Year's. It was Saturday afternoon, and Henry had just finished not returning Debbie-Steve's phone call from earlier that day. He was going to be good, damn it. This time he was going to be strong.

"She did tell me a pretty upsetting story about her stepfather, though. Apparently, he still lives in Ottawa," Rachel continued.

"Certainly sounds like an interesting girl," Henry offered, only half-paying attention.

"Yeah, and since she started working at some café, she's had some money coming in and she's helping out a lot. Pretty much like having a real live boarder." There was a pause. "Are you okay, Henry? You sound a little far away..."

Henry considered this for a moment, lit another cigarette, deciding whether to tell Rachel about his recent amorous slip-up. But what had happened with Debbie-Steve wasn't all that was on his mind. More to the point, he was thinking about what it meant for the future. Sure, he still had feelings for Steve, but did he really want to spend his life being dragged along by an emotional syphilitic? On the other hand, let's face it, Steve was going through a phase, a period of his life (albeit a particularly destructive period), and when he came out of it, wouldn't he see why he had been with Henry in the first place? On the other other hand, didn't Henry have a life to live right now? Near the end of his conversation with Rachel, Henry realized that the math was simple. He had too many hands, and too few balls.

"Hey...," she said, and he could hear a coy smile in her voice, "any luck with that Andre guy at work?" Henry froze. *Right.* He had mentioned Andre's name to her back in the fall. But she didn't...I mean there's no way she could...

"No," Henry said through a wince-smile, "nothing going on there." After they got off the phone, Henry threw up.

***

In the final week of January things were in full swing for everybody: Henry was getting laid, Marie-France was getting laid, Cheryl was getting laid, and Andre was not. Henry and Debbie-Steve were seeing each other about three times a week, and mostly at the bar. Marie-France seemed to be moving steadily along with Josef, particularly after their weekend in the Gatineaus. Cheryl was now seeing some guy she picked up at the health food store–an aerobics buff, or personal trainer, or some damn thing, she would tell Henry later.

Andre was getting much better at smoking, given all the time he had with his hands. He had gone out once or twice since the beginning of the month, but otherwise had tried to lie low.

"I called you after New Year's, but you never called me back," she said. The voice on the other end of the phone though wasn't just any woman. It was a woman Andre had history with. It was his mom.

"Yeah, well, it's been a pretty busy month, ma." Andre sighed.

"How's Melissa, dear? Is she there? Wish her a Happy New Year's for me, will you?"

"No, ma, she's not here. We, uh, split up a few weeks ago, and I don't wanna talk about it."

"JACK!" she yelled. "COME TALK TO YOUR SON!" 'Come-talk-to-your-son' was Joanna's way of saying 'you-won't-talk-to-me-about-this-so-it-must-be-a-guy-thing.' There was a pause as the phone switched hands.

"So, what did you do?" his father said. No 'hi.' No 'how are ya.'

"Dad, I..."

"Did ya give 'er the boot? Naw, you wouldn't't'a done that. Lemme guess, you were screwin' around with another one on the side, right?" Andre could hear his father chuckling under his breath. "Boy, when are you gonna learn that..." and on Jack went. Andre held the phone away from his mouth while he tried to light another cigarette, waiting for it to end. "Why, your mother married me cuz I was a real gentleman, a real man's man, understand what I'm sayin?" Andre winced.

And it hurt. The vice around his chest was making it hard to breathe. Andre lifted his head like he was trying to keep it out of water, trying to sound calm or normal or whatever. It just wasn't something he could say. Not now. He closed his eyes and pressed two fingers to his temple and tried to sound...like he was expected to. *My insides have been scratched out, my throat is closing, I can't focus on anything, and I hurt. And I can't point to the place that hurts, but oh god it hurts.*

"Dad, it's fine. It's just been a rough start to the year. But it's good. Work is going well and I've got lots of things to keep me busy. Seriously. It's good.

There was a pause and, in another moment, Jack sighed and said, "Well, I guess you know what's best for ya." There were goodbyes then, but just before he hung up the phone, Andre heard his father whisper, "Just remember–don't smoke too many of those."

By the final days of January, Ottawa had fallen into the solid vicious grip of winter. The canal was rock hard and more and more skaters flocked to it each day. And this was at the heart of the curious relationship you could have with Ottawa in winter: The skaters were out in droves, screaming, yelling, and flying up and down the length of the city–but you didn't go unprepared either. You'd be aware of the toll on your body, the way the cold sticks in your nostrils and throat, the slow, sure advancement through your gloves and coat, up your fingers and into your skin, until your body says 'no more–get home, something dangerous is happening.'

Part Five
February 1998

CHAPTER 15
A game of Clue

February lurched on through the wet and cold, the slush a thick, dark soup. Dirty had been working for almost a month, schlepping coffee at the shop where she had first met Ruben and Marina. It had been a strange New Year, that first week of January; it was as if everything was falling into place, somehow all at once.

The New Year's party had been wonderful. Meeting up with Marina at the subway, they had veered off into the east end to the house party. When they first got there, they didn't immediately see Ruben, so the two of them scurried off to a bathroom to get to work. Sitting on the toilet with Marina crouching in front of her, Dirty still marveled at how much Marina looked…like a dude. Marina showed her how to lightly drag mascara across the peach fuzz on her face to make the hair look darker, like stubble. And it really did.

"If you just smear it over your face to try to make it look like you have a beard, it doesn't work." Marina instructed. "It just looks like you have a dirty face. You gotta brush the hair that's there—that's the convincing part."

Dressing was easier, since there wasn't anything particularly feminine about Dirty's flannel shirt and jeans to begin with. But Marina put a hat on her, too, pulling it low over her eyes. Then she stood back to look at Dirty's whole look. Satisfied, she said "you are now Don Manson, undercover cop. I'm your hard-bitten partner...Man...Donson...or something." And then she handed Dirty a wad of fabric. "Now stuff it, bitch."

"What?!" Dirty giggled.

"Stick it in your pants. You got a dick, now." Marina patted her crotch proudly. Just then there was a gentle tapping at the door. Marina opened it slightly, and then flung it open. Ruben was standing there, and he looked...not as good as the girls did. But still not bad. He had a monocle, an awful drawn-on mustache, and a corduroy jacket with patches on the sleeves.

"Hellooo," he announced. "I am professor Langley P. Cabbage, Ph.D., Doctor of Awesomeness." Ruben waved his arm in a flourish, then bowed gracefully.

"Why do I feel like this is turning into a game of Clue?" Dirty snickered.

"Yeah, me too," Marina said. "Get in here, professor. Maybe I can do something with your make-up."

Once it got started for real, the party was loud and obnoxious, and after about an hour the three of them found some quiet in the attic with a few others, pleased with the reprieve from the crowd.

Sitting in a circle, Dirty watched the conversation bounce from person to person, but she said little herself. Even when Marina announced that she was taking a job at a bar downtown, Dirty smiled and congratulated her and went on listening and drinking and nodding to the music. Ruben and Marina stared at her, waiting for Dirty to take the cue, which she didn't, and only became flustered when they simply stared at her.

"What...?" Ruben placed his hand on Dirty's knee, a motion she found both exciting and a little uncomfortable.

"Well," Ruben said smiling, "with Marina leaving, that does mean there's an opening..." There was another pause.

"Oh!" Dirty exclaimed, finally getting the job. "Wow. Great. You mean me, right?" Marina laughed and poured Dirty another drink from her flask.

By 4 am, most of the crowd had left and Dirty had moved through giddiness and into feeling positively sick. So, with a wave to the rest of the bodies on the living room floor, the three tramped out into the snow to try their luck finding a cab.

Dirty spent the night at Ruben and Marina's back on the floor as she had before, more passed out than sleeping. And that meant that Scooter and Rachel were the first to come home. They, too, had gotten home quite late and had been so tired that they went straight to bed. It wasn't until the next morning that Rachel found the little drops of blood in the hallway.

"Oh my god...," she said, leaning closely to the floor. "Honey, I think Seeger's hurt!" The two ran around the house calling to him, only to find him sitting serenely under the kitchen table, whiskers licked clean. Picking him up, Scooter inspected him closely. Setting him down again, they watched Seeger walk across the floor, checking for an appreciable limp or anything else that would suggest an injury. At a loss for an explanation, the pair went back to the hallway, puzzled at what nevertheless appeared to be blood on the carpet, just as Dirty walked in the front door. It had only taken a moment for Dirty to clue in to what had happened, hearing what they had found. Racing down the basement stairs, they found a few more drops of blood, and the significant absence of Pickles.

CHAPTER 16
Rowena Glass

There are times when you don't immediately realize there is sand in your mouth. Then you bite down and feel it. Shitty, unwelcome grit that sends shivers as it skitters between your teeth and then out into your spit, only to show up again somewhere else in your mouth, even after you thought you had gotten rid of it all. That was what it was like every time Rowena Glass would come to the cafe. So, when the door opened once more just as Dirty had closed it and Rowena blew in, Dirty bit down.

Nothing seemed to be good enough for her. Not even her own daughter, Diamond, seemed good enough for her. Rowena had a glare and an enormous mole on her upper lip, and when she ordered coffee it was as if speaking to Dirty (or anyone, for that matter) was physically repulsive, if not painful. Her toque cocked to one side, Rowena launched the stroller forward through the café, slush-muddy tire tracks leaking a trail.

Diamond was two, and lovely, even if Rowena didn't see it. She would gurgle and point and laugh, often to herself, and today she was a red bundled marshmallow, her hazel twinkle eyes the size of snow globes.

Rowena Glass was standing at the counter staring at the chalkboard menu high on the wall; her mittens were off and she was absent-mindedly caressing the zipper on her own coat with her finger. She spoke without ever actually making eye contact with Dirty.

"How old is the coffee." She was actually asking a question, but with her it almost always sounded like an accusation.

"I've just made a fresh pot." There was a long pause.

"Tea. I see lots of weird tea. Don't you have regular tea!"

"Sure," said Dirty, so far unflappable. "How do you take it?" Rowena scowled past Dirty, then scowled at the pastry case. Dirty then realized that Rowena Glass wasn't looking for something to order. She was looking for something to complain about.

"A glass of water with a single *biscotto* on a clean plate. Make sure it's clean this time." She spun around and pushed the stroller to an empty table. Customers weren't supposed to get table service here—you order your stuff, then you take it to your table yourself. But Rowena Glass had different expectations.

"Cow say mooooo, cow say mooooo."

"Hi Diamond!" Dirty enthused as she wiped down the table.

"Hi Dymun!" Diamond repeated. She really was a lovely creature, and the mole on her lip to match her mother's didn't seem to faze her at all. She was two, after all. There wasn't much that could.

Rowena was ignoring both of them and staring out the window. Not even that appeared to please her.

"What does a cow say?" Dirty quizzed.

"Moooooooo."

"What does a sheep say?"

"Baaaaaaa." Diamond was on her game today.

"What does a firetruck say?"

"Beedoobeedoo."

"What do cowboys say?"

"Giddup!"

"What do mummies say?"

***

There was something on Dirty's mind. What was on her mind was the attention she had been getting from Ruben. The way they had been together of late—it wasn't sexual, exactly. Evening after evening had been spent talking during their shift, not about the two of them, but about everything. And little by little, they were getting close. Not that there was heat exactly, not like what Ruben seemed to have with Marina. It was a softness, a safe feeling they had with one another. Still, as Dirty stood behind the counter, alone for this shift, leaning against the cooler and thinking about Ruben, she realized it wasn't softness that was on her mind.

Why do things always taste better when someone else makes them for you? Christ, even toast tastes better when it's given to you. Every time Dirty took a cup of coffee from Ruben and let the smell of it stroke her face, she couldn't figure out why his coffee always tasted better than hers.

As it turns out, it really should be so. When a person makes something like toast for themselves, their nose is already taking it in during preparation. By the time they get to putting it in their face, they're already half-used to it. But when someone makes it *for* them, they're smelling and tasting it for the first time, so the impact of it is so much more powerful. Maybe that's why Dirty was starting to spend more time thinking about fucking Ruben. He belonged to Marina by rights, and Dirty had no place in that kitchen, that was for sure. But goddamn that toast smelled good.

"Hey." Dirty hadn't registered that someone else had come in, and as she turned to greet the person she snapped back to reality. It was Marina.

"Where were you just now? You seemed pretty far away."

"Uh... just thinkin'" Dirty said weakly.

"Uh-huh." Marina smiled. "Anyway, I just stopped in to say hi; I'm heading down to the bar soon." There was a pause. "Umm..." she continued, "has Ruben talked to you at all, y'know, about anything...?"

Dirty suddenly felt a sharp pang of guilt and horror, as if her daydream had been announced over an intercom.

"Like what?" she asked innocently. Marina looked down, weighing her words carefully.

"Hmm..." she began. "I'm not sure I can express it clearly, but...." She paused once more and then her face changed. It was as if a thick blanket had been laid over her thought, waiting to be pulled back, but not now.

"Come meet me at the bar tonight, after close." She said with finality. Dirty wasn't sure if she wanted to be down that way at 2:30 in the morning, but it was clear Marina needed to see her.

"Okay," she nodded. "I'll be there. We'll talk." Marina wore a partially natural smile. They re-affirmed their plans, and then Marina was gone.

***

That night, Dirty took the streetcar across town. She had spent the afternoon shift with Ruben, which had been uneventful except for the uncomfortable moment when he said how much he 'enjoyed spending time with her.' The wind had picked up, and as she made her way to the bar from the corner, she was chilled deep. Stepping inside the place, she found herself under the gaze of seven or eight pairs of red-rimmed eyes–these were the kinds of men who had been drinking a long time and had little intention of stopping. Most of them were balding; the two gentlemen in the corner had gone grey-white. The man at the bar was in a suit–albeit a cheap one–and wearing lightly tinted prescription glasses. Not because it was bright in the bar, but because they were the only glasses he owned and, when he had bought them 12 years prior, they had been pretty cool.

The rest of them ranged in age from 45 to 80, most in dirty jeans and flannel shirts, down on their luck and high on their spirits. Dirty had a brief moment of panic that she was in the wrong place, when Marina came out of the back room, energizing the place as if she were made of pure oxygen. She had pulled her hair back, and her skin seemed brighter than Dirty had remembered from earlier that day. Maybe it was just that she seemed so fresh in comparison to her patrons, but Dirty was overwhelmed with the desire to undo the elastic, put her face in Marina's hair, and breathe deeply.

"Hey peach!" Marina called. Dirty slid over to the bar and sat down, leaving a good deal of room between herself and the cheap-suit guy. It didn't work.

"Heyy peach," he said, smiling out of the side of his mouth.

"Finish your drink, Marty," Marina scolded, then turned her attention to Dirty. "Glad you made it." Her face turned serious for a moment. "I should be out of here in half an hour. Then we can run down the street and get a bite. Cool?"

Before Dirty could answer, Marina had put a drink in front of her, but she wasn't sure what it was. She pointed to it and threw a quizzical look at Marina, who shrugged and said simply, "Special of the house, baybee," and wandered off into the back again. Sipping carefully, Dirty's nose was at once struck by the pungent bite of scotch, but her mouth found an unexpected sweetness in the taste. This stuff was magic. This stuff was dangerous.

Forty-five minutes later, Dirty was through her third Rusty Nail and was feeling dreamy and warm. Marina had kicked out almost all of her drinkers, except for Marty who was standing at the door, waiting for the cab Marina had called for him.

"C'mon," Marina said, "let's take off. They'll lock up for me." She motioned behind her, but Dirty could see no one through the glass of the back-room door. Sliding off of her stool, she steadied herself on Marina's arm as the two blew out into the street, past Marty who was now waiting in the cold, trying not to be sick.

It was a short, crisp walk to the diner, and although it was late, the city still had life to it. The two women walked arm in arm as Marina talked about how things had been between her and Ruben. An old Platters song was playing in the diner, and it seemed a fitting backdrop for two women talking about broken hearts.

"He doesn't love me."

"Marina!"

"I can see it." The late hour seemed to energize them both, but these words weighed heavily in Marina's mouth, her resignation giving them a dry texture like their plated eggs. "I think he's bored. Or maybe he's seeing someone else. Or wants to. I dunno…"

Dirty's throat tightened at this, her back straightening slightly. She threw on an expression of innocent concern, with a little surprise thrown in (*I'm shocked! Shocked!* Her guilty brain teased). She reached across the table and took Marina's hand.

"Have you talked to him about it?"

"I can't." Marina sucked hard on the cigarette she had just lit. The thing was, Dirty knew exactly how Marina was feeling. She had felt it too, with Peter. When she had arrived in Edmonton, she could feel a tension, a vibe when they were alone together. He would say nothing, or worse, would speak in that halting manner that suggested he was being civil just for civility's sake. Goddammit.

Marina was looking at Dirty now, looking into her. It was a look the innocent would see as searching, the guilty as accusatory. "Has he said anything to you?" Plop. In the middle of the table. Dirty widened, then narrowed her gaze, pretending to scan her mind for a phrase, a look, a feeling.

"Honestly hon, he's seemed pretty chipper at work." And that was, of course, the truth. They smoked in silence then, their coffee getting cold, when someone in the back changed the music to a radio station that was farting out track after track of old 80's songs. Just then it was 'Wrapped Around Your Finger'.

Dirty's eyes brightened. "You are not going to believe what happened at work today!" Marina raised an eyebrow. "Two words:" Dirty continued. "Rowena. Glass." As she said it, Dirty shoved her tongue just inside her upper lip, making it bulge in reference to Rowena's impressive facial feature. Marina did as well, at exactly the same time.

Marina's sweet face glimmered as she motioned for Dirty to get on with the good stuff. Dirty told her how Rowena had been her regular crabby self, but that Diamond was there and

Dirty had been playing 'animal noises' with her. Marina's eyes narrowed as she tried to imagine how this could go wrong. Leaning in, she waited for the punch line.

"So, I was just running down a list, what do dogs say, what do sheep say, blah blah blah. You know?" Marina nodded, the fingers of one hand curling against her bottom lip, as if she were trying to eat the anticipation. "So then," Dirty kept going, "I said something like 'what does the fire truck say', or 'what does the car say' or whatever. But *then*..." Dirty took a big gulp of air, her eyes on the table in renewed disbelief. "But then I say 'what do mummies say', and she goes--" and here Dirty puts on her best Diamond Glass voice, "Fucking Immigrants!"

"SHUT.   UP!"   Marina   nearly   fell   over. "Shutupshutupshutup. That did not happen!"

"I swear to god, Mar, I swear to god. In her voice it was more like 'fackin immygants', but still!" They were both left shaking their heads, giddy and friends, and for a while Dirty felt like she was on Marina's side again.

"You wanna hear a kinda creepy Rowena Glass story?" Marina asked with a cocked smile.

"Hell yes..." Dirty said, eyes bright and palms together.

"So, one day I was working at the cafe, reading this crime novel and talking about it to one of the other regulars at the counter. There was a part in the book where the killer is trying to take out someone in a hospital bed, and he decides to use, like, potassium chlorate in a needle. This regular, Eddie, says that that would be a good idea, as long as you could hide the needle mark."

"K..."

"Well, in the middle of that discussion Rowena comes in and is standing at the counter, and as soon as Eddie says that thing about the potassium, Rowena, like, sneers and says 'nooo...' and shakes her head. And all of a sudden, she goes off on this thing where the best way to kill someone in a hospital isn't by injection. She said that what you really want is kleenex..." Dirty's eyes bloomed and she pulled her head back in sharp, almost confused disbelief.

"What?!"

"Yeah," Marina continued. "She said that if the person was unconscious or debilitated or something, you could easily shove a kleenex down their throat with a tongue depressor or something, and they would aspirate it and choke to death. You have to close the mouth and hold the nose for a sec, so they take a big breath, but..." and here Marina leaned in for effect, "pretty soon after, the kleenex dissolves, and away you go." Marina raised her hands like a magician.

"What. The. Hell."

"Right?! And she said the best time to do it in a hospital is around shift change. The nurses are exhausted and making notes for the next team, or running around after code..." Marina looked up and away, trying to remember the right colour. "Blue, I think. I think that's what she said. Anyway, they'll generally be ignoring the central monitors. And she said it's how nursing homes get rid of old people all the time."

"What?!" Dirty almost shouted.

"I. Know. And then she orders her tea and goes and sits down at a table like nothing happened. Creeeepy. Oh, and she also said that the injection thing in the book was stupid because when you're about to kill someone, chances are you will be too freaked out to hold the damn thing straight. Unless you've got training. So use a tissue instead."

CHAPTER 17:
Aeaea

Wiping his nose with a tissue, Scooter rode the elevator up to the 4th floor. It's true that Scooter did not enjoy the company of Rachel's mother, Marjorie; she had always seemed equally unimpressed with him. She probably felt that her daughter could do better than living with a grocery store employee. Still, it had been some time now that Rachel and Scooter had been together, and her daughter did seem happy. Or at least unwilling to listen to Marjorie's constant haranguing. Marjorie was no doubt hoping for grandkids at some point, just not from a man named Scooter.

Two thousand dollars. She was giving them a gift/loan of a couple thousand dollars to start an investment portfolio, and maybe just to see how the dynamics of money would affect their relationship. Who knows? Maybe there was more to him than Marjorie gave him credit for. Or, the stress of money would shake her daughter out of whatever dream world she was in, and she would see this man for the loser he was. Who knows.

"No. No. Rach, I really don't feel good about this. We

don't need money. We make rent, we can buy food. We're good." Scooter crossed his arms and scowled.

"It's not about money we *need*. Think of it as a little springboard for the future." Rachel had spoken to Marjorie earlier that day, and the more trouble she had trying to convince Scooter this was a good idea, the more she seemed to sound like her mother. "Please." In his head Scooter was laying in to Rachel with a battery of arguments against this crazy fucking idea. As if there was any way he would ever want to have any kind of debt to that woman, gift or no gift. With Rachel looking at him, he lowered his voice to a stern rumble, and gave her his final word.

"Fine. I--fine." Scooter was pursing his lips in that way that he always did.

"Okay." Rachel smiled brightly. "When you finish your shift tomorrow can you swing by her office and pick it up?"

Scooter twitched. He had been planning to short his shift tomorrow so that he could....

"How bout this: I'll jump over there on my lunch break and then keep the check in the safe at work til I'm done."

***

When Scooter got to Marjorie's office, he was still wearing his smeared deli smock. On purpose. She didn't like him and he didn't like her, so he would occasionally take the opportunity to bug the shit out of her.

But just below the level of Scooter's intentions was, of course, a fear and embarrassment about being a grocery store employee, and especially one that was going into an architect's office. Marjorie wasn't an architect, but she was the office manager, and the place was fucking intimidating. Showing up in his smock was his childish way of owning the feeling of being out of place. Mind you, Marjorie still didn't help.

"Why, Eliot! You didn't have to get all dressed up for me!" she cooed. She couldn't even be bothered to call him Scooter. He gave her that smile that was still fifty percent grimace.

"Marjorie...always nice to see you."

"To what do I owe the honour of your company?" she asked sweetly.

Son of a goddamn bitch she's going to make me ask for the money. Are you fucking serious? Scooter's face blazed red in embarrassment. *Okay*, he thought, *let's do this.* Speaking loud enough for the others in the office to possibly hear, he said

"Rachel told me that you were being gracious enough to help us out with the cost of the abortion! That's really kind of you."

"Well," she winced, handing him a bulging envelope. "Try not to lose it." Scooter lost his breath for a moment when he realized that she wasn't giving him a cheque; this was two thousand dollars in cash. Then he composed himself. She was testing him.

"Thank you very much. I'll give Rachel your best."

Shitshitshitshit he thought as he walked out. He had planned his detour with the idea that all he was going to have was a cheque, not the actual fucking money. He paused in the lobby of the building, about to walk out to the street, when he turned and headed for the washroom. *It's fine*, he thought. Closing the bathroom door behind him, he unceremoniously jammed the envelope down the front of his pants. *No safer place*, he assured himself. And now, for a treat.

Scooter had gotten the address of the theatre, the Aeaea, from an ad they ran in one of the magazines he kept hidden in the car. They advertised like that because they offered a particularly...uncommon product. When Scooter got there, he had already balled up his smock into his bag, ready for the show, but suddenly he wasn't sure he had the right place. No marquee, no ticket booth, what the hell was this place? The only thing possibly marking it as a public place was the shiny, chrome, sand-filled cigarette butt container set just aside from the door. He checked the address twice more with what he had written down, and it really was a match. So he pulled on the door, gently. It gave.

Peering inside, he looked at the wall to his right and knew he was in the right place. Hanging there was a life-size poster of his biggest fantasy, Furlania.

Furlania was a cartoon, of course, but not in the way most people think. She was tall, gorgeous, lithe, delicious, waiting. And she had a tail. And fox ears. And whiskers. Furlania was a strange human/animal hybrid, enough person to make her seem humanly sexy and available, but enough creature to turn the crank of those who were into that sort of thing. And Scooter was.

The magazines and videos were filled with drawings and short vignettes of these furry human-animal things in every sort of sexual situation you would care to think of, and a few more that would probably shock you. But this theater claimed to have full-length movies.

Stepping inside fully, Scooter brushed his fingertips over Furlania's belly as he walked past, down a ramp/hall that had a single bare bulb dangling from the ceiling. Ten paces further he came to an opening in the wall, almost like a window, where an unimpressed old woman sat on a rickety stool. "Twenty," she whispered, not even looking up. Scooter's palms were sweaty as he slipped the bill to her, and then he continued down, down the hall.

The film had already started, but just barely, so Scooter grabbed a seat in the back row near the middle. There were only 7 rows in the whole place, 5 seats in each. This place wasn't makeshift, but it wasn't glamorous, and there weren't more than 6 other people in the whole theater. But dear god it was just like he had hoped. The screen lit up with paws and tails and fucking, and sweet jesus there was Furlania standing above them all, watching, like some glorious fox-queen.

In the row in front of Scooter and two seats to the left, on the end, sat a youngish looking guy who, while he looked nervous, didn't look any more nervous than anyone else in there. The others were loosely gathered further to the front and to the right.

Scooter put his bag down in the seat to his left, tucked up close to him, just in case. As he looked and watched, it was like the movie dug its fingers directly into his body, finding the holes that had never quite been filled, and fitting them perfectly. Perfectly.

It was getting uncomfortable in his pants now, what with the extra padding in there, so Scooter decided to move the envelope over to his bag, but still keep it close. The fact that his pants were undone now, though, turned out to be the signal for the theater's premium service, which Scooter had no idea even existed.

"Premium service..." she whispered over his shoulder. "Premium service, twenty bucksss...." Scooter covered his crotch in surprise and looked over his shoulder to see who was talking to him. He couldn't see much in the dark, but if he had been able to, he would have said that the woman was probably 45, or maybe 32 with a really bad habit.

In a swift motion, she moved into his row and took the seat next to him on the right and showed him what was on offer. It was a handjob, simply enough, but in this case she would be wearing large, almost cartoonish fur gloves. Complete with plush claws. She placed one paw firmly on his crotch. Scooter's eyes widened in a brief moment of confusion, but just then Furlania was getting down on all fours on the screen. The timing was delicious.

Slipping her the last twenty out of his pocket, Scooter eased his jeans down a little and held his breath. Furlania was on her knees now, looking up at an eagle-like dude who was pushing his enormous eagle-cock (?) towards her face.

Scooter's premium service was getting to a fevered rhythm when the manboy in the next row oozed himself out of his seat, his eyes locking with Scooter's, which got weird for a moment when neither of them looked away while Scooter was getting jerked off. Now sweeping in behind the last row, the young man grabbed Scooter's bag, barreled through the door and back up the hallway. For a moment Scooter couldn't actually believe what was happening, as if the gods of luck and mothers-in-law were taking turns pissing all over him. He had almost been able to grab the bag back—if he had just been able to snag a strap, he could have easily overpowered that kid. But no, it had skittered out of his fingers.

Scooter peeled himself away from his premium service and tore off after the guy, but when he hit blinding sunlight the chase was already over. Breathing heavy and trying to get his zipper up, Scooter turned to the corner of the building and vomited.

***

"Forget it, okay?" Dirty heard Scooter say through the vent several days later. Whatever it was he and Rachel had been talking about, it was heated and getting hotter.

"Don't you think I...," she heard Rachel say, but the rest was lost to poor acoustics. *They're situbicating,* Dirty thought. It was a word she had made up as a little girl. When she was 7 years old, she wanted to know what the word was for *whisper-yell,* that thing that parents do when they are reprimanding children in the middle of polite company, when they can't *actually* yell. *Sally! Get. That. Finger. Out of your nose! Nowww.*

Dirty was annoyed when her mother told her there wasn't a word for it, so she made one up. Her mother thought it was hilarious. Her mother had always thought she was funny, how she would mix up words, sometimes by accident, sometimes on purpose. Dirty had mixed up the pronunciation of her own name at a very young age, so it came out as *Dirty.* Her mother thought it was a riot. So it stuck.

Dirty didn't think Rachel and Scooter were arguing about her–in fact, she was positive they weren't–but lately a part of her felt like she was starting to overstay her welcome.

A door slammed, then silence. Dirty would have been happy to stay in the basement for the rest of the evening. The problem was, she was getting hungry. Treading lightly on the stairs, she listened carefully for movement in either camp, but could discern nothing. Pressing her ear to the door, she thought she could hear a faint shuffling in the kitchen, which she was sure was Seeger.

Carefully pushing the door open, she found herself frozen in the threshold, looking at Scooter's wide back, hunched over the kitchen table. She was stuck. She didn't want to barge in, not now. But turning around and closing the door again would catch his attention anyway, and wouldn't that just defeat the purpose of going back downstairs?

Just then, as if by curse or by grace, Rachel swept back in

the kitchen, index finger raised in an "and another thing" gesture, but stopped short of saying anything when she saw Dirty frozen in the doorway. Silence. Dirty had no idea what they had been fighting about, and she wasn't sure that she wanted to know.

"I–I just..." she said sheepishly, but Rachel was gone again, to another part of the house, and Scooter just turned away. She stood there for a second, and then in a moment of boldness went over and sat at the table. Though he had his head down, Dirty could see Scooter's jaw working, which meant that he was grinding his teeth again.

"Do you wanna tell me about it?" Silence. "The anal warts came back, didn't they?" she said teasingly. Caught off guard, Scooter looked up and cracked a smile in spite of himself.

"Oh man...," he muttered, shaking his head in frustration. Dirty waited. "I lost some money," he began.

"How much?" she asked.

"Two."

"Hundred?"

"Thousand." Dirty swallowed hard. "I'm such an asshole," he continued. "What the hell was I thinking?"

"What happened?" Dirty tried to calm him down. Scooter proceeded to give her a (somewhat vague) story of a guy with used stereo equipment over in the Junction area of town, equipment which turned out to be just empty, weighted casings in brand new boxes, which he hadn't bothered to check before the guy drove off.

"So," Dirty said, "you bought used stereo equipment from some guy, out of the back of a car?" Scooter winced. "Well," she continued, grabbing a cookie out of the bag on the counter, "you're right about one thing. You're an asshole." Scooter cradled his head in both hands, sliding his fingers through his hair and scratching his scalp.

"What the fuck am I going to do?" he whined. Dirty sat for a moment, and then a tiny spark lit in her mind. She rose quietly from the chair and went over to the drawer by the sink, pulling out a little plastic sandwich bag.

"Scooter," she said, sidling up next to him. "I need you to do something for me. There might be a way to fix this. Just trust me." Scooter straightened, his face a mixture of confusion and faint, faint hope. Handing him the baggie, she said "I need you to go back to where this happened and get something for me."

CHAPTER 18:
Shitknife

Scooter had gone and retrieved what Dirty had asked for, as weird as it was. When he came back, Dirty had taken the bag from him, studied it briefly, then placed it in her pocket. Then she announced that they should all get in the car.

"Where are we going?" Scooter asked as he pulled the car out onto the street. Dirty was in the back, giving directions while Rachel sat, arms crossed, in the passenger seat.

"Kensington Market," Dirty said.

"Why, to see a loan shark?" Rachel said dryly.

"No," Dirty replied, "but we are going to get your money back."

As the car pulled into one of the vacant spots on the side of the street, Dirty leapt out of the car, then leaned through Rachel's window from the curb.

"I need two cigarettes. I won't be long. Twenty minutes–tops." She knew Rachel had a pack in her purse. Dirty cradled them carefully as Rachel released them into her hand. Pounding up the stairs, she mashed the buzzer to the building's security door.

"Mmrphl?" the intercom belched.

"It's Dirty. Lemme in." Once inside, Dirty climbed the next set of stairs, a freshly-lit cigarette dangling from her lips. As she turned the corner on the landing, she saw that the apartment door was already open. Fern stared at her for a moment, then focused his gaze on the cigarette between her lips. His hair had somehow gotten crazier, wilder, bigger. He made a motion for her to come in, and the stench hit her like a hammer.

"Sit," he said.

"I need your help, Fern," Dirty said, purposely licking her cigarette. Fern stared. She took a deep drag. "I need to find someone."

She looked at Fern and noticed that his left eye was saggy and weepy--no, gooey. It was gross, but she supposed it was no more so than anything else in that place. He looked tired, like he had lost a lot of that energy she had seen before. The kind that made him seem so unstable. Maybe he still was, but it seemed to be wearing on him.

Dirty told him that her friend had had a big wad of money taken from him by a guy in the Junction offering used stereo equipment. The stuff turned out to be bogus, but he still lost all of his money. The same story Scooter had given to her.

"I had him go back to where it happened to get some evidence." Dirty produced the baggie from her pocket which contained three little cigarette butts, which she took out of the bag and placed in the middle of the table.

Fern stared a little longer at her mouth, then reached over and moved an ashtray towards her.

"Ahhhh. Mm." he said. He leaned over the table, his eyes barely an inch from the butts as he inspected them closely. Then he slid his hand forward and took one of the cigarettes, holding it almost inside his nose. He breathed in lightly, then put it back down. Fern sat, just looking. Dirty held her breath, fascinated and anxious. Then suddenly Fern was up, pulling two jars down from the shelf nearest the stove.

"Bold, but nervous," he said flatly (belly, lips). "Look here." He pulled two butts out of the first jar. "All these I found outside a bar on Parliament. Look how chewed the filters are. These cats are tough, but jonesing for somethin'. And they ain't real happy. Now this one," Fern opened the other jar, "if ya look, most of 'em are Player's King size an' shit–hard smokin' and," Fern sniffed one of them, "hard drinkin' too." He held out the butt for Dirty to smell, which she politely declined.

"But *some* of these...," Fern dug in the second jar a little deeper, then mashed his palm against his forehead and pushed it straight up into his hair. Twice. Dirty noticed that his tic had changed, and pushing the oil from his forehead straight up was making his hair gnarled. "Some of these are roll-your-own, see, and they haven't been crushed underfoot: They've been left to burn out, like he has things on his mind." By now Dirty had finished her first smoke and was well into her second. "Are you sure these are from the Junction?"

"Yeah..." Dirty frowned. Fern thought for a moment.

"It's nothing definite, but if you want my opinion," Fern said, eyeing the ashtray, "I'd put my money on jar number two." Dirty raised her eyes to meet his. "Go to Parkdale" As Dirty got up and moved for the door, she thanked Fern quickly.

"Dirty," (belly, lips, hair, hair, HAIR) he said, "does your friend like music?" Dirty stopped, her head cocked to the side.

"Hell ya," she said, "he's got a kick-ass collection."

Fern's face darkened. "So...," he ventured, "why does he need used stereo equipment?"

***

Back in the car, Scooter and Rachel were still not speaking to one another, but they were both feeling out of place in the market that late at night. As Dirty leapt down the front steps and jumped back into the car, there was a quick, quiet sigh of relief. From them, anyway.

Parkdale, Dirty thought, grimacing. It had been awhile since she had been there, since she had even thought of Alan, but now she was thinking of the kind of danger she could be in. As the car glided west along Queen Street, the silence coming from the front seat had morphed from tension and anger to tension and nervousness. "Where are we going?" Scooter asked, feigning benign, idle curiosity.

"I'm not positive," she said, "but my friend gave me a couple of places to check–here! Here!" Dirty pointed through the window and Scooter pulled the car into a spot a few doors down from a questionable-looking bar.

"Just wait," Dirty said, though she realized she didn't even know what this guy looked like. That part would be on Scooter. Half an hour later not much had happened, and Rachel had to pee.

"Look," Rachel said with an edge to her voice, "let's go. Just–forget about it!" Almost a full minute passed before Scooter spoke.

"Dirty, I gotta admit, Rachel's right. B'sides, if I barely know what this guy even looks like, how could your friend even know he'd be here?" There was another pause.

"Do you guys really wanna go?" Dirty asked, deflated.

"Wait," Scooter said. Everyone in the car froze. "Your friend was wrong, Dirty. The guy wasn't at this bar. He just got out of a cab across the street."

All eyes were on the small, dark-haired manboy on the opposite sidewalk, walking away from them to a darkened side street. Scooter was shocked to even see the little bastard again. Rachel was shocked that this guy could even be found. Dirty was shocked that they were following Martin. Scooter turned the car on and pulled back onto the street, following at a distance.

"Does this seem insane to any of you?!" Rachel said nervously. No one responded. Dirty's heart was racing faster than anyone else's, not just because of what they were doing, but because of where they were. She knew this street, and she knew he would be close by.

Scooter pulled the car over again, and shut off the lights and engine as they watched Martin climb the stairs to his apartment. The building was immediately familiar to Dirty, not because she had lived there with Alan, but because it was twelve doors down.

Watching from the street they saw a second-floor light come on after a few moments, and Martin breeze by the window. In a flash Dirty was out of the car and down the alleyway– (she had come this far, why stop now?), despite the whispered yelling of the others. The fact was, all of the buildings in the row were laid out the same, with the same shitty fire escapes, and the same crappy latches on the windows. Not that Dirty had figured out what she was going to do on the next fire escape landing, but it was worth having a look. So she climbed.

Peering through the glass, she could see little. The window opened on the kitchen (where the lights were off) and she could see down the hall to the living room, where both the TV and lights were on. There was also a light coming from under the door halfway down the hall, and if the layout was like

Alan's place, it should've been the bathroom. She slipped off her shoes and left them on the landing, believing she would make less noise in her socks.

Shaking from the cold, Dirty dug her nails in the soft, rotting wood of the window, both to test its weight and to see if it was latched (it was not). There was, of course, an actual door next to it, but a pile of beer and wine bottles had fallen over in front of it. Pulling with her shoulders, she raised the window enough that she could swing one leg through, half-straddling the frame. If he came out of the bathroom now, all she would have to do is fall back onto the landing and then run like hell.

She listened, but couldn't be sure of exactly what she was hearing. Was he blowing up a balloon in there? Lifting heavy furniture?

Dirty didn't know it, but what Martin was actually doing was trying to negotiate some of the problems that come with having an abnormally large colon. He sat there gripping the sides of his head, sometimes twirling the hair at his temples through his fingers as he got ready for another push.

Between the toilet and the wall next to him was a small bucket, and in the bucket was shitknife. It was a proper chef's knife, but Martin had been using it for a year or so now to break up the fecal matter he would deposit after great labour. Too big to be flushed down and too gross to be removed, he opted for cutting it up into smaller pieces that could be flushed. It seemed like the best solution to an uncomfortable problem.

Dirty quickly brought her other leg over the window sill and slid inside, frantically looking for something to prop it open with. Nothing. Gently (and using up precious seconds) she brought the window back down to its original resting place. She stood only for a moment before she comically soft-stepped her way down the hall, past the bathroom and the balled-up jeans on the floor, and into the living room.

"Jesus," she thought. Old pizza boxes, beer cases, Kleenex, cigarettes, porno mags, and an envelope on the table. "No fuckin' way," she thought, hoping the money was inside. Poking it, the envelope seemed only to contain thumbtacks and a long piece of red thread. Fuck.

Making a quick circuit of the room, she could see nothing that looked like it might hold a wad of—. Spinning around, she looked again at the jeans left on the floor in front of the bathroom door. Dirty crept over and toed them open, grimacing as she stuck her foot in Martin's underwear. But there it was. The bulge in his pants *had* gotten bigger. She reached down to grab the roll of money, being careful not to touch the (not-so) white cotton undies.

"ohgodohgodohgodohgod----hunhhhhhh!" Dirty didn't want to listen as Martin tried to pass a cantaloupe, but there was only a thin wood door between them.

For a split second she thought that this was her one chance to see him naked, but then slid down the hall in her socks as if she were skating, pushing the money into her own jeans. She was in the middle of the kitchen when the bathroom door opened.

Quickly, she swung herself around the fridge and froze. Listening, she could hear him moving around, sort of. What Dirty couldn't see was that Martin was still on the toilet, and had just pulled the door open to give himself some cooler air.

Despite the full light from the bathroom now, the kitchen was still quite dark. She knew it was only a matter of time before she was caught, so she had to move. Sliding over to the window and gripping the wood again, she raised it an inch. It creaked softly, but to Dirty it sounded like a foghorn. She froze.

Martin was still moaning and gasping, so Dirty went for the next few inches. At a foot, she felt a gust of icy wind push against her stomach, realizing he would feel it soon enough, too. She decided to pull the window back down for a moment, but it stuck. She tugged lightly, and then a little harder, but it didn't move. She even pulled her hands away completely, and it just hung there. She was absolutely fucked.

Martin was in such pain now, but there was no going back. He had to bear down and launch this one. Which was when he heard the window come down. And holy fuck was it loud.

Not knowing who or how many were out there, Martin grabbed shitknife and threw himself forward onto the floor. His giant turd was still crowning, so all he could do was pull himself along the floor on his elbows, a grotesque scatological chimera.

Hauling on it again, Dirty reefed the window high enough to push her upper body through, when someone grabbed her by the collar.

Pulling her onto the landing like a doll, Scooter had stuffed Dirty's shoes into his pockets and was now pushing her forward down the fire escape. At that same moment Martin had reached the window and pulled himself up and halfway through, out far enough to lunge with shitknife and just barely nick Scooter as he fled. Which is when the window came down once more, this time right on Martin's lower back, and with enough force to help him shoot out his bloodied turd-baby, right onto the kitchen floor.

Racing around to the front of the building, Dirty stared in disbelief–the car was gone! Hauling her up the street, Scooter told her that he had given Rachel the car, and she would meet them at the corner.

"You gave her the car while I was still in there?" Dirty was hopping on one foot, holding Scooter's arm and shucking one of her shoes on.

"Well, she had to pee," he said sheepishly.

"So?!"

"She really had to pee!"

The pair ran back to Queen Street and saw the car back in front of the bar, the original bar they had waited at. Out of breath and adrenaline-rushed, Scooter and Dirty walked into the beer-busy place and stood awkwardly in the entrance, scanning the room for Rachel who was fast-approaching from the rear of the bar, by the pool tables.

From across the room, sitting in the corner, someone watched as a woman (cute) walked from the bathroom to the front of the bar, to meet up with a guy (huge) and... her.

"Jesus shit!" Alan said through a mouth full of fries and gravy. He wanted to jump over the table and ring her little fucking neck. He wanted to, but now wasn't the time. Besides, the guy she was with was bigger than him.

Outside, the three piled into the car, with Scooter revving the engine triumphantly as he pulled a U-turn, heading east. In the shadow of the bar's lights, Alan was taking down the license plate.

Part Six
March 1998

CHAPTER 19:
Trying to shake off the cold

On the first Friday in March, Cheryl and Henry were sitting in the breakroom, with Cheryl giving Henry a run down of her latest theory.

"So, something has hit me recently."

"Herpes?" Henry teased.

"No fuck-o. A realization" the last word emphasized with a philosophic eyebrow arching. "What is the difference between 'sensual' and 'sexual'?" Henry thought for a moment, but came up empty.

"Ya got me."

"Okay," Cheryl continued, "let's say you have a lover and..."

"I wish," he pouted.

"Shut up. Hypothetically. You have a lover, and they take their finger and..."

"This is getting good!"

"Lemme finish! So, your lover takes their finger and draws it along your skin on the inside of your forearm towards your elbow. Feels nice, right?"

"Oh, my yes," Henry agreed.

"So, the question is, is that sensual or sexual? And the answer is: intent. If they're doing it as part of some lead-up, even foreplay, and it's somehow clear that you're interested in screwing, then it's 'sexual.' But if they're doing it because it feels nice, like you're on a beach, or walking down the street, or lying there after sex, with no intention of getting it on, then it's 'sensual.'"

There was a pause as he considered Cheryl's proposition.

"Question," Henry said. "What if you're in a bar and someone you don't know comes up and runs their finger along your arm—how do you know if it's sexual or sensual?" Cheryl gave him a pitying look.

"Dollface, you're in a bar. What do you think? And besides, the real question is, what if it's someone you *do* know?"

Henry seemed pleased with this, but was suddenly distracted as he looked over Cheryl's shoulder at the clock.

"Fuck. I need to get in on a phone conference for the next hour. See you in a bit!" Henry scrambled out the door then, but Cheryl was alone for no more than three seconds.

Andre came in then, and it was obvious to Cheryl that he had been waiting for Henry to leave first.

"Hey." he said, sitting across from her, both of them at one end of the long lunch table.

"Hey you," she replied. She was going to say more, but the look on Andre's face said that it was his turn.

"I have a question. A puzzlement, really."

"K..." she ventured.

"How can you be friends with that guy?" he said, not with derision exactly, but certainly with disappointment.

"Henry?" Cheryl said, her face scrunching in a what-are-you-talking-about way.

"Yeah. I mean, after what he did...."

Cheryl sat for a moment, not quite sure what to say next. She knew what had happened that night. She was there. They had a thing in the bathroom, it went south, they hashed it out, and there you go. But she couldn't just say that. It seemed too dismissive of whatever it was Andre wanted to tell her.

"So... why don't you tell me what he did...?

Andre sat up and back as if he had been poked with something hot. He actually hadn't been prepared to return to specifics. Not knowing what to say, it just fell out of his mouth. "He assaulted me."

Cheryl turned in her seat to face Andre squarely and then asked him to repeat what he had said.

"Henry assaulted me in the bathroom that night. I was too drunk to know what the hell was going on; hell, I was too drunk to know where I was. And he didn't care. He did not care. And he did it anyway. So what would you call that?"

When Andre had first said 'he assaulted me', Cheryl's first thought was that this guy is trying to save his straight-guy status card by saying he didn't like it. But when he started talking again about being too drunk to know what was going on, Cheryl began to go back in her own mind, to ask herself if she had been misreading that night this whole time. I mean, had she?

"Andre, I..."

"Look, I'm not bringing this up for the hell of it. I'm bringing it up because if I had a friend who had done what that guy did, he wouldn't be my friend anymore. And I like you, and you seem like a good person, so I was having a hard time figuring out why you are giving him a pass on this."

"Andre, I..."

"I'm guessing that this is the first time you've realized what it was that happened that night. And that tells me that maybe you didn't know. So I'm sorry this is kind of appearing out of nowhere. But even if you didn't know, he did. So the question is, what now?" Except he didn't really say it like a question.

"Anyway. I... I gotta go." As Andre walked out, Cheryl was left staring at the table, gripping her dress with her sweat-lathered hands. The knot in her stomach hurt.

***

Marie-France had spent almost all of February lost in new love. He called her all the time, she thought about him all the time. She thought it was exciting and adorable that he always wanted to know what she was doing. And the way he held her when they were together, it was exciting and exhausting and consuming. A bit rougher than she was used to, but to be honest she wasn't used to much. She had had two steady boyfriends in her entire life, and only had sex with one of them. But Josef doted on her when they were together. He bought her things and was always brushing her hair out of her face, cradling the back of her neck when they walked around in public.

He had that little temper flare, though. Sometimes he would get off the phone from a business call and start throwing things or hitting the wall. The first couple of times it happened had been quite startling to Marie-France, but she was beginning to get a handle on the lead-up signals. The way his voice would rise slightly, but his breath would shorten, sharpen even. She felt weirdly proud of being able to anticipate his mood, like she was connecting to him, even if he didn't always see it or appreciate it. Maybe being in a relationship was something she could be really good at.

***

At the end of the second week of March Henry was sitting in a different bar waiting for Cheryl. The snow had come back (again), and though the wind had dropped, the evening was a chilly mistress. Pulling another cigarette from the pack, Henry looked across the room at a man he swore he knew. Careful not to stare too long, Henry went through his mental roll-a-dex to try and place the face. Just then Cheryl came in, and Henry couldn't tell if her strange expression was simply from trying to shake off the cold.

"Hey," she said, distracted. Concerned, Henry leaned in.

"What's up?"

After a pause, she began again. "I just saw Marie-France outside, in a car. She was just sitting there like she was waiting for someone. When I went over and knocked on the window, she barely recognized me. A little smile and a wave. That's it."

The pair frowned, Henry giving (a token) consideration to what Cheryl had said. He was distracted, too. Nodding politely, he said "Well, she must be a busy girl. So how's... um, 'fit guy'? Whatever his name is...."

"Henry!" Cheryl spat, feigning insult. "It's been almost six weeks that I've know..." —Cheryl went pale, embarrassed in the forgetting — "known, um–... Charles!" She smiled and then covered her mouth with the lip of her glass. "Ah... I don't' really give a shit. We see each other every week or two. We ball, and —" Henry cut her off with a wave.

"'Scuse me, did you just say 'we ball'?"

Embarrassed, she murmured, "What...?"

"Who talks like that anymore? 'We ball...' Did he 'do ya,' too?!" Henry teased in his best tough guy voice. In a moment, though, the conversation would turn to something much more serious, while across the bar Josef had ordered another drink, as a few more patrons shuffled in to shake off the now brutal cold.

"Henry," Cheryl said with a kind of heaviness, "I need to ask you."

"Then you should ask me," he said playfully, not getting the change in her tone.

"I need to ask you about... Andre."

Henry swallowed hard.

"What do... you need... to know...?"

Cheryl looked down, took another sip of her drink that she really didn't want anymore, and then went for it.

"Henry. Was it consensual?"

In seconds his back was bathed in sweat, his throat dry. Then he nodded and said,

"Yes. It was a messy-drunk kind of sex. To be honest, it was over super quick, and I may have even passed out for a bit, I'm not sure. But we both seemed into it." And then Henry took a gamble. A gamble that Cheryl wouldn't be aware of the conversation he and Andre had had back in January.

"But I think... I wonder if Andre isn't so sure." Henry said. Cheryl's eyes widened, listening intently, wanting Henry to say something redeeming. "He was super drunk. Maybe too drunk. But so was I. It was sloppy on both sides. And maybe we shouldn't have. Maybe when two people are that drunk, it's best to just keep your pants on and go to bed. So yeah, it wasn't good decision making on either of our parts, but I wouldn't say there was anything nefarious."

Cheryl nodded and placed one hand in her lap. What Henry said seemed to make sense, on the surface. And part of Cheryl, the part that would eventually win, just needed to hear that surface plausibility. There was a little voice in her head that was saying things like, *you say you were that drunk, and you think you shouldn't have, and you did it anyway.* And, *don't think I don't see how you chose the words 'on either of our parts', and how that pushes blame onto Andre.* But enough of her wanted to believe what he was saying. Because if she didn't, if what he was saying now wasn't true, if he really had assaulted Andre, what would that say about Henry? What would that say about her, as his friend? Too much was at stake to not buy what he was selling. She drank a little more and said,

"Okay. Thank you. That helps clarify some things."

In Henry's mind, too much was at stake to think about what had happened in any other way. *Fuck! Why do I have to think about it at all? It's over. That's it. It just wasn't like he said it was. It isn't like he said it was. Everybody just needs to shut up about it. Jesus.* Henry ordered a double, hoping the alcohol would get rid of the bile taste. *I am not that person.*

***

"What are you doing?" Steve asked as Henry brushed his finger along the inside of Steve's forearm.

"Testing a theory," he said flatly. The bar was starting to get crowded, mostly with regulars. Hell, given the size of the community in Ottawa, who wasn't a regular–and Henry wanted to leave. Someone breezed behind them and leaned towards Steve's ear.

"Kitchen, 5 minutes." And walked on.

"Steven, no," Henry pleaded. "Can't we just go?"

"Yeah, yeah, no problem. I'll just tell them I'm bailing." Steve got up and jogged up the half-flight of stairs to the kitchen and restrooms. Henry ordered a quick soda water to clear his head and waited for Steve's return.

And waited.

Fifteen minutes later, Henry knew what had happened. "Mother fucker," Henry thought. He knew about Steve's little group of 'friends'—a bunch of guys who hung out at the gym, fucked, occasionally rented themselves out, and spent the money on coke. Pissed off, Henry got up from the bar, hopped the four stairs and turned right.

The layout of the bar was such that you could enter the front door and be on the dance floor almost immediately. Directly across the room was the main bar, and beside it, the stairs in question. Climbing them, you were met immediately on the right with the swinging door to the kitchen, and on the left (directly across from the kitchen) was the first bathroom. Technically there were two, but of course one could use whichever was less full—both doors said "ladies." Pushing the kitchen door open, Henry found exactly what he had expected. Leaning over the stainless-steel counter, which was covered in white powder, was one of the gym-monkeys, with Steve standing behind him with hands on his head, bouncing up and down with increasing rapidity.

Henry just stood there. Watching. Then the big one stood up and looked at Henry. Steve had turned to him, too. And with only a slight shake of his head, Henry walked over and took a face-full. Pulling deep through his nose, Henry's hands gripped the straw and the counter, tight. He had no idea what he was doing, but he was done being on the outside.

Everything lit up; his body burned. It felt like his heart was going to come out of his chest.   Steve grabbed him by the shoulders and stood him up, cackling.

***

As insidiously as winter had crept in, it finally began to recede. It was a cruel older sibling finally preparing to leave home, and all those days that you lived in fear of bodily harm were finally coming to a close. You could breathe again, without the looking-over-your-shoulder worry of another boot to the arse. But just as the rain started to seep into the pores of the city, thawing bones and buildings, the cold would sweep back in, bursting through the front door to inflict one more skin-twisting arm burn, before it left for good.

Rubbing her forearm gently, Marie-France sat on the couch in Josef's apartment, looking at her soggy boots lying limply in the hall. Josef had just walked through the room, not saying a word to her. She had arrived 40 minutes earlier, had driven out from the other side of town just to see him.

When she arrived though, Josef had acted like she had distracted him from diffusing a bomb, tearing into her verbally: how dare she arrive so presumptuously (*Hadn't he invited me?* she thought). Then he had pushed her to the couch and spat,

"Stay here." And there she sat, while once or twice he came through the room from the den to collect some papers or some such thing, only to go back again, shutting the door behind him. The third time he had emerged, she must have looked exceptionally pathetic because he finally stopped and muttered, "I'm just finishing some business—I'm on the phone with Australia. Stay here." And off he went again.

"Australia," she thought, and briefly considered (while still rubbing her arm) how odd it was that in one part of the world a summer could be starting, while in another part a winter could be setting in.

***

Steve left town a few days after the bender at the bar, without word to anyone, not even to Henry. Steve had come by to borrow some money and had said he would swing back in the evening. And that was it. By the morning after that, Henry had called the two or three of Steve's friends he could actually have a conversation with, but Henry seemed to be the last one to have spoken to him.

By the end of the third week of March, Henry passed through both panic and anger, and settled comfortably in simmering hatred. So that now in the last few days of the month, by nailing a series of men 10 years his junior, Henry managed to forget Steve for sometimes hours at a stretch.

Steve had done it before, of course. A year ago, he had disappeared for 10 days. It turned out he had been chasing some tail in Vancouver while on a bender. After putting the plane ticket on Henry's credit card. And the hotel. And there was that time just last October. But this time was different. This time Steve's friends weren't trying to keep his whereabouts hidden from Henry. They really didn't know where he had gone, or if he'd be back.

***

"Wanna smoke a joint?" Joel grunted, barely out of sleep and blinking at Henry.

"No," Henry sighed, sliding out of bed. "I have things to do today, and you have to go." Joel pouted, then scratched what little hair there was on his chest.

Trudging down the stairs and into the kitchen, Henry tossed enough grounds into the coffee maker for one and then, feeling bad, adjusted for two. Behind him, Dave the Smartest Dog in the World waited patiently beside his bowl, head on paws. "Shit! Sorry!" Henry exclaimed, dumping kibble quickly and unceremoniously into the dish. Munching slowly, Dave lifted an eyebrow to watch Joel come into the kitchen dressed in his club-wear from the night before, complete with bright green t-shirt emblazoned with the number 69.

"Coffee?" Henry asked, then regretted it almost immediately. Joel nodded enthusiastically, but because it was still brewing, they just stood in the kitchen silently, uncomfortably.

"Well..." Joel said, "mind if I smoke a joint?"

"Fuck it." Henry sighed. "Spark it up."

CHAPTER 20:
Play a game with me

Sitting at her desk, Marie-France tried to relax and take the weight off her bruises at the same time. Sore from Josef getting surprisingly physical, sore from the sex, she pressed her breasts against the wood, the only part of her where there was still feeling, but little pain. Strolling down the hall, Andre swept into her office and was stopped dead.

"Don' you fucking knock h'anymore?" she snapped. She had jerked back when he surprised her, and the pain made her react more harshly than she had intended.

"Okay..." Andre retreated several steps and stood in the doorway. "Sorry Marie-France... I was wondering if you had finished editing that copy I sent you last week. I needed it today." She squinted at him for a moment, sneering slightly, not knowing what the hell he was talking about.

"Muh? Shit Andre, I'm not finished yet," she muttered, waving him away with the back of her hand, leaving him wide-eyed.

"Well get it done, fuck! It's overdue already!"

Walking back out, Andre sent a shrug and "what the hell" look through Cheryl's open door, directly across the hall.

At lunch, most of the office went across the street to Andre's favourite bar, except for Marie-France who sat at her desk, and Henry, who had taken the day off (or as Cheryl had put it, had 'called in laid'). Marie-France tried to work through lunch but found herself staring off, wondering how she was going to make rent at the end of the week, with all of the money she had given to Josef. When she had asked him about it the day before, he suggested simply that she should move into his place, where she wouldn't have to worry about rent at all. Gently, she ran her fingers along her rib cage, feeling how real the soreness was, and wondered how long it would take her to pack.

Marie France thought about what it could be like sometimes. How beautiful and sweet Josef could be, buying her things and fawning over her. They could be sitting together watching a movie and he would brush her hair from her face, so delicately, and whisper things like 'I burn for you even when we're sleeping'. No one in her entire life had ever said such things to her. It felt almost...relieving. Like she didn't have to keep looking anymore. And sometimes love and care boils over, like you can't control it. Like he can't control it. But it's always still him. He's still in there. And Marie France was sure she could help him.

After lunch Cheryl came to see her, gently looking for clues, something to help her understand what Marie-France was going through.

"So...," Cheryl began, sitting squarely across from her. "What's up, duck?" Marie-France smiled a little and tried to sit back as casually as she could.

"I jus ave a lot on my mind lately. Tings are going well wit

Josef, and he wan' me to move in wit 'im. Jus a little nervous, I guess."

Cheryl looked surprised at the news, unsure how to proceed. She really didn't like Josef herself, but she wanted to be supportive just the same.

"Wow, that's a big step, hon." Immediately she felt stupid. "Uh, anything I can do to help?"

"Non, non, I th--ink I'll take a few days nex' week to pack and move, but my m--ind is m--ade up." There was a pause. "Sorry Cheryl. I don't wan to be rude, but I ave a file to fin--ish for Andre..."

Pursing her lips with nothing left to say, Cheryl got up and left with a forced "Good luck."

✳✳✳

By 3 o'clock Henry had accomplished little. He had then half-straightened the bedroom, half-cleaned the kitchen, and half-heartedly made himself lunch. "You're brooding, my boy," he told himself, rolling smoke around his mouth. Sitting on the couch, he watched the rain through the window and decided he would be better off in a public setting. Throwing on his coat and leaving Dave in his favourite chair, Henry got in the car and drove down to play some pool.

Puk! went the balls as Henry walked in, Josef breaking another game by himself. Their eyes met, each not quite recognizing the other, but Henry thought he would be polite nonetheless.

"I'm sorry, I think we've met before, but I'm not sure where." It was out of his mouth before he realized it sounded like a come-on.

"Yes... I think you work with Marie-France." His memory

sparked, having met Josef once before in the parking lot at work. Henry's hand shot out to Josef before he remembered he didn't really like him.

"I've just broken. Play a game with me." Feeling too awkward to decline, Henry ordered a scotch and grabbed a cue. Josef ordered another one for himself, specifying again that it should have one-and-a-half ice cubes.

"So, how is Marie-France?"

"Ugh, you know women," Josef grunted.

"I suppose..." Henry ventured, not really sure where this was going.

"Anyway, she's helping out with my business, not that I really need it now, but it gives her something to do." Henry's brow furrowed.

"What about her job?"

"She's going to quit. It's not good for her anymore."

"Is that what she said?" Henry asked. Josef held up his hand for silence as he attempted a shot, and made it.

"Anyway," Josef began again, "as my business grows more, I'll need her around. As I say, not now, but later."

"And until then...?" Henry asked.

Josef shrugged. "It's a big apartment. Things get dirty fast."

Puk!

Henry swallowed his scotch hard, too hard, stifling a choking cough as he put his glass down.

"Sorry Josef, I'd like to stay, but I have to go and let the dog out." Henry felt foolish and transparent.

"It's okay. Game's over anyway." Puk!

Driving home again, he had to swerve several times as his windshield was drenched in the wake of oncoming trucks on the bridge. Henry thought about Marie-France—it was quarter to five, but he didn't feel like going to see her at the office. It could wait until morning. She would probably be okay, anyway.

By the time Josef got home, Marie-France was asleep on the couch. She had gone over there to ask him what she should do about this month's rent, since she couldn't just give two days' notice. She had waited but, her body stretched thin, fell unconscious almost as soon as she sat down.

"Get up," he nudged her. "Get up or I swear I'll burn you where you sleep." Slowly she roused, not comprehending what he had said.

Josef smiled. "Want some tea?"

***

Marie-France phoned in on Friday morning, both to take the day off and to give her two weeks' notice. Hugo, in personnel, had thought her voice had sounded funny–not sick or congested, but somehow swollen.

Part Seven
April 1998

CHAPTER 21:
Always

It had been almost two weeks since Dirty had slept with Ruben. Twice. And God it was sweet. *But bad! So bad!* she told herself. *Very Very Bad!* How could she do that to Marina? What was she thinking? Well, she really hadn't been thinking, because they had been drunk. But how could they have known that it would work out like that? The first time….

Mind you, two days later he went to her place after Rachel and Scooter had left for work. She remembered barely getting the door closed when he spun around behind her, his hands on her hips and his mouth on the back of her neck. They stood there together, Dirty leaning against the door, pushing back into his body as his hands found hers and...

So yeah. How could she have known that it would happen again?

The first time started at a bar. Innocently enough, to be sure. Mostly. It was a bar they had been to before, once with Marina and Scooter and Rachel as well. (They weren't all fast friends, but they knew so much about one another through Dirty, they all had to get together at some point.)

But it had only been her and Ruben that first time that it ended up happening, when Marina had gone to see her parents in Orangeville. So, they talked and drank. A lot. By closing time, they were staggering out the door and they walked closely, holding hands and holding each other up and holding their breath. Finally, she turned to Ruben, placing her hands on his face and kissing him hard, their bodies pulled into each other, their bodies so close not even the silly gobs of falling snowrain could seep between them. She remembered his bruised lips and the shape of his hip bone in her palm, and he took her home to the couch, the floor, the hall, the bed, the morning.

And as her body lurched back towards consciousness with the sunrise, she was horrified at what she had done. Then she slipped from his bed, pulled on her still-wet clothes and gingerly descended the fire escape, pulling herself along Roncesvalles in sunlit, rain-wet guilt.

She needed to make sure it wasn't going to happen again. It was a mistake. They were drunk. She regretted the whole thing. And she was going to be strong now. And the guilt was heavy and terrible.

So how could it have happened again? Marina was supposed to be back on Monday night, but Monday morning Ruben called Dirty, and 45 minutes later there he was, the two of them leaning against the door, his hands finding hers.

Two weeks had passed now, and Ruben and Marina, and Dirty and Marina, and Ruben and Marina and Dirty were all getting along normally. Mostly. But there were times when it seemed like Dirty's brain would burst, the tension so thick in her head, and Marina didn't have a clue. And Ruben–stupid-assed Ruben–sits there smiling innocently, occasionally caressing Marina's shoulder like she was the only thing in the world. Not that Dirty cared, mind you, but goddammit, could he show a little bit of regret? Remorse? Tension? Satisfaction? Dirty wasn't sure what she wanted from him–maybe just to know that she was still on his radar, that at least he thought about her sometimes.

***

About two or three days after the fiasco in Martin's apartment, Scooter started having problems with a cut on his butt. It was red and puffy and, yeah, probably infected. As soon as they had gotten home that night, he had been semi-careful to clean it and bandage it (although at the time he told neither Rachel nor Dirty that Martin had actually managed to get him with the knife). He hadn't bothered putting some kind of antibiotic something on it; but then, he had no idea that the knife he had been clipped with had fecal matter on it.

By the third day his upper leg and ass were red and sore, which is when he started slathering the wound in an antibiotic cream he found at the back of the cupboard in the bathroom. By day five he was running a steadily high fever, and Rachel was wondering what the hell was wrong with him. He showed it to her when she asked what was wrong. It was alarming to look at, and Scooter suggested that he must have sat on something sharp at some point, but he couldn't remember what.

So as they crept closer to the middle of March, Rachel and Scooter ended up in the walk-in clinic at the end of their street. Which is where they had their first meeting with Dr. St. John Always Callan. His mother had been an occasional Buddhist, and thought that the middle name 'Always' sounded mystical and important.

Scooter was almost delirious by this point, and so he wasn't really in a position to get a good read on the doc. Rachel, however, had a very clear impression after the first five minutes of him speaking. She didn't trust him. She didn't even know him, and she didn't trust him.

Dr. Callan was tall and lanky, except for the small, round pot belly that looked completely out of place with the rest of his body. His jawline angled sharply down to the point of his chin where some scraggly whiskers lingered.

He had an odd demeanor that was unsettling not just to Rachel but also to most of the people who worked in the clinic. Every time he spoke, he would smile that non-smile, an almost textbook non-Duchenne smile. But it wasn't like he was trying to hide something—more like he was looking for legitimacy or validation on every fucking thing he said. It was as if he was saying 'did I pass?' 'Did that come off as something a regular person would say?' Every. Time. It was creepy. Rachel was sure she would be reading about him in the newspaper at some point. And not in a good way.

"Okayyy...we should have a look, huh?" St. John Always Callan was rubbing his hands with sanitizer. Rachel wanted to leave, go somewhere else, but she knew this was probably the best chance to get Scooter some strong antibiotics right away. Scooter dropped his pants, wincing.

"Well that's a doozie, isn't it?" St. John Always Callan looked from Rachel to Scooter and back again. But then he seemed disappointed. "Mm. Uninterestingly bacterial. Not catastrophic, though. A little infection gets a little antibiotic. No need to amputate your bottom, eh?" He started writing on a pad.

"That's it then?" Rachel asked, trying to hide her incredulity. "Not going to...check anything else? At all?

Temperature? Medical history? How he got it?"

"He probably sat on something. I don't imagine you were knife-fighting with your bottom, eh?" St. John Always Callan had a smear of perspiration over his balding head and was giving that smile again. "500 mg Flucloxacillin, 4 times a day until finished." And then he got up and left. Rachel was getting ready to protest, but Scooter really did look like shit. She sighed.

"I'll drop you back at home and then go and fill this." Scooter nodded droopily and said nothing.

***

Dirty had been trying to find a time to talk to Scooter about what really happened that day that he lost the money, that she didn't believe that it was about bogus stereo equipment. But every time she thought it was the right time, he seemed to look worse and worse. At least he was on antibiotics now. And anyway, there was another part of her that maybe just didn't want to know what had actually happened.

"I have to talk to you," Rachel whispered to Dirty in the hallway. Dirty motioned with a nod, and the two of them slid down the stairs to the basement apartment. Scooter was sleeping upstairs, as was Seeger, so there wasn't a need to be whispering. Except Rachel was knee-deep in shock and embarrassment, and it felt like a whisper was all she could muster.

They sat on the ratty couch as Dirty rolled a joint for the two of them. Rachel didn't smoke terribly often, but occasionally. And this certainly was an occasion.

"Look what I found," she said to Dirty, handing her a small, black plastic bag with what felt like a catalogue inside.

"What is it?" Dirty asked, her voice pinched as she held in the smoke. She passed the joint to Rachel.

"Just...just look." Dirty pulled two magazines out of the bag, her brow furrowing.

"What...the...fu...?" she breathed. And then she started to laugh. "What is this?!" she said, her nose scrunching with each page she turned. "Where did you get this?" Dirty was holding the book in front of her, looking at it like it was in another language she couldn't decipher. And each time she thought she was getting the measure of it, she would turn the page and it would get weirder. But then she was laughing again, because the pictures were just so absurd. Clearly, they were supposed to be titillating, but they were just so deeply unsexy.

Rachel was starting to feel a little less tense, thanks to Dirty's laughter, but her heart felt heavy.

"Scooter's car. I was looking for a CD I thought I had left in there." She waited. "What do you think this means?" She was pressing her hands down on her knees, trying to wipe the sweat away.

"Does he..." Dirty didn't know how to finish her own sentence. "I mean have the two of you…?"

"NO! God, no! I had no idea that he…that there even was…" and then she pretended to make a retching sound.

"Dude, that's fucking weird." Dirty paused. "What are you going to do? Are you going to ask him about it?"

"No. I mean, how can I? What am I supposed to say? What is he supposed to say?" Dirty hadn't even looked at the second magazine. But then she did, and it was worse.

"What does it mean if he gets off on cartoons...?" Dirty wondered out loud, which sent Rachel into a new tunnel of revulsion. *What the fuck have I been doing with him this whole time?* Rachel thought.

"How could I have missed this?" Rachel curled her fingers into almost-fists in front of her mouth, her eyes glistening and wet.

"Should you put it back and pretend you never found it?"

"How can I? How can I look him in the eye and pretend I don't know?" For a moment neither of them said anything.

"C'mon," Dirty said, grabbing her hand. "We've gotta get some air."

***

They walked for almost an hour, the evening breeze easing Rachel's tension headache, but only slightly. And then they came across the sign.

"Ooh!" Dirty stopped and read it through. "Oh my god, this sounds terrible. Let's go in!" Dirty said, bouncing up and down.

"What is it...?" Rachel asked, reading. The sign read Discover the Secrets and Threats of the Relationship Virus! A Free Public Seminar, tonight 7pm. And then she read the last line. *Dr. St. John Always Callan.* "No. Absolutely not. That guy is a creep and a weirdo and probably several other things. No way."

"EVEN BETTER. And look--he even managed to fuck up that medical symbol thing: It says he's a doctor, but he put that stick with two snakes on it." Rachel, her eyebrows peaking, gave her head a small shake as if to say 'so...?'

"A stick with *one* snake is the symbol of medicine. A stick with *two* snakes is called a caduceus. It's the symbol of Hermes. Two snakes bad. One snake good. For medicine, at least." Dirty was pretty pleased with herself.

"Yeah, this still isn't selling it for me," Rachel complained.

"Come awwwwn," Dirty pleaded. "Think of the cringey story it will give us to tell people! COME ON!" Dirty was so insistent that Rachel let herself be dragged inside.

Up at the front of the seminar room was a stroller where Diamond Glass was sleeping, while her mother Rowena talked to the evening's special guest speaker. Finding two seats near the aisle, right in the back row, Dirty and Rachel settled in, with Dirty still gleeful at the prospect of seeing a train wreck.

Dirty was about to explain to Rachel that she knew the woman up near the front from the cafe, and Rachel was about to explain to Dirty where she had seen this guy before, but at that moment Dr. St. John Always Callan stood up from his crouched position with Rowena Glass and addressed the room.

"Friends, welcome," he said, clasping and unclasping his hands. His baldness still glistened like before, and he punctuated everything he said with a slightly forward-leaning tilt of his head, as if to say 'riiight...?'. He made Rachel queasy. Dirty, on the other hand, positively vibrated with anticipation.

"Oh god, he's so weird!" she whispered to Rachel who smirked in agreement.

Although many people in the room had assumed that his first name was pronounced as it seemed— 'Saint John'—he pointed out that the proper way to say it was to give it a good British mashing, turning it into "Sinjun". And then he went on.

"Tonight, I want to talk to you about relationships. All sorts of relationships" (riiight?) "Many of us believe that when we meet other people, we just come together, find each other compatible (or not), and that is the end of the story. But I am going to tell you about—" He stopped. Rowena Glass had her hand up. "I shall begin taking questions in a little while," he said, making a lowering motion with his hand as she then lowered hers.

"But before I say more about relationships, I want to tell you a story. A few months back I was in a little shop to buy a coffee, when I noticed a customer being quite rude to the person serving her. Quite. Rude." For emphasis here he peered over the top of his glasses. "There was some issue with the drink that had been made, but I shall tell you, I have never before nor since been witness to a rudeness of this magnitude, particularly over such an insignificant thing." He paused, and the room held its breath. "I decided at that point to do something to salvage the dignity of the young person receiving this abuse. So I walked over to the rude customer and... stared at her hair." There was some laughter, but more out of confusion than anything else. Because no one had any idea what that was supposed to mean.

"You probably don't have any idea what that is supposed to mean, but I will tell you. She looked at me with the same anger and derision with which she had been looking at the server person, and she said something like 'What the gosh-darn heck is your problem?'. And I said to her, very innocently, 'Please take no offense, but I could just swear that I saw two things in your hair, crawling'. And I continued to stare, as if to look for them." The people in the room were now tittering with disbelief.

"From that point on, she could not regain her former anger and rudeness; her hand shot up to her head and began to scratch, and she looked around nervously, over and over. Dislodged from her perch, she gathered her things and left." A few people near the front, including Rowena Glass, applauded lightly. Dirty and Rachel did not.

"What I want you to pay attention to is not that someone's bad behavior was halted, although it was. Rather, I want you to think about how the mere suggestion that there was something in her hair--and I assure you, there was nothing actually there--made her sensitive to every little feeling on her head, and that every itch and vibration would thereafter be interpreted as, quite possibly, being a bug of some sort." At this point both of the doctor's hands flourished upward, as if he were preparing for some big reveal.

"What I want you to think about is how changing this woman's interpretation of various sensations on her head made her experience those sensations in a very different way. When I suggested that there might be something important to pay attention to, her perspective changed, and so too her focus and priorities." Dr. St. John Always Callan placed his hands on his belly then, but not in a haughty sort of way. It just looked like he couldn't find any other good place to put them. It looked awkward.

"And so, what I want to do for you this evening is to suggest a different way to look at the relationships in your life and, in so doing, to consider how changing your perspective may change your interpretation of your relations, and perhaps also your priorities...." He seemed to delight in a weird, condescending intonation on this last point, as if he were finally opening a box of ancient wisdom.

"I think my Weird Meter just went to DefCon 3," Dirty whispered. Rachel gave her a 'tell me about it' look. She was going to say something witty in reply, but just then the doctor started up again.

"I want you to think of each other—and yourselves—like viruses. Not necessarily bad ones, mind you. There certainly are bad ones in the world, but that is not quite what I mean. Instead, I want you to imagine that when you meet a person, you begin to receive part of them in yourself and they part of you. Not some mystical thing, like their soul or some such, but some characteristic of them that makes them who they are." Rowena Glass's hand shot up, but this time she didn't wait to be called upon.

"Is that like when people come to our country and pretend to be one of us?" The room stopped, and even St. John Always Callan seemed confused.

"Erm...no." Then he continued. "Have you noticed how older couples seem so much like each other that they even start to look alike?" Most of the room nodded in agreement, but Rachel crinkled her nose, thinking that was kind of banal. "These people have acknowledged many of the new interests and characteristics of the other person and, as so often happens, they take them up as their own. Your new friend likes comic books and, soon enough, you find yourself lingering over the comic book section in the bookstore, since this other person has opened up for you the possibility of enjoying such things. And so you have, in effect, endorsed those characteristics by taking them up as your own. Sometimes it is just a turn of phrase that you start using, sometimes it is a preference for a certain food or activity the other person endorsed first. Who knows?" (riight?)

Dirty was pouting. This was way less goofball than she had wanted. She was hoping Rowena Glass might say something else hilarious. Anything.

"And so, when we become close to another, we exchange this kind of metaphorical virus that is us, really, and we begin to endorse the way of living they have, and they ours. So, if I am now a friend of Willy, part of my evolving self-identity is as a Willy-friend, in addition to being a Mary-son, and a Veronica-brother, and so on." At this point Dirty was giggling madly at the thought of being a willy-friend. Finally, it was getting good. Rachel was trying to punch her into silence.

"BUT!" and here he waved his finger at the crowd in a cautionary gesture. "What happens when we find something about the other person that we dislike, or that we cannot endorse?" Dirty and Rachel exchanged looks. St. John Always Callan continued.

"Isn't there a risk that we might be infected by this bad thing? Well, if it is a small thing, our healthy selves—our strength of character—can swamp such a bad germ. We can see and acknowledge that this new consideration is not a good fit for the person we ourselves are or want to be, and we may hold it at bay. I like you, Willy, but this is not a thing I can get behind, as it were. BUT when it is a big thing, something that matters, that there is something important…." He wiped the sweat from his head and mashed his now-wet hand across his pants.

"When we reject someone we previously endorsed, we are also attacking part of ourselves, because they had infected us in many different, still-compatible ways. (riiight?) If we begin to reject Willy, we must also begin to reject that part of ourselves that we identify as 'Willy-friend'. It is that part of us that had come to own or identify or internalize part of this other person. That excision—" and here he paused for sharp emphasis, "that self-amputation is why it hurts to reject the person. But that excision is good for us nevertheless, assuming it turns out that the other person really should be rejected." In spite of her intention to avoid any sort of contact with this man, Rachel's hand shot up.

"So what is a good reason to reject someone?"

"Ah!" St. John Always Callan paused for just a moment, as if he recognized Rachel, but then continued. "Perhaps because some part of them is something that you yourself cannot endorse, something you cannot or will not allow to infect you, because of the person you believe yourself to be. A person might be very open-minded, tolerant, accepting—perhaps she is a vegetarian, but acknowledges and accepts that her good friend is not. She decides that they can continue being friends, despite this difference.

"But maybe there are some things she just cannot imagine herself being, cannot imagine herself endorsing so closely to her own sense of goodness. She may discover subsequently that her friend also attends dog-fights, or cock-fights, or some other kind of animal abuse. And on this matter, she cannot continue to endorse this person, nor indeed to endorse *herself* as someone who is friends with that sort of person.

"But just know!" he exclaimed, "a weaker immune system—a person of weaker moral character—can be infected by just about anything. Such a person does not have a sense of which things are good for them, which things should be endorsed and which rejected. And so, they just carry along, accruing and accommodating and allowing such an infection to grow."

Rachel grimaced. Dirty was still stuck on the phrase 'cock-fight'. But they both wanted to leave.

"A person's strong character is like a strong immune system. She would be able to fend off or reject the contagion of another's poor character. But a person with a weak immune system would quickly become infected by the depraved influence of others, and he would have no way of fighting it off."

"So who is worse?" a young man somewhere in the middle piped up, although without raising his hand. "Is it worse to be a bad person, or that weak kind of person?"

Dr. St. John Always Callan smiled broadly, even enthusiastically. "I must say that I find the depraved person less revolting. At least he stakes his soul on the moral weight of his actions! The weak person will not even say that he is committed to that! Because he cannot say he is committed to anything!"

"What if—" a sixty-something woman in the front row, near Rowena, had her hand up. "What if the thing you get from the other person turns out to be a lie? If you believe a person is one thing, and that thing is good, but then it turns out to not be true. What if—"

"You mean just like all those immigr—" Rowena cut in, but was cut off herself.

"Ah!" Dr. St. John Always Callan responded. "We can only take up and endorse what we believe to be true. We can do no more and no less. Even if we are wrong, or we are deceived, their words are all we have to go on...." He inhaled sharply. "Let us pause for a moment, perhaps for coffee, perhaps for some biological imperatives." And with that Dr. St. John Always Callan clapped his hands, as if concluding a magic show.

CHAPTER 22:
Home to roost

Tink. Spoon in cup. Rachel sits in the kitchen, staring over her cup at the table. The mid-morning sun is stretching through the blinds, easing a single beam across her forehead. *Maybe this is how it ends. Maybe I just say 'enough' and he says 'I know', and we just wrap it up. Maybe it's easier than everyone says. Maybe.*

But there was something else that Rachel was thinking about, something that Dirty had said on their walk home from the seminar last night. She said that maybe it wasn't as big a deal as Rachel was making it seem. He has a kink. So what? Lots of people do. And it's not like he's into kiddie porn, or poop stuff, or something. Maybe just let him have his thing. Maybe it can still work.

Rachel tried to think about that; she tried to think like that. Why did this have to be such a big deal for her? Maybe it didn't have to matter so much.

But it does fucking matter. It just does. And I can't let it go. I can't just be in the same room as him and think 'here is the man I love and I love everything about him and even the stuff I don't I still kinda like'. Because I don't. I just don't. And because I can't. And because I... won't.

Tink.

Rachel's mind wandered to making another trip to Ottawa. She wondered what Henry would say about this bloody mess. She wanted to get away. She could see Scooter's shadow in the living room from where she was sitting, and hadn't realized he had come home so soon. And she had no interest in talking to him right now. She just couldn't look him in the eye, and he didn't even know that she knew.

Just then, like a blessing, Dirty came up from the basement and looked gently into the kitchen at Rachel. Rachel sighed. Dirty gave her a 'just relax' hand motion, and then stepped softly into the living room to say hi to Scooter. A minute later, she called Rachel to come in the room. Rounding the corner into the living room, Rachel noticed that Dirty was sitting on the couch right next to Scooter, pulled in quite close. And what she noticed after that was that Scooter wasn't Scooter, but some other person with a terrible ponytail. A man was holding a knife to Dirty's throat, motioning for Rachel to take a seat across from them. Rachel's eyes had grown so wide they almost hurt, her mind spinning to understand what the hell was going on and why.

"You're going to go upstairs and dig into your jewelry box or your penny jar or whatever you're going to do and you're going to give me my thousand dollars." He nudged the knife closer to Dirty's skin to make the point. "Or I'll ventilate her throat." Rachel was terrified, shocked, and also quite confused.

"Um, who are you again...?" she asked bluntly. Almost hilariously, both Alan and Dirty gave the same 'oh come awwn' look, although neither knew the other was doing it. Dirty answered.

"Long story, hon. Best if we just do what he says." She

paused, then said to Alan with a tiny tilt of her head, "I thought it was like, six hundred or something."

"Keep talking, bitch, and we'll just make it twelve hundred." Alan had lost weight, Dirty noticed. Not a lot, but his face was a bit thinner.

Rachel's mind immediately went to the money she and Scooter had gotten from her mother. That would have solved this problem easily. If they still had it in the house. When they had finally gotten it back, Scooter was so adamant that they get it out of the house and into a bank, somewhere he wouldn't have to worry about it going missing. So it was sitting in a bank account she had. Not invested yet, but safe.

"Why would I keep that kind of money just lying around the house?" Rachel ventured cautiously.

"I don't really care where you keep it," he said, "but you better figure it out quickly, or you'll be spending a bunch more on cleaning this couch when I ventilate her throat." Rachel's chest tightened. She thought for a moment and then said

"There's a corner store down the street with a bank machine in it. I can run down there and take the money out." Alan stared and frowned, apparently thinking. Then he set his jaw and growled,

"You got 9 minutes to get back here with the money." He glared at Rachel. "me and this miss are going to sit here and have a chat while you do that. But you've got 9 minutes. And when that nine minutes is up, if you're not back I'm going to ventilate her throat. And if anyone but you comes in through that door, at any time, I'll—"

"Ventilate her throat." Rachel and Dirty groaned in unison. "You know..." Dirty continued "it might be helpful to take on a few different versions of that expression, just for the sake of variety. Like, puncture her windpipe, or give her an impromptu tracheotomy…."

"Ooh! What about 'torture her trachea?'" Rachel offered, a little too excitedly.

"I think that's a blowjob, Rach." Dirty frowned.

"Alrighty," Rachel blushed. Alan looked confused, like he was having trouble keeping up with the conversation.

"Nine minutes," he grunted at Rachel.

"But it'll take me five minutes just to walk there!" she protested.

"Well I guess you better run."

Rachel had her purse in a chokehold as she bounded out of the house and across the lawn. Nearly tripping over the edge where the grass meets the sidewalk, she sprinted down towards the corner store (now with video rentals!), with her right shoe in danger of flying off. On her way she suddenly realized that she had a $500 daily limit on withdrawals on her bank card. Which meant she'd have to take money out of two different accounts. Which meant two separate transactions. Rachel tried to figure out how much more time that would take, but there was an even bigger problem waiting for her at the bank machine in the store when she got there, by which time two minutes had already elapsed.

At 82, Lottie Dymott stood 4 foot 11 inches, plus an additional 8 inches of white, beehive hairdo. Her eyes were quite good, but the arthritis had gotten to her knuckles, so her hands weren't quite as deft as they used to be. Still, they were good enough to hold a Camel-ultra-light-cigarette-in-the-blue-and-white-package-thank-you-very-much, and she needed to take out some money in order to buy some. And she didn't trust those darn machines at the cash register that take it right out of your account. No sir. So Lottie carefully blipblipped her way through the instructions on the screen, sometimes pressing the button, always muttering under her breath.

As Rachel came barrelling into the store, she headed straight for the cash machine near the back, white-knuckling her card the whole way there.

When she got there, she found herself staring into the back of Lottie Dymott's hairdo, which also blocked Rachel from seeing how inept Lottie was at getting her money out.

"Oh...," Lottie was making that old lady cooing sound. "Oh you...." Rachel's eyes were bulging now. "Chequing... or... savings...."

Rachel was feeling so much pressure in her chest that she thought she was going to pass out. Gripping her card in her teeth, she did what an up-til-now Rachel would have said was terribly rude and shocking. Pulling Lottie aside, Rachel stepped in and finished the transaction herself, stuffing two fresh twenties into Lottie's hand and tossing her card up in the air and back, coming down to nest right in Lottie Dymott's hair. "Oh my!" she said curtly. There were four minutes left.

By the time the old woman had processed what had happened and had placed her money in her black patent leather purse with the gold top snap, Rachel was already finished with her first transaction and was working on getting the other $500. Outside the store, Scooter was just driving past and up the street to the house.

Eight minutes had elapsed when Rachel came running back out of the store, which made it almost impossible for her to get back to Dirty in time. She just hoped this guy's watch ran slow.

But she ran, and she ran hard, and with about fifty meters left, Rachel could see something she hadn't anticipated. Two things, actually. The first was that she could see that Scooter had come home, because there was his car in the driveway. The second was that the front walk was covered in blood.

***

Scooter was driving with one hand, because in his other hand was a brand new video he had gotten delivered to his post office box near work. And this one was supposed to be unbelievable. But what happened when he pulled into the driveway of the house was a total boner killer.

Scooter had just turned off the car when some guy with a stupid pony tail and covered in blood came staggering out of the house, bouncing across the hood of the car. The guy had already rolled, fallen, and scrambled back up by the time Scooter got the car door open. Whoever he was, he had made a goddamn mess of the front walk. Scooter probably could have caught the guy, but as far as he knew, Rachel was in the house, so he went slamming through the front door at full tilt. And what he saw inside was blood. So much blood and gore.

***

Moments after Rachel had gone streaking out of the house eleven minutes before, Dirty and Alan sat on the couch in silence. Weirdly, Dirty felt like she should say something to break the tension, but couldn't really come up with anything. Behind the back of the couch, however, there was some excitement brewing.

His pupils had become the size of dinner plates, and whatever it was that Seeger was looking at, it looked delicious. Seeger's face was pointed straight up, ears back, as he carefully watched that stupid ponytail of a thing twitch and swish every few seconds. This was his moment.

In a moment of comedic timing, both Alan and Dirty opened their mouths simultaneously. For Dirty, it was because she was about to idly ask how Alan's little brother was doing, the one who used to get her weed when she was in the 11th grade and he in the 10th. For Alan, it was because a set of cat claws had just been driven into the back of his skull.

Alan screamed and squealed in a way Dirty had never heard before, and it wasn't until he reached back and grabbed Seeger by the head that she realized what was going on. In that instant, her brain clicked over and she made a move. Alan had moved both of is hands up to grab the cat, dropping the knife behind the couch in the process, so Dirty made a desperate grab for the oversized ash tray on the table in front of them (Cuba Libre!) and brought it around full force into the side of Alan's jaw. Again. And then up over top of him, bringing it slicing down through his forehead. Blood. Everywhere.

Alan stood, hazy but enraged, and ready to twist Dirty's head off. But the cat was on him again, bounding from the floor to the couch and then up to his ear, slashing with his claws. Alan grabbed at the cat again, spinning in place, but catching his shin on the corner of the coffee table and stumbling toward Dirty.

Another bash sent the ashtray bursting through Alan's orbital bone. The crushing pain sent him down on all fours between the couch and the table, down low enough that Dirty could take one more giant swing, this time at his lower spine, hitting him so hard that he actually felt his legs tingle. And that was enough. He stood, wobbled, lurched for the front door and stumbled through, smearing blood and bits with every step.

Dirty stood there for what seemed like minutes, and what must have looked like a horror film, as Scooter walked in fully prepared to vomit.

***

The police stayed for hours, going over again and again what everyone knew about Alan, what Dirty's relationship to him was, what it was that he wanted. Over and over. None of them had any real answer for how this guy could have known she was there, but Dirty gave them a gloss on Alan's history and where he lived and usually hung out. The whole time she was talking to the cops though, she was petrified that Rachel and Scooter would be thinking that this was the sort of person she was, someone who would be involved with a guy like that. Someone who would bring problems like this into their home....

When Rachel had come running in with the money, the first thing she thought was that Alan had killed Dirty because Scooter had walked in unannounced, upsetting the whole situation. No one was supposed to come through the door except for her. That was the arrangement. But when she saw that Dirty was alive, she figured that Scooter and beaten the crap out of the guy. But when she saw how nauseated Scooter looked, she realized that was unlikely. And it took a little while longer for her to get Dirty to tell her what exactly had happened. Rachel wanted to hug her then, but she was really, really gross.

CHAPTER 23:
Do what you have to

Embarrassed. Small, and needy, and embarrassed.

"I am a tire fire," Dirty said quietly to no one, since no one was in the room. She felt so ashamed about what had happened, about what she had brought to Rachel's front door. It was all her fucking fault. It was like everything that she touched turned to shit. She had even been stupid enough to think she was actually getting somewhere, building a life or some shit. But it always comes back. The fact that she was a useless piece of shit wreck of a person. Not even a person. Just a walking mistake pretending to be a person.

Rachel and Scooter kept saying that it wasn't her fault, that Alan was the wrecking ball in the situation. But Dirty knew. And more than that, Dirty knew that they knew. Alan had come there because of her. And the police, and that weird cleaning company, and the shake in Rachel`s voice, all of it. All of it there because of Dirty. And what about what she did to Marina? What she did behind Marina's back? How could that not be her fault?

Dirty had spent almost every minute down in the basement

since the police had left; she stayed curled up, ashamed and tiny.

"You know, you can come up...," Rachel said gently, taking three steps down the basement stairs. Dirty was sitting on the couch and didn't meet her eyes. Rachel looked and waited, took a deep breath, moved down the rest of the stairs and slid in beside Dirty. She looked at Dirty then and waited, trying to not even make a sound in the hopes that the empty space between them would make Dirty want to say something. Something.

Dirty sat, her hands turning over each other, pressing and wringing, trying to squeeze the pressure of shame out of her body. Impossible, globby tears hung in her eyes, waiting, and she wanted to say it all, say how it was her fault, how she didn't know that any of it would happen, that she was so scared and alone and she just wanted to disappear from everyone's lives so she wouldn't burn anything else down.

"This wasn't your fault, love. That guy came after you, and he did what he did because *he* was in control of his actions. Not you. You are not responsible for what he does or did. And what he does or doesn't do doesn't say anything about the kind of person you are. And you're good, Dirty. You're good."

"No," Dirty replied, squeezing her hands tighter. "I mean, I know what you're saying, *here*," she said, motioning to her head. "It makes sense. I get it. But..." Head shaking, palms upturned, defeated. "But I can only go so far in my life before I start to see how things like this happen *all the time*. How long should I go before I look around and realize that *I'm* the common piece to all of these fucking catastrophes? I mean...." Here Dirty paused, not positive that she wanted to share this next piece of information even though it was practically out of her face anyway. "Maybe I'm not responsible for other people's behaviour, but I am responsible for mine. And would a good person…would a good person…jesus, I fucked Ruben behind Marina's back, okay?" Dirty crushed her eyes shut, wincing, half-expecting Rachel to do something like punch her in the face. Or maybe wanting her to.

Rachel was quiet for some time, her mouth turned down in a I-did-no-see-that-coming expression.

"Well…," she began. This was not the sort of thing Rachel could really get behind. She liked to think of herself as pretty open minded; there were lots of things she could totally be okay with, even if they weren't the sort of thing that she might choose to do herself. But then there were other, firmer lines that were forged in her head, lines that you just didn't stomp on. And for Rachel, this was one of them. And Dirty knew that, too.

"Well…," she began again, "does Marina know?" Dirty shook her head. "Are you going to tell her?" Rachel asked. Dirty's eyes grew wide in horror at the suggestion.

"Good god, no! How could I? That would seriously destroy her." Silence between them.

"There you go, then," Rachel said, enigmatically.

"There I go then, what?"

Rachel gave her a small smile and rubbed her leg. "Remember that when we started talking you said you were doing things wrong. All sorts of things. And I suggested that you were still a good person. And you said that that is probably not true, since you've done some things you think are bad. But being a good person isn't about always doing the best or right or awesome thing. You're going to get things wrong. Everyone's going to get things wrong. But how you react to it, how you think about it, how you regret or revise or correct or cry over it because you recognize it as something that maybe you shouldn't have done—that's what a good person does. And the fact that you're horrified at the thought of hurting Marina, and that you see what you did as something that might be hurtful, that's the mark of a good person. Bad people don't worry about being better." Dirty stopped crying and slowly pushed her fists up and down her legs in a massaging motion, thinking about what she was hearing.

"But I *could have* done the right thing. I could have. And I didn't."

"Look," Rachel said softly, "you've spent probably half of your life just trying to keep your head above water. And when you're spending all of your energy just trying to do that, you don't always have the luxury of being able to know what the absolute best choice is. You're just trying to get through. So you do what you have to. And when you've got that solved, *then* you do what you should. And in the in-between, when you're moving from the 'have-to' to the 'should', you're probably going to get some things wrong."

"Do what you have to, *then* do what you should." Dirty repeated, mantrically. Secretly, Rachel wasn't absolutely sure that she believed her own words. Surely there were times when, even in the direst of circumstances, there were things that she would never do, even if her own life depended on it. Weren't there?

Still. It seemed like it helped Dirty. So maybe it was good enough.

Part Eight
May 1998

CHAPTER 24
Like a lead blanket

When Rachel called to say that she needed to come and visit for a few days, part of Henry just added her to the list of crisis cases in his life. There had been some dude in her house, like a home invasion or something, but kinda not really, he wasn't totally sure. And things seemed to be deteriorating with her and Scooter. Henry wasn't really listening to that part. But between Rachel, Marie-France, what had happened to Cheryl, and Steve missing in action, Henry was close to not giving a fuck any more.

He hadn't ended up calling Marie-France that following Monday afternoon back in April. He had wanted to, or at least he thought it was something he should maybe do, but then he just let the chance slip away. But why was it his job, anyway? People need to sort their own shit out. He can't be everything to everyone.

Marie-France had spent the week emptying her apartment and recovering a little, and had ended up telling Henry quite bluntly to stay out of her life. Cheryl was in her own mess, although how it happened was a bit silly. She had had a fight with fit-guy and had broken up while they were sitting in his car. She got out and went to get her bags out of the trunk. What he didn't know was that the strap of one of her bags got snagged on the trailer hitch just as he floored the car in anger. Still holding the other strap, Cheryl was dragged quite a way before she let go and he realized what had happened. It could have been worse, although she did break her elbow.

The thing was, Henry felt bad for her, but he just couldn't gather enough care to actually do anything for her. He spoke to her on the phone, but no visit, no checking in as she was recuperating.

Rachel arrived that Friday night, glad to see Henry and determined to get drunk.

"Fuckin' assshole...," Rachel rambled.

"Yeah!" Henry drooled. They had killed an entire bottle of vodka and he had had several fat joints that Joel had left behind. Then they finally got around to talking about what was going on with Rachel at home, going on with Scooter and his...preferences.

"If he thinks I'm going to just sit back like this..."

"Yeah...," Henry repeated, tilting precariously.

"Do you think he still loves me?" Rachel asked weakly.

"Yeah!"

"Hen?" she asked.

"Yeah," He repeated.

"Are you going to be sick?"

"Yeah!" And then he was.

They slept in the same bed that night, mostly so Rachel could make sure he wasn't sick in his sleep, but also so she could feel the kind of body warmth she hadn't felt in a long time. Even though Henry was passed out, the feeling of sleeping next to someone she wasn't angry at or suspicious of was something she had forgotten.

***

The semi-circular burn on Marie-France's face had begun to heal nicely by May. When Josef had pressed the kettle onto her face the round bottom had described an arc from her eye, back towards her ear, then down across her jawline. The inside of her mouth had been swollen from the almost boiling water for several weeks, which affected her speech to a good degree. But by May, the only thing that remained was the arcing red line.

She had a feeling that even Josef thought he had gone too far because he hadn't laid a hand on her for weeks after. In fact, he had been almost sweet. It had only taken a few solid days of packing to have all of her things ready to move, and by mid-April the deal was done.

Marie-France lay in bed Saturday morning, feeling better than she had in a while. As she rubbed her eyes, her fingers touched the raised scar there and she realized that she had completely forgotten about it for two or three full seconds. She tried to pull it back to her, to be back in that feeling of before—she had just tasted it, dammit—but it was gone.

Josef was sitting in his office, thumbing the wad of cash Marie-France had given him—most of her vacation pay from work—before sticking it with the rest of the cash in the box, totalling $15,450. Not a lot, compared to what he was used to playing with, but enough to help him make a move if he had to. And it looked like he was going to.

If they ended up freezing his assets, he'd at least be able to get out of the country for a while. On the other hand, with some quick signatures on the paperwork he had been preparing,

Marie-France would be able to provide him with ample support. In fact, if he did it right, he wouldn't have to leave the country at all.

Sunlight streamed in the bedroom window, and Marie-France could feel the warmth through the sheets. Wiggling her toes, she scrunched and un-scrunched the sheets, feeling the cotton move over her skin slightly. Sliding her hands along her hipbones, now feeling skin on skin, she thought about being made love to. Not being fucked (like it so often was now), but being moved into gently, slowly, luxuriously. She didn't know what kind of mood Josef was in this morning, but one thing she could lay was odds. It looked like she would have to do it herself.

Sliding her left hand over her stomach and then holding it there, she pressed down gently as the palm of her right hand lightly brushed her nipple. Bringing the tip of her fingernails down her torso, she started to rub smooth circles on her thighs. The room was bright and warm and she could almost smell the sunshine on her, bare and easy, her limbs loosening for the first time in what felt like decades. She breathed out lightly, happily, feeling tickling and trickling back into her body. Sliding a finger inside of herself she was surprised, remembering the feeling of actually being wet before penetration; the feeling of being ready, of anticipation, of wanting.

Flexing her left hand, she pushed a little harder on her stomach, her wet fingers sliding up to tease her clitoris. She could hear Josef moving around in the living room and she prayed to be left alone, just a little bit longer. If he came in now, she didn't know what she would do. Give up? Pretend to sleep? Keep going? Let him in? No, not now. She knew he would strip her of the feeling—not cheapen it but obliterate it.

She knew the feel of his cock inside her, the way it curved—not like love but like a scar. Marie-France knew she had been sent a reprieve. Just one more minute, god, just let me have this, god, I'm close I'm so close I'm getting so close just one...

More.

Minute.

***

Sitting in the living room with Rachel, Henry felt like he had a tiny bit of shelter. It had just been the two of them, not going out, not having to deal with shit. And Henry could pretend that there wasn't anything wrong, that he hadn't fucked up in yet some other way that would bring down people's disappointment. He felt like old Henry for a little while. And then Andre floated back into his head and he felt sick.

When he closed his eyes, Henry could see Andre's spider-hand on the table; he could feel the guilt, scarring him from the inside out. The memory of...the thought of it pushed down on him like one of those lead blankets they give you during an x-ray. But the looks that Andre was giving him went right through anyway and burned him up. And it was always there now. It wouldn't leave.

Henry was shaking. He got up to go to the bathroom, to douse his head in frigid water just to maybe forget for a moment. Rachel didn't notice that he had gone.

***

She was thinking about how she had been able to forget about things at home. Not for a long time, but for a little while here. But now she was circling back. Why couldn't *they* have Sundays like this? Lord knew they used to in the beginning, sort of, but now she wondered how they could even possibly get that back.

Not with this thing between them. It was gross. And weird. The pictures she had seen were...animals but not quite animals. They had human faces and human...bits. But they were like cartoon creatures and Rachel kept coming back to the idea that cartoons were for children, and if Scooter had a sex-thing with cartoons then—

She shuddered.

No. Absolutely not. She no longer cared what his excuses were. This was a deal breaker. Part of her wondered if she was being prudish, but that part of her was nowhere near strong enough to convince her to give it more time and energy.

The coffee she sipped seemed to be the warmest thing in her now, and that's when she knew it was over. She would drive back home tonight, she would go to her house, and she would have to end it.

But there were so many details to consider, the thought of the process made her feel ill. God, would they be separating their things like an actual divorcing couple? Of course they would; it would be stupid to think otherwise. And what about Dirty? Should she take Dirty with her? Of course not, she's not a fucking child. But there has to be another way. But there isn't. And it has to be done.

"Hen," she called, bouncing her pencil on the crossword puzzle and now noticing he had left the room, "I'm stuck here. I need a four-letter word."

CHAPTER 25:
One good hand

At work on Monday everyone seemed quiet and industrious. Henry had sent Rachel off late on Sunday afternoon, and she had promised to call later in the week with an update on how things had gone. As time had gone on, people asked less and less about Marie-France, although Henry still thought about her quite a lot. How she had looked in those last few days he had seen her. And his conversation with Josef in the bar that day. He should have called her. He should call her.

He held the receiver in his hand, cradled it, thought about what he would say. What if Josef answered? Was she even still at her number? Did she want to talk to him? And as the courage left him once again, he replaced the phone, his shoulders slumping guiltily. She could probably handle it anyway. Henry's stomach tightened.

Henry sat for quite a while then, alternately staring at the phone and out his window. Breathing deeply, he grabbed the phone and dialed quickly, before he could stop himself. Waiting through several rings, the machine finally picked up, and all Henry could do was leave a message.

"Joel, it's Henry. Just wondering if you're free tonight. Gimme a call."

***

Sitting in the living room together, across from one another, Marie-France watched him intently. Slowly her hand flexed—not the damaged one, the bruised one. Open and closed, to a fist and watching. She was tired, so very tired, but she had stopped sleeping whenever he was around. Just to be sure. Whenever he was in the office, she could count on him being in there for an hour and a half, on average. She almost always dozed then; not right out, but enough to recharge a little. But now she watched and waited, watching the sun cut through the window as it settled further and further toward the Gatineau Hills. And she remembered when he had been gentler with her that day. Sweet and suggestive, when they had been together, actually together. Not like now, not like it had become, and not like it would be very soon.

He had gone out several times in the last few days, always spontaneously (so it seemed to her), always for 40 minutes. And when he went, she had seen the box, had seen where he kept the money. She tried flexing the bad hand but it was still too swollen. That was alright. If all went well, she'd only need the good one.

***

"Five guys in seven nights, Henry. And you only missed the sixth one because you threw your back out." Cheryl was sitting across from Henry in his living room, she nursing a scotch and he nursing his sore muscles. Henry was glum, tired, and angry. He didn't know why, but it burned when he thought about what she was saying.

Cheryl rolled him a pin and lit it, handing it to him like tummy medicine for a child who should have known better. "You've got a hole in your life, Hen. I don't know how it got there. Maybe Steve, maybe something else, maybe lots of things. But you're trying to fill it with things that just don't fit. They aren't big enough. And when one isn't a satisfying fit you keep adding to it, hoping it'll work when they're all added up." Henry's red eyes blinked at her. "Where is it that you want to go, man? Where is it that you think you *should* go?"

Henry took another drag and then tried to pass it, wincing as his back sang to him. Steve was gone, Marie-France had needed him and he had failed, Joel was no longer speaking to him, he couldn't help Rachel, his body was failing him, and his best friend was giving him shit. Oh, and according to Andre, he should just be locked up or something because he's a goddamned rapi—.

Fuck. Thirty-two fucking years old, and Henry was losing his grip on his world. It felt like his life was just happening to him.

***

Somewhere down in a cold, dark, rainy alleyway, Henry stood slouched in his jacket, waiting. Then the back door of the club opened, and one of the bouncers stepped out and handed him a bag of ecstasy that Henry jammed into his pocket. And then he gave the bouncer a blowjob. Not because he couldn't afford what he was buying; he had the money for god's sake. It's just that he wanted to.

But even that wasn't completely true. What was going on

for Henry was much *emptier* than that. It's not that he wanted to. He just did it. Without thinking about it at all. Empty. Directionless. Hollow.

And he just didn't know what he was supposed to...do? Hope for? What is it that people do after they have what they need? How do they know what to do next? What to go after?

It's not that he had high ideals when he was younger that somehow got lost or forgotten when he got older and sold out. Fuck that. No. Standing in the return of the rain, with cum on his shirt and high pressure in his chest, he tried to look at himself. He looked and there was nothing there. A lump in his throat, he tried to stop from crying. His dick hurt; that poisoned arrow that would go on to make him much sicker. And in all of it, together, he was left with a sad little question: What am I supposed to *be*?

***

Rachel had left that first weekend with a promise to call right away if anything happened between her and Scooter. And things had eventually happened.

And it was awful.

When she had gone back to Toronto from Henry's earlier in the month, she had gone home to Scooter and lain in bed that night, neither of them saying much. In the middle of the night she had mouthed the words, thick and miserable, but couldn't make them form in his ears. She wept and he slept.

But she had done it, finally, when they lay beside each other a week later. It had happened simply, cleanly. The evening had been tense, as if they both knew this was it. It was like the unspoken tension before lovers have sex for the first time, before they are actually lovers. But this situation would probably require more tissue.

"I can't do this" she whispered. Scooter said nothing for a long time, just as he often did. At one point, Rachel had to look to see if he was awake, but as soon as she saw his face, she knew he had heard her.

***

All of this she recounted to Henry over the phone—Scooter was spending the weekend at his parents' place now—sitting in her living room, Seeger sleeping on a pillow beside her.

Although she hadn't discussed any of this with Dirty, Rachel said, Dirty had come to her just yesterday to tell her about her own plans to move out. Henry listened as she droned on and on. Something about Winnipeg or maybe Vancouver, or some such thing. She herself was concerned, Rachel said, because she was afraid that Dirty would feel like she was being pushed out. The whole thing was a fucking mess, she said.

Henry was barely listening to what Rachel was saying, but good god she was talking a lot. And so he found his mind wandering back to his own life, to his own fucking mess. Rachel had just said something about coming to visit again, next weekend or something and Henry said sure, of course, anything you need, but he just wanted to pour himself a drink.

"—which is just the part I couldn't understand. What do you think, Hen?" Rachel had finished talking and Henry was caught not listening.

"uh, well," he feigned "I don't quite know what to make of that—you?" He had managed to pull the cork out of the wine from last night and pour a glass with one hand.

"I don't know, I…," Rachel continued. Henry was tired and needed to get off the phone, but instead he sat and half-listened, drank and felt bad about being a poor friend. And the more he thought about that, the more he realized he still wasn't listening, and the worse he felt.

"Oh Henry, I gotta go" she said. They said goodbye and Henry hung up the phone. He poured another glass of wine and looked at the dog in the living room.

***

"Your hair is a mess. Fix it." Marie-France was in the bathroom, looking in the mirror when Josef passed by the door. Slowly she lifted her hands, drawing her fingers through her average brown hair, feeling the texture and holding her hands against her head. There was the scar, her swollen lip, the paleness of her skin and the redness in her eyes. She smiled then, pulling her hair away from her face and wondered what there was left to do. Could she just leave? He'd be going out again soon, and she could grab the money and race out the door and be free of him. But he'd find her again. She was sure of that. And where would she go? How long would she last, conspicuous, looking like she had been hit by a truck? Her smile faded.

"Marie-France!" he called down the hall. "I need you to sign those papers we talked about." Pulling her robe around her tightly, she padded down the hall in her bare feet.

"What are these, again?" she asked. Josef glared at her.

"I told you, I'm making you a partner in my business. Now sign the goddamn things!" She heard his voice rise slightly, as it always did just before an outburst. She took the pen in her hand and signed wherever he pointed—three, four, five different places; afterwards she wasn't really sure how many there were.

As soon as it was over, he went out again and she was alone. It was the middle of the day and the city was beautiful once more, and Marie-France thought about going out on her own. She didn't care about how she looked anymore; she just wanted to be around people once more. She pulled on her jacket and boots—*my god!* she thought. It was spring and all she had were these damn boots. When she moved in, Josef had purged her belongings of the things he felt were...unnecessary.

So here she was standing at the mirror in the hallway, brown boots and dishevelled. I look like a bag lady, she thought. Fuck it. I'll just go. Opening the door and making sure it stayed unlocked (Josef had refused to give her a key), Marie-France plodded down the front steps and onto the street. It was a bit cloudy now but warm--warm enough with her jacket--her fingers tingling with the touch of the air.

She was going to buy shoes, dammit. New, gorgeous, elegant, slick. A little smile hit the corner of her mouth, but faded before she hit the corner of the street. She needed money for that. How could she—

The box.

She stopped and turned. She didn't need much and there was lots in there. Piles, really. How could he miss a hundred bucks? Like he didn't owe it to her anyway. Christ, it was probably mostly hers to begin with.

She walked back to the house and in through the front door. Slipping off her boots, she crept into the office (creeping, even though she knew she was alone) and stood over Josef's desk. Gently opening the bottom drawer, she lifted the lid of the box. The tips of her fingers brushed the cash. Looking carefully, she realized it had been placed in neat, crisscrossed piles. Fuck she thought. He's counted it all, that anal-retentive prick. He knows how much is here and he'll know how much is gone--

She heard the front door open.

"Marie-France!" Josef called, "why are your boots in the middle of the hall?!" Sliding the drawer closed, she looked around quickly, trying to decide where to go. He would come in and find her in his office with her jacket on.

She leapt across the room and flung herself into the leather armchair in the corner, curling her feet under her. The door opened just then and Josef stalked in, barely glancing at her. He went to his desk, standing in front of the drawer, she knew, just to see, just to check. Then he looked at her, hard.

"What the hell is going on?!" Before she knew what was happening, all the words she needed tumbled out of her mouth.

"I missed you, Josef. I wanted to go out and find you—I got all the way to the front door when I lost my nerve. I don't like going out there. Being here in the office seemed like the closest I could get to you before you came home. Please forgive me." Even she was surprised at her performance.

Josef stood for a moment, then came over and took her by the shoulders, lifting her. He held her there, the two of them standing face to face, and he stared at her as he did that first night in the bar for what seemed like hours. Then he kissed her, hard. This is what she had to do; she knew. If her words were going to carry, to keep her safe, she had better show it. She kissed him back then, surprising him.

CHAPTER 26:
Get over it

Henry was filthy. He hadn't shaved in several days, nor showered in as many. He had managed to let Dave out into the yard once or twice a day, but had done nothing with the shit. His clothes reeked, and his cock had started to itch badly.

There had been a party at his place—last night or maybe the night before. So many people from the club, most of whom he didn't really know or care to. Through the haze of his hangover—or buzz, or both—he looked at the mess of his living room where the orgy had been.

Such an ugly word.

But then, it had not been pretty. And what the hell was all over the floor?! Was that cum? Lube? Bile?

Rubbing his hand over his stubbly cheek, Henry thought he might cry. *Nothing in my life is worthwhile*, he thought. He reached over and dug a roach out of the ashtray, chastised himself for being so pathetic, and then felt even worse for feeling sorry for himself. *No wonder Steve left,* he thought. *I can't even get through my own life.* He wondered how other people did it—got through each day. They all seemed to be going after something,

something that kept them going. And he, he had nothing.

Rising from the couch, he shuffled to the bathroom to take a piss. Standing over the can, he found himself staring at the shelves, or rather at the bottles and jars on the shelves. *Fuck it*, he thought, *I could just end it all now. Swallow something or—open my wrists with—* he stared at his electric razor. He finished pissing, and only briefly remarked on the sickly red of his dick. Then he stumbled back into the living room to turn on the fan because *why is it so fucking hot in here?*

***

As Andre hung up the phone, he stared at the blank television screen. It was a warm-ish evening, the kind that was great for lovers, sometimes. Which, of course, was not why he had called Cheryl, but it did make him want to see Melissa.

He had called Cheryl because of what he had seen that day. Or rather, whom. He had been walking downtown when he could have sworn he saw Marie-France. Maybe. It looked like her, but it seemed like it couldn't have possibly been her. Not like that. Her hair, her clothes, her face—although the woman he saw did have the same boots. He had wanted to cross the street, to call her, something, but what he had seen had left him without words. Then she had turned and had gone back the way she had come, and then she was gone. Cheryl had thought it was weird, but also that maybe he had been wrong, that maybe it hadn't been Marie-France. Maybe.

Andre got up and walked to his balcony—more of a fire escape landing, really—and watched the traffic all the way down Elgin Street. He thought about Melissa again. God, had it really been 5 months? He wondered what she was doing right then. He looked at the phone. Should he call? What's the worst that could happen?

Andre sat down again and dialed the number he found in the white pages. Five months had passed, for god's sake. He--

"Hello?" Damn, Andre thought. She must have a roommate. He hoped it wasn't Loretta. She had never really liked Andre. Probably hated him, after what had happened,

"Hellooo?" the voice repeated. He was pretty sure it was Loretta. He held his breath.

"Hi," he said finally. "Is Melissa there?" There was a pause at the other end.

"Hold on." Andre could hear the muffle of clothing against the receiver as Probably-Loretta held it against her body to talk to Melissa. He could hear her voice through the vibrations in her body, both hollow and hard at the same time, like Charlie Brown's teacher on a bender. Finally, Melissa's voice came on.

"Yes?" It wasn't edgy. That had to be a good sign.

"Oh hey. It's, uh, Andre"

"Oh. It's you." This was not a good sign.

"Uh, yeah. Hi. How are you?" he said weakly. There was a pause.

"Fine. What do you want?"

"I just called to see how you were doing." He was sinking fast.

"Well, I think I just told you. Is that it?" Andre bit his lip.

"I just wanted to tell you that I—" the words stuck in his throat.

"Oh, and how is Henry these days?" she asked snidely. Andre winced. He took a breath and started again.

"I guess I wanted to let you know that I will probably never be able to tell you honestly about what happened that night. And that no matter how much you believe you know about it, you don't. Because... just because. I know that that probably doesn't take away your anger or hurt. But in my own pain from what happened, I can still say that I am poorer for having lost you." And then it was Melissa's turn to fumble.

"Th-thank you. I—I mean...thank you." Neither of them spoke then, and with nothing left to say Andre wished her luck and then hung up. Walking back to the 'balcony', Andre thought about going out.

***

By the end of the week, Henry had gone into work three times, had half-heartedly wiped some things from his kitchen counter, and successfully avoided Cheryl's pointed questions about his deteriorating appearance and demeanour.

That Friday, Henry walked into the breakroom, nearly barrelling into Andre. Andre stepped back, repulsed, while Henry moved in a wide arc away from him. And then something in him snapped.

"Would you fucking get over it?" Henry said, throwing up his hands. "You've made working here feel so shitty, I can't even walk in here without feeling smothered in your death-glare." Andre stared at him in disbelief.

"'Get over it'. Is that what you said?" Andre spat. "I'm making things uncomfortable for you? For you."

"Oh, my god. Just forget I said anything." Henry raised a dismissive hand. Andre turned to leave, and then stopped.

"Maybe that feeling you get, maybe it ain't coming from me. Maybe it's your own conscience giving you exactly what you fucking deserve." And then he left.

***

Driving home that afternoon, Henry's hands were shaking so badly that he could barely hold his cigarette. He had three bottles of wine waiting at home, and he intended to burn through every single one of them. So when Rachel arrived on Friday night as Henry had forgotten she would, his embarrassment only made him feel worse.

Rachel couldn't hide her surprise. In the entire time she had known him he had been organized, neat, even meticulous. What she saw when she walked in was something she would have expected more from Steve after one of his mega-parties. Henry stood in the corner of the room, looking sheepish and small, about to burst into tears. She went to him then, held him, and he cried hard, half-collapsed, worn-thin, spent. She soothed him and they sat in the dark through most of the night, breathing.

In the morning, Rachel awoke two full hours before Henry and set about the repairs. Dave was eager to see her, following her from room to room in her cleaning vigor. By the time Henry woke at nine he was no longer sure where he was. The kitchen still looked like hell, but the living room was immaculate. He felt stupid then; the sleep had cleared his head enough that he could catch a glimpse of how far he had fallen.

"Sit. Drink." she ordered as she handed him a cup of coffee. He sat. Dave watched.

Henry sat on the couch, protecting his mug as if it were a child or a jewel, but he could not raise his eyes to meet Rachel's when she moved through the room. The pressure behind his ribs was back, and it began to dawn on him that maybe now Rachel, or even everyone, might be able to see through him, see him for the shell that he was. He had lost his ability to be and do all those outwardly proper things: the dressing right, the saying things that people want to hear, the organization and efficiency, all the things that are supposed to be part of navigating the world. Now, maybe they would see him for what he was, or what he wasn't. Barely even a person.

Rachel came back in the room and sat down.

"I'm going to tell you a story, goofball. So just listen. You know that friend who is staying with us? Dirty?" Henry nodded. "She's been through some pretty serious shit, and I don't just mean recently. She lost her dad, she's estranged from her mother, or maybe she's dead (I'm not sure), and a whole bunch of other stuff. I mean, her stepfather was controlling this girl's mother, and then he stole a bunch of money from them, and then kicked her out *at twelve*. I mean, jesus, mary, and joseph, who does that?"

Henry snickered at this last. Rachel cocked her head and stopped.

"Sorry," Henry said "it's just that you're describing the kind of guy that my friend Marie-France is involved with. And his name is *actually* Josef."

"Lemme guess," she said sarcastically, "he takes his scotch with exactly one-and-a-half ice cubes." Henry's face dropped.

"How the fuck did you know that?"

"What? What…"

"The ice cube thing.

"I was kidding. It was just something Dirty said about her step-father, about how he always had a drink like that."

"Oh my god." Henry said semi-enthusiastically. "That's exactly what he ordered when I met him that one time and we played pool. He was really specific about it with the waitress." He was hoping this little revelation might distract Rachel enough to stop her from driving the advice-train any further. "Marie-France is dating that girl's step-father. That's fucked up."

"Okay, that is fucking weird." She paused. It *was* weird, but what was more pressing for Rachel just then was how terrible Henry seemed, how far he had fallen, how little he resembled what she had known him as. "Anyway, what I'm trying to tell you is that this girl who has been through god knows how many things still manages to pick herself up and keep going. She's a fighter. Even when things are terrible, she seems to find a way to get out of bed in the morning and push on. And if she can do it, so can you. Don't worry about where you are right now. Just pick your head up and move forward." She was trying to put heart into him, but she wasn't sure it was working. Henry was frowning.

"What if I'm not strong enough?"

"You'll find a way." Rachel was particularly dissatisfied with her answer, but she felt like she needed to say something. In a way, Henry had a point. What if a weaker person gets knocked down? Does it mean they never get up? Do they just crawl away? She didn't know. But for now, she needed to get him going again because he was a fucking mess.

CHAPTER 27:
So goddamned heavy

Marie-France sat in the kitchen, staring at the creamy circles in her coffee. It was 9am and Josef was still in bed. She had wanted a cup of coffee but was worried that the scent would wake him, so she made instant. Tasted like shitstant. It was Saturday, the end of the roughest week yet, but she felt like she was ready. If he would sleep for just another 15 or 20 minutes it would be done.

He had ended up buying her a pair of shoes that week. She hadn't said a word to him to hint, but there they were. And, oh lord, were they ugly. The low, square heel and those stupid laces--they were the farthest thing from elegant that she could have imagined, and so goddamned heavy. Josef had made her put them on so they could walk around the block together--she would have much rathered her boots than those beasts.

She walked into the hallway and picked them up and, bringing them into the kitchen, she placed them squarely on the table. She slipped the lace out of the left one, slowly, but found her fingers more eager on the right. Her heart was racing now, because she knew she would have to finish it. Looping the laces into slipknots, she took the left shoe into the palm of her hand and slid easily down the hall, into the bedroom.

He lay in front of her, half on his right side, half on his stomach. His left hand fell loosely at the side of the mattress, but his right—*fuck!*—his right was curled under the pillow.

Placing the shoe on the ground, Marie-France carefully pulled one of the laces through the slats of the headboard, then gently easing it over his hand. Looking at the angle of his body, she realized her only other choice was to bind his right foot; she prayed it would be enough.

She tried several angles but nothing seemed to give her enough slack to tie it to the bed. She felt she might be sick now, and she knew she was running out of time. Abandoning his foot altogether, she dropped the lace and picked up the shoe, swaying slightly over his head. She raised it and brought it down, hard, the heel landing squarely on his cheekbone.

The pain woke him of course, but his mind stayed foggy long enough for her to get in two more strikes, the last crushing his nose completely. She was wild then, raging in anger and gore. Understanding now, Josef pushed his right hand out to grab her shirt. Panicking, she pulled away, but tripped over her own feet, bashing her head on the wall where she fell.

Through her own haze she saw Josef yank at the lace, snapping it, then rise from the bed. He stood over her for only a moment, dripping, then left the room. Marie-France scrambled to her feet, still holding the shoe. Peering around the door into the hall, she could hear him in the kitchen, in one of the drawers. When Josef came back into the hall holding the hammer, they found themselves staring at each other: he, standing square, she, still tentative around the side of the door.

He was a mess, and his left eye had closed, but he raised the hammer and smashed it into the wall next to him, crushing the drywall. Before she knew what her body was doing, Marie-France burst out of the bedroom and into his office across the hall, slamming the door behind her with Josef closing in.

Josef was still naked, leaning his body against the cool wood of the door. With one quick strike, he knocked the doorknob off, but it was still fucking locked goddammit. He whacked and bashed at the mechanism to break the latch, then leaned in to push the door open against the weight of the couch Marie-France had shoved in front of it.

Grunting and shoving against the wood, he yelled and cursed while digging the claw of the hammer into the wood. Then he bashed and bashed at what was left of the door latch. It finally started to give.

When he stepped inside though, she was gone. The window behind his desk was open, and from where he was standing, he could see that one of the desk drawers was open. *Bitch*! he thought. He strode to the window and peered out, then turned toward the desk.

Just before she struck, Josef could see that that the drawer was actually still full, the box unmolested, and then he saw her crouched beneath the desk.

She brought the letter opener up--straight up--into his scrotum. He let the hammer go and fell to the ground shaking, his palms pressed flat on his thighs. He was leaking all sorts of fluids now, and only the handle of the opener was visible, the tip of it 10 inches away somewhere up in his body.

Marie-France yanked the letter opener out again, then grabbed the hammer and backed away from him. His good eye was rolling up and down, his mouth gaping like a dying fish's. She wanted to finish him then, but she walked over to the door and dropped the hammer. Standing for only a second, she picked up the shoe from where she had dropped it earlier, when she had moved the couch. Then she took the shoe and walked back to Josef, stood over his ugly head, and began again.

***

Henry and Rachel had finished off the kitchen by 10:15, after Henry had gotten off his ass and managed 10 good minutes without being swallowed in self pity. Even when the pity came back, he had enough caffeine in him to at least wipe down the counters. Henry was shaking though, a fever blooming more fully, pulsating through him. And he smelled.

"Take a shower and take some time. I've got this." Rachel said, and she sent Henry upstairs to do his business, and then let Dave out into the backyard to do his.

***

Marie-France looked horrific as she needled her car through traffic. She had managed to wipe most of the blood from her face with the edge of her shirt, and the bits of gore on her fingers had come off in the fur of her boots. Her hair was wild with sweat, what Cheryl would have otherwise called sex hair.

But she had to get to Henry's first. Before the rest of it. She would give him the money because she owed him some, and maybe he would know what to do with the rest. And maybe that would let him know... know something she didn't know how to express. Turning onto a side street, she panicked for a moment, forgetting which house was his. It was one-hundred-and-something, but all the ones around here were in the twenties and thirties. She drove slowly, becoming more and more aware of how she must look from outside. When she hit the end of the street, she realized that she had misjudged by one block; after making two quick rights, she was bearing down on his driveway.

She reached over to the passenger seat and gripped the grocery bag stuffed with bills. Turning the car off and sliding out, she walked up to the door and could feel how stiff her muscles had become from sitting in the car. She was about to press the doorbell when Rachel appeared at the door, and Marie-France panicked again that she had the wrong house. Rachel was clearly alarmed at her appearance.

"Ar--are you looking for...Henry...?" Rachel asked, attempting to sound calm.

"Yes. Yes." Marie-France said weakly. "You must give this to 'im. Tell 'im it's from Josef. No. Tell im it's from me." Rachel's eyes grew wide.

"Are you Marie-France?!" she asked. Marie-France didn't answer.

"Rachel!" Henry called from the top of the stairs. He thought he had heard voices, or something, so he plodded down in his towel to see what was going on. Standing ten feet behind Rachel, he could see over her shoulder that there was someone....

And then Marie-France saw him there, clean and shining and everything that was the opposite of how she seemed at that very moment, and he was perfect. She half-smiled, not sure what to say.

Except that his face said it all. Clear and utter revulsion. His mouth was a grimace, his eyes partially squinting. Henry's nostrils were flared as if he were trying to get fresh air to avoid a smell that wasn't actually there. His left hand was clutching

his towel, but his right had curled to a fist on his chest like a
starlet, aghast.

The thing was, he *knew* it was Marie-France and he *knew* he
shouldn't feel that way. Or, at least he shouldn't be fucking
showing it. But he couldn't help it. It was just kind of there, on
his face, and he couldn't figure out how to hide it.

"Henry...!" Rachel scolded, the way a parent scolds a child
caught masturbating in public. Firm and a bit alarmed. And
through gritted teeth. Henry looked at them both, realized how
awful he was being, and then fled back up the stairs.

In that same instant, Rachel turned back to offer Marie-
France something--help or gauze or something--but by the
time Rachel had turned towards her, Marie-France was already
down the driveway and getting back into her car, the bag of
money left at Rachel's feet. Marie-France yanked the car into
reverse, and there was a wince-inducing thumping as two tires
flubbed over the curb.

Now the tears came for Marie-France. Not for what she
had been through, and not for everything she had lost. But
because of... the look. The look he had given her. Like she was
a disgusting wretch. Not just that she meant nothing, but that
she was actively repulsive to him. Two streets over, she hit the
curb again because she could barely see out of her smeary wet
eyes, that same flub flub of the tires. Except it wasn't the curb
this time. Not that she knew that, because she kept driving. It
just felt like the curb. Unknown to any of them, Dave had
gotten out of the backyard after Rachel had put him there that
morning.

Marie-France turned back onto the main road which led to
the bridge to Hull, no longer worried about the trucks that
barrelled toward her from both directions. Pulling over just
before the start of the bridge where there was still a shoulder,

she sat for a moment and watched over the bridge and into the hills beyond. It was almost June and green there, but it didn't really matter anymore. And why did she even buy this Volvo in the first place? These things are too damn safe.

Pocketing her keys, she got out of the car, careful to look both ways. When the timing was right, she stepped out into the path of one of those trucks, which hit her so hard she flew right out of her brown, fur-at-the-top, ugly, ugly boots.

CHAPTER 28:
She's gone

Henry and Rachel sat and looked at one another, the bag between them.

"Well, she said it was for you."

"Well I don't want it!" Henry squeaked. He had meant to be even more animated than that, but it was so goddamned hot.

"Well it ain't mine," Rachel said, crossing her arms.

"So what do we do?"

"You don't understand. She's in trouble, Henry. We should just give it back to Marie France."

"I don't even know where to find her...," Henry demurred. It just seemed like a lot of work to him. They stared at each other again.

That evening, after they had hid the money under Henry's bed, the police came. Rachel and Henry had called them, as soon as they had seen it on tv--they had each recognized her car at exactly the same time, Rachel because she had seen Marie-France drive away just that day, and Henry because he had helped her buy it in the first place. Rachel had reached for the phone, but Henry stopped her.

"What are you going to tell them about...." Rachel hadn't thought about the money.

"The victim's name is being withheld until next-of-kin can be notified." the television blurped. Rachel's eyebrows raised.

"That's it!" she exclaimed. "We give the money to the next-of-kin!"

"Marie-France's?" Henry asked, confused.

"No. Josef's." she answered, smiling.

***

When the detectives arrived, Henry was nervous. When they hinted at the horrific scene they found at Marie-France and Josef's townhouse, he was ashen.

His surprise made everything he said much more believable, Rachel thought afterwards, and as they began to talk, Henry poured out all he had seen. His voice was strained but earnest. He talked about the changes he had seen in Marie-France, his conversation with Josef months ago, and Rachel filled in most of what had happened when Marie-France showed up at the door. Rachel remarked (silently) that it was so easy for them to just drop that one little item from the story, and it all seemed so clean. Except that then the police asked, and it seemed to come out of nowhere.

"And did she give you anything?" the detective asked Henry pointedly. Rachel felt her breath catch and then realized the other detective was watching her carefully. Coolly though, Henry cocked his head to the side in prepared confusion, a move that reminded Rachel of Dave. It was an innocent look that asked 'What the hell are you talking about?' without saying a word. After a pause he said

"What would she give me?" The detectives looked him over slowly, then said simply

"I dunno. Just trying to fit all the pieces together. I mean, why would she even come here in the first place, y'know?" The other detective just looked at Rachel.

"I dunno, either" Henry said flatly. "Maybe she just wanted someone to know she was sorry."

Or that she wasn't. Rachel thought.

Things seemed to be wrapping up, and then the doorbell rang. Henry gave a 'what the fuck is it, now!?' look to Rachel. He went to answer the door and began a quiet conversation. And then it was not so quiet, as Henry went tearing through the house to the back door. Rachel and the two detectives sprung up in alarm. And then the horror hit Rachel. Henry was yelling Dave's name out the back door. Something was wrong.

One of the detectives had gone to the front door and was now talking to the neighbour who had found Dave. He had come here with Dave's tags because the address was on the yellow one.

Henry was now fully across the backyard, at the back fence in his sock feet, while Rachel stood in the patio door, explaining to the detective who Dave was, but still not completely sure how he could have gotten out.

But Henry was. There was a patch of dirt that had been dug out by the fence. The space it created under the fence honestly didn't look big enough for a dog like that to get through, but apparently dogs judge such things differently.

***

That night they got drunk. What was weird about it was that it felt different to Henry than other times he had gotten blitzed. Henry felt like it was *about* something. *Did that make sense?* Henry wasn't sure. Of course it was about something: it was about the fact that his goddamned dog was dead. Sweet, adorable, snarfly Dave.

This kind of drinking seemed to mean something, seemed to have a point, seemed to be anchored in the loss and the hurt. Henry felt like he could do it—the drinking—without feeling like he was falling down a hole with no bottom.

Anchored in the loss. Anchored. Like there was a place to stand. At least for as long as the hurt would allow. So they sat together, he and Rachel, and drank together, and were sad together. Then they went to bed and tried to forget.

***

On Monday, Rachel called work and explained (vaguely) what had happened and that the detectives had asked that she not leave Ottawa for the next couple of days until they could wrap everything up. They had come back on Monday afternoon, and one last time on Tuesday asking the same questions, sometimes in a different order, sometimes asked first by one detective, then the other. They left not quite satisfied, that something unseen didn't quite fit, but there seemed nothing left to look for.

That evening Henry and Rachel sat in the living room saying little. They hadn't actually counted the money (the prospect made Rachel feel like they really were getting away with something), but Henry guesstimated that there might be ten or twenty thousand.

She called Scooter that night to tell him she'd drive home sometime Wednesday afternoon, the first of June. Just dialing the numbers to talk to him made her feel sick. She told him what happened, why she was staying longer than expected.

"Wow. That's bad," he said flatly. *Like he was trying to care more than he could,* Rachel thought. *I think I could hate him if this went on,* she would tell Henry later.

"Do me a favour," she said to Scooter near the end of the conversation, "just tell Dirty that I have something for her." She glanced at Henry as she said it, and they shared a smile between them.

"I can't," Scooter said. "She's gone."

"What are you talking about?" Rachel's back straightened.

"She said she was heading out of town—I forget where—yeah, her bus leaves 6am tomorrow."

"Well, why didn't you stop her?!" Rachel yelled, regretting her volume immediately. "I know she was thinking of going, but why now?" She lowered her voice and stared at the bag. "Scooter, please. It's really, really important that you not let her leave til I get there. I—"

"She's already gone" he said again. "She left this morning; said she'd be crashing at a friend's place—her name was something... nautical...."

"Marina," Rachel said.

"Yeah! But she didn't leave me the number," he said, gruffly. "Why is this such a problem?" he challenged. Rachel frowned. She could feel it starting again.

"I have to go," she said, pausing briefly to listen for a response, then hung up. It was 10:45pm.

Rachel explained the situation to Henry as she dashed about the house gathering her things; he lingered in the doorway of whatever room she moved to.

"It's a five-hour drive, Rach," he said gravely. "That'll get you there around 4am, I guess."

As she loaded the car, the plastic grocery bag was still there in the bedroom, almost daring them both to forget the whole thing. Rachel tried to play it cool, eventually sweeping the bag up with the last of her clothes. By the time she was ready it was 11:10pm, and Henry was nervous.

"Do you want me to go with you?" he asked.

"Thank you, luv. But to be honest, this isn't the only thing I've gotta do when I get back." They were standing in the doorway. "I've still got to finish up some things with Scooter…." She trailed off. She hugged him then, and by the time she got in the car it was 11:20pm.

Pulling out of the city, she had to decide if she was going to take the highway or the two-lane. *It's late*, she thought. *No traffic. The highway should be the way to go.*

***

Sitting on the sofa, Henry thought about everything that had happened. When he thought about what happened to Marie-France, and the money, and the cops, it was exciting—horrific, sure—but he had felt a jolt to his life, a spark; for a brief time he had a kind of direction because it was clear what needed to get done. It was clear. But now that Rachel was gone—finishing that work, he supposed—he felt like he would just fall back into his regular life. Crossing his arms, Henry just stared at the floor.

He reached over and grabbed the tv remote. He knew it would ultimately make him feel worse, the avoiding, but he was drawn to it, the quietness in his head that would come. This was also the time when he would have cuddled up to Dave, or at least have him flopped on the floor in front of him. God, he missed that dog. God, his body hurt.

Pressing the button, the tv burped on and he settled in. Half an hour later he would be watching a news bulletin about an accident on the highway.

Part Nine
June 1998

CHAPTER 29:
Wherever you're going

The clock on the dash read 12:01 and Rachel was stopped dead on the southbound freeway out of Ottawa.

Fuck. There were lights, sirens, cops everywhere, while Rachel eyed the bag warily. Reaching over, she tucked it underneath the passenger seat. Twenty minutes later she had not moved an inch and several cars both in front and behind her had made a U-turn over the grass median in order to head back north to find a route around the wreck. She was thinking the same thing when there was a tap at the window.

"Ma'am," the officer said, shining a flashlight in the car, "it's pretty messy up there; no telling when we're going to be able to get it cleaned up." Her eyes danced over the interior of the car, to Rachel's face, the back seat, the dash. Rachel smiled innocently.

"Is there any way to go around?" she asked sweetly.

"Technically I can't recommend it, but the folks turning around seem like they have the right idea…."

Fuck. Looking up, Rachel realized that the officer's eyes had settled on the part of the bag that was sticking out from under the passenger seat.

"Well I guess I better get hopping then, huh?" Rachel said quickly, trying to re-engage the cop's eyes. There was a pause.

"All right then," she said, clicking her flashlight off. "Drive safe."

By the time Rachel had re-traced her path to get to the much smaller and often much slower two-lane heading out of the other side of the city, it was already 12:50. It was going to be close.

***

Lying on the floor of Marina's apartment, Dirty stared at the ceiling, thinking about the trip. It felt a little clichéd, taking off like this, but she really didn't know what else to do. It was like the little ball of yarn that was her life was unraveling, out of control. She wanted control back. She wanted to start over. She wanted to cry. Marina was lying on her side listening to the room, listening to Dirty breathing.

"Hey," she whispered. "You okay?" Dirty didn't answer. Marina inched to the edge of the bed and reached out to take Dirty's hand. "C'mere" she said, pulling her up. Dirty climbed under the covers, curling herself into Marina's arms. "Scared?" Marina asked. Dirty didn't answer, but pulled in closer. "Don't wanna talk about it?" Dirty shook her head. Then she mumbled

"What do you call a flock of crows again?

"A murder." Marina answered. Dirty wrinkled her nose. "What about peacocks?" Marina asked.

"I think it's a bevy" Dirty said.

"No," Marina offered, "I think that's a bevy of bartenders." Dirty laughed.

"Is that like a gaggle of schoolgirls?"

"I think that's a giggle of schoolgirls." Marina smiled.

"A whisper of rabbis..."

"Ooh, good one" Marina said. "A superfluity of nuns."

"A scruff of boys" Dirty said.

"A cuddle of lovers." Silence. "I'm never going to see you again, am I?" Marina asked.

"You never know...," Dirty said, but not even she believed it.

***

The problem with highway 7 coming out of Ottawa was two-fold: one, except for the smattering of small towns, there really were no lights along the way, save for the headlights of the other cars. Two, it was two lanes, and winding at that, which made it very difficult to pass. Tonight was doubly so with all the overflow traffic after the accident. Rachel was near the back of that train of vehicles, which was headed up by a small car traveling about 12 kilometers below the speed limit.

Indeed, as Lottie Dymott negotiated the next curve, she was concerned that she had been traveling too fast; she assumed that the car behind her flashing its high beams was warning her that she was in danger of a speeding ticket. Carefully lighting another Camel-ultra-light-cigarette-in-the-white-and-blue-pack, she slowed to a steely 52 km/h.

By 2:00am Rachel was cranky, tired, and out of patience. Turning south on increasingly lesser roads, she tried to make her way down to the freeway that would carry her into Toronto. Twice she lost her way, veering into subdivisions or just down weird, dirt country roads, having to backtrack to the road she had been on to begin with.

The night was cool enough that she had to have the heater on, but she found that if she really cranked it up, she could cruise with the window down and still be comfortable. The sounds of crickets and gravel in one ear. The annoyed hiss of the car's fan in the other. The radio losing stations, only to pick up new ones on the same frequency later on. With just enough distraction around her, her mind drifted to the pictures in those magazines. Weird, over-sized dirty bits and furry faces staring back at her. Her stomach lurched.

By 3:00 am she finally hit the 401, the freeway, and it was going to be a three-hour trek to Toronto, which would get her there just as Dirty would be leaving. And that wasn't good enough.

***

At 4:30 am Dirty was naked. Standing in the bathroom, she had taken off all of her clothes and stood in front of the mirror. Gripping the edge of the sink, she lowered her head to try to catch her breath. She had woken with a tightness in her chest that she thought would kill her. Feeling it ease slightly, she tried not to think about what she would do. She knew she needed to start again but her faith was thin and her wallet thinner.

What would she do when she got to Winnipeg? It didn't really matter, ultimately, just as it hadn't the other times she had done things like this. But she was tired and she knew that at some point she would just have to stop. Pulling on her jeans and a Sophomore Level Psychology band t-shirt, she shoved the rest of her things into her backpack and then laced up her boots.

Stalking across the living room, she stood over sleeping

Marina, watching her, listening to that weird nose-whistle she sometimes got. Leaning over, Dirty gently kissed her forehead, touching her hair lightly with her fingertips.

"I'll go with you...," Marina said wearily.

"No," Dirty said gently. "Please don't." They looked at each other for awhile, in the dark.

"You could stay. We could figure it out. I could help you build a life here." Then she smiled. "You know, *hand in hand is the only way to land....*"

"*Always the right way 'round.*" Dirty returned her smile. And then more silence.

"Here." Marina handed Dirty a small, crumpled piece of paper.

"What's this?" Dirty asked.

"It's my email address. I just made it a couple of days ago. When you get to wherever you're going, send me a ping."

"Uh...how do I...do that?" Dirty asked. Marina looked at her and smiled sleepily.

"You go to a computer and type in that part there. Then it will walk you through how to make your own. Then you can send me an email."

"But I don't have a computer. Wait. Neither do you!"

"Go to an internet cafe, luv. It's like a cafe. But with the internet. It's also an easier way to find a job, too." Marina rolled onto her back and draped her arm lazily over her forehead. "Just write me when you can."

***

By 5:30 Rachel had reached the city's edge after not quite obeying the speed limit. She reasoned that if she ended up with a speeding ticket, it would be (1) earned in the service of a good deed and right action (and so, justifiable), and (2) paid for, possibly, off the top of an object of that good deed.

Peeling through the downtown core, she found that the city was already awake and the traffic was becoming snarly. Rachel was looking for the parking lot she thought was across the street from the bus station on Dundas St. It was around there somewhere; she just had to find it. When she was a block away, she realized she was approaching from the wrong direction and that she would have to make a (technically illegal) u-turn.

"Fuuuckiiiitttt," she muttered, and launched her car across oncoming traffic, narrowly missing two joggers and vaulting over the low curb that bordered the lot. Slamming it into park, Rachel grabbed the bag and ran toward the booth, tossing the attendant a 20 from her pocket. That was out of habit, of course. She was so wound up by that point that she had forgotten about possibly taking it from the bag. The attendant blinked, unsurprised, and set Rachel's change down beside the register for when she came back. It was 5:47 am.

***

If you enter a bus station looking like you haven't slept in almost 24 hours (which Rachel hadn't), carrying a rumpled grocery bag and yelling the word "Dirty!", people will think you are out of your mind. Thankfully, the only other person in the station even remotely interested in the noise was, of course, Dirty.

She had been standing behind the glass overlooking the platform, waiting for her bus to arrive. When she heard her name, Dirty didn't turn but instead watched the figure approaching in the reflection of the window. The reflection was distorted, but it looked and sounded a helluva lot like

Rachel. Dirty turned and blinked.

"Hi," Rachel wheezed. She had been going for so long that she wasn't sure how to slow down, and she realized that in all the rush she had no idea what she wanted to tell Dirty.

"I'm sorry, I—" Dirty motioned out the window at the bus that had now parted its doors, waiting to be entered.

"No, no—" Rachel waved her hand. "I just needed to...." She was breathing hard. "Okay, there isn't much time to explain, but here it is: something horrible happened in Ottawa, and it has to do with your stepfather. See, Josef was--" Rachel realized that Dirty was already not quite following. "Just trust me and listen, okay? He was seeing this friend of my friend Henry—you remember me telling you about him? Anyway, there was a horrible—" Rachel realized that she didn't know what to call it. "—situation. He—he was killed." Dirty's eyes narrowed, pursing her lips as Rachel continued. "Some money was taken from his apartment and given to Henry and I for safekeeping, and so—" Rachel gulped air again. "I guess this, technically, is yours." She held up the bag. It was 5:55 am.

Slouched in a blue plastic chair, watching the two women motion to the grocery bag between them, Steve saw his chance. He had been in Toronto for some time now, and he had moved on from coke to crack. His face was drawn, eyes sunken, hair stringy and unwashed. The look on his face said every inch of his body hurt.

Had he been in a clearer state, Steve might have actually recognized Rachel (although she too was not at her finest), but his real focus was on what they were pulling out of the bag. And that was all he needed to know.

Dirty stared at the bag, then at Rachel, wide-eyed. Rachel smiled. Then Dirty spoke, and Rachel wasn't smiling anymore.

"I can't have anything to do with that man," Dirty said

flatly. Her fingers curled around the pockets of her jeans, sweat and anger seething. "I won't. And you should fucking understand that. Of all people." Her voice was quieter now, rumbling.

In shock and confusion, Rachel dropped her hands (and the bag) to her sides, and so Steve made his move. Jumping from the chair, he went barreling towards them. Rachel barely registered the movement in the corner of her eye, and when she turned, he was already beside her, a flurry of matted hair and the smell of urine. She felt the pull and then the bag was gone. Steve was streaking toward the doors.

The two women stood motionless, Rachel in shock because in the instant that he came up she thought she was about to be attacked. They stood that way for what felt like forever and then, as if someone had actually hit her, Rachel took off after Steve—not knowing it was him—leaving Dirty standing open-handed and open-mouthed. As she watched Rachel motor for the door, Dirty looked up. It was 6:01. If she was actually getting on the bus, it had to be now.

***

Fern never realized what had hit him. He had been lurking around the bus station for several hours, needling the ground for cigarette butts he might have missed, waiting for people to drop more. The 6:00-8:30 slot was always fruitful. In any event, he had been watching a trio of bus mechanics (a number small enough to qualify as a 'tinker' of mechanics according to Marina), waiting for them to finish.

Casually, he slid over to where they had been standing, now leaning over to inspect the goods. One had been a chewer, but all three had only finished three-quarters of their respective smokes, the grease from their fingers leaving the remaining bit less-than-savory. And that was really all he would remember later; Fern probably had heard the station door slam open behind him, but then there was the impact as Steve inadvertently sent him flying into the wall head first, while Steve himself careened into a newspaper box. And in that pounding of flesh and brick and metal the bag went high into the air, barfing out little pieces of paper now gliding to the sidewalk everywhere.

From a window seat in the bus Dirty watched the street intently. She was embarrassed or surprised or afraid or something she didn't know what. Her elbow jammed into the windowsill, Dirty pressed her hand into her face.

As the bus yawned around the corner she could see through the window; there was Rachel on the sidewalk, kneeling, cradling someone's head in her lap.

Rachel had run out of the building after Steve, and got outside just as the money was falling from the air. She looked at the ground by the wall at a young man, a boy really, whom she guessed had been knocked over in the shitstorm. The boy was crying, weeping. His head was scraped with flecks of brick and flesh, and her impulse was to soothe him. A few feet away several people had gathered to grab what they could, and a few blocks away some sirens had begun.

CHAPTER 30:
Homecoming

As the bus pulled out of the station and onto Bay Street, Dirty could see the whole mess out on the road. Gripping the backpack on her lap, she thought about something— something real and earth-shaking. Just wait a goddamn fucking minute. Rachel had given her a gift. Not the money; that disgusting pile of garbage that had been touched by his sweaty disgusting fingers. No, the real gift: Information.

Maybe… maybe I don't have to keep going away. Maybe I… oh god, I can go home. This was something that she hadn't anticipated putting in motion for another many years. Like, after the bastard had died of old age. But now this. He was dead, and maybe she could go home.

Her fingers thrummed the armrest. *You can do this. So, fucking do it then.* Dirty dug into her pack looking for the schedule she had stuffed in there hours earlier.

This bus is going west. But I need to be going east. Come on. There's a way to do this. There has to be.

And there was. Her bus heading west had to travel north first, up to Barrie, the schedule said. She could get off there and trade in her ticket for one to Ottawa; she could maybe even be there before the end of the day.

It was only an hour's ride to Barrie, but Dirty had to wait an extra two hours there for the Ottawa bus that would be headed in the other direction. It was warm though, and she waited by a wall outside the building, slowly smoking and thinking about her homecoming. Finally, after burning through half a pack and two doughnuts, Dirty climbed aboard the new bus and sat, vibrating, finally ready to be aimed in the right direction. She had no idea what was left for her in Ottawa, if anything at all from her previous life; she just knew, finally *knew* that she could be the hand steering the ship. That her life would no longer just happen to her. She was going to get hers.

Dirty's bus trundled into the city close to 4:30 that afternoon, burping her out right at the mall downtown. Her insides felt gross, mostly from the greasy food and coffee she had been picking up at stops along the way. She needed information, but more than that she needed a place to land, even for just a night or two. And then she had it: dorms.

Just up the hill from the mall was the campus of the university of Ottawa. It was summer, and sometimes universities rent out dorm space to people. It was worth a shot.

The woman at the desk of the residence building looked sour and unimpressed, not just with Dirty, but with everything.

"Are you a student here?" her mouth squirted.

"No, not yet. I mean, I'm enrolled for the fall, but I haven't actually started yet. I came to town early because there isn't much work at home, y'know, at my dad's garage or the Dairy Queen or that new shop that sells candles and things so I thought I could get here early and find a job before I start school but to do that I know I gotta have a place to live which I have downtown but I can't get in there until the end of the month so I was thinking that—" Dirty could have kept going, but the woman behind the desk cut her off. Her eyes were bulging with delirious boredom.

"Fine. Fine. Do you have your—never mind. Fill this out. You're on the 12th floor, 1208. Here's the key for the room, and this bigger one is for the front door at night. Payment for the week due now." Dirty handed over a dishevelled wad of bills from her bag. It hurt to part with that much all at one time, but at least she had a place to sleep.

The room was basic: Cinder block and concrete walls, a single curtain over the window, the single bed stripped bare. *Shit*, she thought. Of course the bed wouldn't have any sheets or pillows. It wasn't a hotel, after all.

Dirty knew she should get moving but god, she needed to rest. Maybe just for a bit. Danielle would have said something like, 'if you've waited this long, a little longer won't kill you'. But Dirty disagreed with brain-Danielle. If she's waited this long, how could she even think of wasting another fucking second?

Dropping her bag at the foot of the bed, Dirty went back out and down the hall to the elevator. There was no use going to the old house; her grandmother had long ago told Dirty that Josef and her mom were selling it. It was long gone by now.

Settling in to one of the big chairs in the ground floor common room, Dirty hoisted a phone book into her lap. The smell of it was a little bit library, a little bit...beer? Probably. Given how many students over the years would have sat in that same spot in drunken stupidity, cradling the phonebook looking for taxis or pizza.

She first grabbed handfuls of pages and threw them aside as she searched, then more precisely, one at a time, the pages thin like onion skin. And there it was—her stepfather's name and address. She had to know for sure.

The next part should be easy. Except now she couldn't move. She hadn't been this close in... Dirty squeezed her hand to a fist and took a deep breath. *Ghosts can't hurt you. Now, where do you bloody well need to go?*

Dirty had a pretty good sense of where the street was, but she quietly ripped out part of the page to bring with her, in case she needed to ask for directions. Her stomach was knotted again, but not from coffee and grease this time. She wasn't sure what she was going to find there, or what she even wanted out of going there. Maybe a sense of finality. To give the corpse one final stab.

CHAPTER 31:
Terror

At almost 7:00 in the evening the air was warm and the sun still shining as Dirty turned onto Josef's street. *Executive townhomes* a rental sign said, but that was still up the street from where she was going. Almost all the houses on the street looked like that, though, and when she got to number 442, she saw that it was attached on either side with units just like it, like a little three-house family.

She could see from the street that the door had a lock box on it, the kind that real estate agents use to secure the keys on an empty home. Climbing the stairs to the front porch, the metal of the railing felt cool in her hand. When she was almost at the top, the door from the house on the right opened, and a white-haired man came out, quite skinny but not frail looking. He had a friendly smile as he cocked his head to the side.

"Are you alright, my dear?"

"Euh, yes. I just..." Fuck. Get it together, woman. "My uncle used to live here, I think. His sister--my mom--got a call that something had happened and that we should come down. She's not all that well, so I said I would do it. Am I right that this..." Dirty trailed off while hesitantly motioning to the door.

"Oh. Oh dear. Oh, my dear. You poor dear." He walked across the shared porch and clasped Dirty's hand in his. "Of course you're here. I understand. Terrible thing that happened. Terrible thing." He was shaking his head slowly.

"Do--do you know what that is?" she asked, motioning to the lock box.

"Oh! Yes. There was a company. A... um... I'm sorry... a *cleaning* company here, and they put that there for when they come back. But luckily, they gave me the combination for just such an emergency! Just let me go and get the number."

Holding the strip of paper gingerly in one hand, the old man carefully tried to open the box. It took him three tries. The whole time Dirty was standing behind him, hands crossed and pressed in front of her, desperately trying not to snatch the paper away and do it herself. But then it was open. And when he pushed the door wide and stood out of the way to let her in, what hit her first was the acrid smell of cleaning products. She had no idea what had been cleaned, but there seemed something about the smell was sinister. And familiar.

It was dark and echo-y, the sheen off of the dark hardwood gave it a kind of professional feel. Professional what, god only knew. Dirty was also aware of the neighbour lingering in the doorway.

"Do--do you know what... happened?" Dirty asked as she cautiously stepped into the kitchen.

"Well," he said from the doorway, trying to give her some room, "the police didn't say too much in the way of details, but I guess there was some sort of disagreement." Dirty couldn't see it, but he was raising his eyebrows in response to his own understatement. "Hard to understand, really. He is such a polite fellow." More head shaking.

"Yes..." Dirty said, not sure if she was speaking loud enough to be heard, and not really caring. "I guess he..." then she stopped. Speaking louder but still staying back in the kitchen, she said "Sorry, did you mean to say he *was* such a polite fellow?"

"Oh heavens, no. We shouldn't speak in such a way about the living! Still, it was a close call, I guess. I remember when they brought him out and the paramedics were shouting 'he's got a pulse! He's got a pulse!'" The neighbour was waving his arms around in pantomimed excitement. "Darndest thing."

Dirty appeared from around the corner, her throat painfully dry. "He's... alive?"

The man was aghast. "Oh, my dear! My poor dear! Had you heard otherwise? Oh, this is terrible! Yes! I do believe he's up at the hospital now, though I can't say how he is coming along. Didn't look too good when he left here, I can tell you. Oh, but I've kept you so long, I don't think you would make it for visitor's hours tonight. Oh dear. Oh, my dear. Still, this kind of news is better than the alternative, wouldn't you say?"

Dirty's jaw was stone. "Yes. For sure. Okay. Well, thank you, I—right. Right. I've just left something here on the counter...." Dirty turned back into the kitchen, her eyes sore from not blinking. Quickly she slid open three different drawers. The third one was the one she wanted. Turning on her heel she bounded around the corner and out of the front door, surprising the neighbour with her speed.

"I do want to thank you again for your help," she said, turning and looking into his eyes. "You've given me exactly what I needed." Gripping the metal rail with her right hand, she carefully but deliberately came down the stairs. Her left hand stayed in her pocket, her fingers tightly gripping the paring knife.

That night Dirty lay in her stripped-down bed with a balled-up sweater for a pillow and the rest of her clothes arranged on top of her like a blanket. Her heart was racing and sleep was not coming. *I can't do this. This is stupid. There is no fucking way I can do this.* Her mind paused for a moment, as if taking a calming breath. She rolled over and looked at the knife she had put on the desk beside the half-eaten convenience store sandwich. *Fuck.*

She looked around the room, her clothes strewn across her, balled up socks sitting benignly by her shoes near the door. And then somewhere in the back of her mind, a plan began to germinate.

CHAPTER 32:
Do what you have to

The next morning was beautiful. Sunny, radiant, cloudless, with the hint of a breeze. Dirty was slightly overdressed, which made her sweat just enough to be uncomfortable no matter how she moved, but at least the bus had air conditioning. The balled-up socks in her crotch were uncomfortable, but when she had first put on her disguise it made her feel like she just might be able to do this.

That morning she had stopped in to a drugstore and bought the cheapest mascara they had, then went back to the dorm to put it on her face, just like Marina had shown her at the New Years party. Pulling her hat down a little lower, her stomach was starting to tighten. She was beginning to lose the confidence she had had earlier. Hints of panic creeping in around the edges.

When the bus pulled up to the main entrance of the hospital, Dirty forced herself out of the rear doors against the roaring voice in her head that was telling her to *just run*.

"I'm looking for a patient by the name of Josef Plouffe." The volunteer at the information desk bent to her computer, looking.

"Mm. Don't see that name here. Maybe he's been discharged?" Dirty went cold. And then another volunteer leaned in to the computer.

"Honey, no, you've done that wrong. You need *F3* for a patient search, and then you *tab over* to the blue area and select the pull down. See? There he is. Room 502, east wing." Dirty was still reeling from the thought that he was out, but she took the little slip of paper with the room number on it from the first volunteer, then wobble-turned on her heel and headed for the elevator.

The chiming of the elevator was making her feel sick. She was about to wipe a hand over her dry mouth but caught herself in time before she rubbed off the makeup. The door opened. Stepping out onto the ward, she scanned the little wall signs for the right set of room numbers. *This way.* But instead of going that way, off to the right, she stepped up to the nurse's station and pretended that she didn't know where she was going.

"Hey," Dirty mumbled. She had no idea how to make her voice believable, so she decided to stick with as few words as possible.

"Hiiii...." the nurse trailed off, clearly trying to get through at least three other things at once. Then she stopped abruptly and looked up. "Can I help you?"

"I'm looking for room 502..."

"Oh! Are you family?" The nurse seemed surprised.

"Y-ya. I--I'm his neph. I just got into town and—"

"No problem. It's just that nobody has been in to see him since he came in. He—" the nurse had already come around the station to take Dirty to the room, and was talking over her shoulder as they went. "He's in pretty bad shape, but stable.

They brought him here from ICU just yesterday. He's—" and here her voice dropped to a whisper as they entered the room, "he's probably not going to be awake for some time; he's just had a sedative."

The first bed was empty as they came into the room, and there was a privacy curtain between the beds so that Dirty didn't get her first look at Josef until she had come around and stood at the foot of the bed. *Thank god he's asleep.*

"There's a chair there if you want to sit for awhile, but I really don't think he's going to know you are here."

"That's fine," Dirty said, far more brightly than she had intended. She cleared her throat. "That's fine," she said in a more sombre tone.

Josef's head was almost completely bandaged up, across most of his face and his right eye completely. His left eye was bruised but otherwise intact, and the bandages continued down around most of his right-side jaw, and then under, to some of his left jaw.

Dirty pulled the chair to the opposite corner of the room from the bed, the furthest she could get from him without climbing out the window. And then she waited.

She wasn't waiting for him. She was waiting for her own courage. The knife was in her pocket. She was alone. He was probably sedated enough that he wouldn't even wake up. So, what was the problem?

Could I actually kill someone? Well of course the answer is yes. I would have killed Alan and probably almost did, but that was because he was going to kill me. That was something I had to do. But what about now?

There was something that Rachel had said a while back. Do... do what you have to and then... do what you have to until you get to a place where you can do what you ought to. Or something. So, what was this? If

I… if I killed him. Here and now. Is that something I have to do, or is it what I ought to do? Is there ever a moment when those become the same thing? Is that now?

"They are MY slippers and they are NOT for public use! Why don't people understand that?! Huh?!" Another nurse was wheeling in a man who seemed both disoriented and quite angry.

"You're right, Mr. Stevens. We'll get your slippers back right away," the nurse said in a monotone, placating way. He helped Mr. Stevens into bed and parked the wheelchair in the corner. He gave Dirty a nod of acknowledgment, adjusted Mr. Stevens' oximeter, and then left quietly.

"Bastards…can't even do…a grphlmbldurg…" Mr. Stevens was mumbling and trailing off.

"Just die already," Dirty whispered. *It would be so much easier.* Dirty sat, watching for twenty, maybe thirty minutes. By then, she had come to some realizations. There was no way she was going to get away with killing him, not with a knife anyway. Too obvious to anyone who would come looking. Blood and stab wounds, generally a tip-off. And she didn't know how to fuck with the IV bags that Josef was hooked up to, at least not in a way that would do the job for sure. So when it came to the question of *should* she kill him, it wasn't really a question anymore. Because there was no good way that she *could*. So Dirty got up and left.

Walking slowly to the elevators, her shoulders were slumped and her face was stone. As she waited for the doors to open, Dirty overheard the nurses discussing when to move Mr. Stevens to the 7th floor. Not that she cared.

CHAPTER 33:
One more look

Sitting in the coffee shop in the hospital lobby, Dirty hovered her nose over her cup, out of habit more than anything else. The knife lay impotent in her pocket. *Do I leave town again? After all of this? Just let him have it? Just let him win?* Dirty looked up at the ceiling to stop the tears from rolling down her face. Then she got up and went to catch a bus back to the university.

Maybe I can do it, she thought. *Maybe I can still live in the city with him around. It's big enough that I would probably never run into him....* And then Dirty almost threw up.

Walking through the university campus, she went into a bathroom to wash off her face. The water was cool on her skin, almost invigorating, but she still felt so goddamn terrible. Dirty crossed the common and went to buy a bag of chips and another pack of cigarettes. As she turned to leave the store, a middle-aged man, much taller than she, was coming in.

"Move." he scolded, shoving in through the door she was trying to exit from. She did, and then she stepped out onto the sidewalk. She stopped and stared at the ground. Her face felt hot. Anger, the heat of rage was splitting her chest.

That. That is what her life was going to be like if she didn't do something. If she let him live. She would always be wondering, fearful, watching.

She turned and went back into the store. The guy who had walked in past her was standing at the counter, his back to her, paying for a drink he had already opened. Dirty walked up behind him. With a godly fire in her lungs she screamed at him,

"MOVE!" The sound she made was so piercing, so otherworldly that he spun and recoiled, falling over his own feet, baptizing himself in his soda. He sat there on the floor of the store looking up at her, frightened, legitimately frightened, saying nothing. Dirty stared, both her hands tensed into claws. Then she turned and left.

There has to be a way. There is always a way and I just have to find it. She resolved to go back to the hospital the following morning, just for one more look.

CHAPTER 34:
Do what you ought to

She stood at the mirror in the dorm bathroom at dawn, gathering her courage and making a plan. She thought about dressing up again, but something had changed. She was done with sneaking around. It was time to take her stand. No disguise. Just her. It was time to go.

Stepping off the hospital elevator an hour later, Dirty was unsure of how she felt (mass transit has that effect on people). Not energized, but not despondent. She felt taut, somehow. She had bought some shitty flowers at a corner store, not as a disguise, but certainly for appearance. Dirty gripped them a little tighter. It was 6:35. She walked past two nurses she didn't recognize, one of whom was telling the other about the new patient in 502 that had the absolute worst case of gonorrhea she had ever seen.

"I mean, I had read about cases like this, but *jesus*."

As Dirty entered the room she had a moment of panic. What if he's awake? What the fuck do I do? Do I talk to him? Do I spit on him? Dirty stopped just in front of the first patient's bed, the new gonorrhea case she guessed, as she decided what to do. Dirty had never actually seen Henry before, so she had no idea that he was the one lying there.

Slowly inching her feet forward, positioning herself so she could just see around the curtain—

Thank god. Asleep.

But it wasn't like she wanted to wait around until he woke up. Fuck that. But if she left again, she'd be right back where she was yesterday. So Dirty stood. She stood there straddling the room, her body lined up with the dividing curtain, just so. Half in, half out.

Dirty crossed her arms and hung her head. Henry was burbling vaguely, but otherwise pretty out of it. *He must have been awake at some point though*, she thought, *because his hand is still gripping a kleenex.*

Dirty blinked. She suddenly remembered what Rowena Glass had said—well, what Marina said that Rowena had said. About using a kleenex to—

Dirty shifted her feet and looked again at the tissue. *I cannot be here in this city with this man. I would spend every day wondering if he was coming around the corner, or if he would be coming into some place I'd be working at. He's taken too much. I would have to leave. But I'm not going to leave. Not any more.*

She walked over to Henry's bedside table and put the flowers down there. His eyes fluttered, but Dirty didn't notice.

***

Oh god, it hurts. It all hurts so much. Henry thought. *God, I deserve this. I deserve it all. I'm useless. No one will miss me when I'm gone.* Henry's eyes rolled up and down, delirious with sickness and medication. Unable to speak, he tried to focus on the young woman who had come in. She couldn't be there to see *him*, surely not. *Who the fuck are you? Why are you bringing me flowers?*

***

Dirty pulled one sheet out of the tissue box on the table next to Henry and gently rubbed it between her fingers. Then she tore a piece from the corner of it and placed it in her own mouth. Immediately it went soft and molded around the tip of her tongue like bland cotton candy. She tried moving it around, and it slid off to the side and started to ball up. It was weird. She found herself chewing on the little ball, her mouth trying to do *something* with this thing. Tasteless and persistent, it was sucking up all of the spit she had. She couldn't even swallow it. She took her fingers and plucked it out, pushing it into her pocket. As she did, she felt the handle of the paring knife and realized she could use it to push the tissue back far enough to do the job.

***

I don't know why this is happening to me. I didn't do anything, Henry imagined himself saying out loud. His throat was so dry, he was unable to actually speak.

***

Dirty was careful to keep the tissue flat in the palm of her hand. Sliding across the room, she eased the door closed with little effort. Then she stood for a moment and looked at the curtain. Her body was taut, her mind was ready, but her hands were shaking madly. Yet from that point on there was never a moment, never a single trembling moment when she thought 'I'll never get away with this'.

She moved smoothly through the room, around the curtain and bed so she was standing right next to Josef's head.

Her mother. Her childhood. Her home. Dirty took out the knife, blade in her hand and the handle pointing straight up at her.

No, she thought. *If he moves, I'll cut my hand open on the blade.* Her eyes narrowed. *But I can use the handle to keep his mouth open.* She draped the tissue over two fingers like a little ghosty puppet, then wrapped it more like a ball or a marshmallow. Dirty eased his jaw open slightly, which was a little awkward for all of the bandages. She rested the plastic handle between his teeth, and readied her fingers.

And as she leaned over Josef's face, she had one final thought:

Fuck.

You.

***

As Dirty walked around the curtain, her job done, she slammed her sleeve over her mouth to muffle a yelp. There was a woman standing there. The woman put up her hand and said

"Sorry, doll. Didn't mean to surprise you."

"I—I—"

"I'm just here to visit someone. You do your thing."

"I was just... leaving...." Dirty lowered her head and moved past the woman, quietly but briskly. She closed the door behind her when she left, leaving Melissa standing over Henry's bed. When she was alone, Melissa walked over beside him, leaned in, and whispered in Henry's face.

"I called Andre last week. He finally told me what happened that night. What you did." She waited to see if anything she was saying was sinking in. "He won't go to the police, but I can't let you get away with this."

Melissa stood up and took a pillow that had been lying at the foot of the bed. Leaning in again, she spoke to him once more.

"You think you didn't do anything wrong that night. But you did. And you had a chance to own up to it, to take some fucking responsibility, and you *didn't do anything.* So I'm here now to say: Fuck you." And in her simmering rage, Melissa shoved the pillow over Henry's face.

CHAPTER 35:
The warmth of the sun

The elevator opened on the ground floor and Dirty stepped out, shaking. She kept her head down and was trying desperately to keep her trembling under control, but she couldn't stop it. Her chest was tight but she didn't feel panicked or scared or any of it anymore. Her mind was strangely still. But her body shook. Taking straight, deliberate steps to the main doors, her chin lifted slightly. She could see sunlight streaming in through the giant windows ahead of her.

"Ma'am? Hey! Ma'am!" A security guard was streaking towards her. Dirty slowed, but kept moving to the door. Her back was bathed in sweat now, her eyes focused directly on the door. The guard was almost upon her.

And then he moved past Dirty to a woman behind her. There was a commotion bubbling up and Dirty turned to look. The woman was half out of a large chair, grasping her throat and turning blue. The security guard reached her just as two other people did—nurses, maybe. In scrubs, anyway.

Dirty didn't look back after that, and put her hand forward to feel the coolness of the metal door handle. It swung out easily, and then Dirty was bathed in the warmth of the sun, and a coolness in the air touched her lips.

CHAPTER 36:
Ithaca, at last

The shaking was the worst part. Standing at the bus stop, her mind felt curiously calm. But her hands, her arms were quivering in a way that felt like they didn't belong to her. She didn't feel scared or nervous or anything like that, so she couldn't connect what her body was doing with anything in her head. It was just shaking. Jamming her hands down into her pockets, Dirty tried to slow her breathing and reconnect with her body. Then she tried to focus on what she needed to do next.

Except there wasn't anything she needed to do next. What began to unfold in her mind was the idea that what came next for her was whatever she wanted it to be. She was free. For the first time in… had she ever felt this way? It dawned on her that maybe this, *this* was the feeling of her life starting. She was broke, ostensibly homeless, but she was free.

From the hospital she rode in silence, the bus trundling its way back downtown. Within the hour Dirty was sitting on a bench in the Byward Market, packed with vendors and restaurants and tourists and glowing sunshine. It was a place she knew from her childhood, although she found it a little overwhelming back then, for all of the people and noise. None of that bothered her now. She sat, filled with relief and shock and elation and god knows what else.

Things in Ottawa had changed—no surprise—but there was a thrilling familiarity to it as she looked around. So many of the shops and restaurants were different, but there were a few she still recognized. As she turned her head towards the Parliament buildings, she caught sight of a small sign on the sidewalk in front of a store. An internet cafe. Dirty scrunched her fingers around in her pockets and found her wallet, and inside that was the little piece of paper Marina had given her.

Pushing the door open, she stepped into the weird, dark space. Rows of computers on tables ran up and down the room, and she could see a second room further back with even more, but that had a crowd of teenage boys in it, yelling and complaining and cheering about something. Dirty looked lost and was about to leave.

"Five bucks for a half hour," a middle-aged man with an enormous gut grunted to her from behind the counter. Dirty looked around the room, deciding what to do next. Slowly she fished a bill out of her pocket, and the man motioned her to one of the machines close to the front. Easing herself into the chair, she stared at the screen, trying to figure out how to do any of it.

She had used a computer before, of course. Peter had had one in Edmonton, and she had been on it a few times, mostly to play pinball and minesweeper, though. She looked over the icons on the screen, then took the mouse and clicked on the one that was blessedly named 'internet'. She did two things then which, together, took her about the full half hour that she had paid for. The first was creating an email so she could send

Marina a message. The second was to look up the address of the cemetery where her mother was buried.

"God-fucking-dammit, are you fucking serious? Without any notice? For fuck's sake, man." The guy behind the counter was situbicating into the phone. He slammed it down just as Dirty was rising from her seat, folding another piece of paper into her pocket, this one with the directions to the cemetery.

"I don't suppose you know anything about computers, huh?" he sneered.

"Not much. But I know a lot about running cafes," she offered as she headed for the door.

"Wait. What? Do you want a job?"

"You've never met me before," she demurred, buying herself some time to get a better measure of the guy.

"Fine. Got any references?" Dirty thought for a moment. She considered emailing Marina again.

"Can I borrow a computer for a sec? I'll have someone send you one." Dirty sat back down, then asked where the reference should be sent.

"If it checks out, when can you start?"

"I've got something I need to do today, but otherwise…." Dirty finished the message and rose again to head for the door, patting the pocket that held the cemetery address.

"Come in first thing tomorrow morning. I'll get you set up."

"Cool." Dirty smiled. They shook hands.

"Uh…what's your name?"

"Deirdre."

***

As the bus rattled along the road, Dirty cradled another

bouquet of flowers in her lap. Twenty more minutes to the cemetery.

An old man was eyeing her from across the aisle. He reached up and pulled the cord for the next stop. Then he stood up. Before moving to the door, he paused next to her.

"You know what your problem is?" he said. Dirty turned her head and looked him in the eye, unwavering.

"Yes. Yes, I do."

"What's that, honey?"

"My problem is that strange men feel the need to offer me unsolicited advice." Then she looked down at his feet. "So why don't you put those shabby-ass boat shoes to good use and just keep walking."

*

EPILOGUE
(Aesop 475/Chambry 110)

"The wait is about 40 minutes."

Fern thanked the nurse and found a seat in the waiting room. His goopy eye had gotten worse—it was so bad that he really couldn't see out of it at all. And now his other eye was cloudy and leaking, which made finding his way to the doctor's office by sight fairly difficult. But his eyes weren't the reason he had come in.

The gash on his head had stopped bleeding, but had been oozing around the edges for a number of days now. And it itched. And it was giving him a steady headache. So, Fern had found his way down the narrow, creaky staircase of his apartment building and across Bloor street, despite not being able to see very well.

Fern did not have a regular doctor, and so he really only visited walk in clinics when he thought he needed to. He had been to this particular clinic once before but he had never been seen by this doctor. And then the intake nurse called him.

"Fern—" He was up and moving towards her before she could say his last name, doing his best to manage the relatively unfamiliar room. The nurse guided him into an examination room and told him that the doctor would be in soon.

Hearing the door close, Fern pulled off his jacket, an unopened pack of cigarettes in the right pocket. In the left pocket was a plastic baggie and two urine sample containers that he used as an interim home for the used butts that he collected, wherever he happened to be.

The door opened and in came the doctor, who seemed unfazed by Fern's unusual appearance. Fern sat, looking roughly in the direction of the doctor but actually past him and slightly to the left. The doctor was writing something, and furiously so, but had not yet said anything to Fern. And then he did.

"Well then," said Dr. St. John Always Callan, "you're here about your eyes, then?"

"Erm...no." Fern frowned.

"The lice?"

"Nope."

"Your apparent nail fungus."

"Not as such."

"..."

"..."

Fern took a gangly finger and motioned to his forehead.

"Mm," said Dr. Callan. He stared at Fern for what seemed like ages. Not that it mattered, since Fern couldn't really tell what he was or was not staring at. "Fern," he continued finally, "why don't you just hop up on the table so I can get a better look at you."

As Fern slid out of his chair and made his way to the examination table, Dr. Callan got a look at the pack of cigarettes in Fern's jacket pocket.

"Just a few questions then...," he said as he adjusted the

blood pressure cuff around Fern's arm. "Do you exercise?"

"Not really."

"Diet?"

"I dunno... pizza pockets and water, maybe?"

"Smoke?"

"Nope."

"Drink?"

"Not on my budget."

"I see." Dr. Callan concluded, leaning in to release the pressure on the cuff. If someone were to have asked the doctor a personal, biographical sort of question, he would have said that he had always had a great tolerance for all sorts of behaviour in others. But one thing he could simply not abide was lying, especially when help is being offered. So, when he asked Fern to remove his shirt, Dr. Callan took the opportunity to slip the unopened pack of cigarettes out of Fern's jacket and into his own. As a lesson.

Fern had a squished up, sour look on his face but not in response to anything in particular. It was just the way his face was going these days, at least sometimes. Stroking his thighs with his open palms, he sat patiently while Dr. Callan checked his ears and listened to his lungs. The doctor was much more cautious about his eyes.

"Have you ever heard the term 'stromal keratitis'?"

"Don't think so." Fern said, not very interested. "How's the cut on my head?"

"Ah!" Dr. Callan replied. "I'm getting there. As for your eyes, I—"

"Just the forehead, please," Fern interrupted. Dr. Callan frowned.

"Yes. Well. Very good then." He gave a cursory look at the infection that was slowly bubbling on Fern's face. "A fairly straightforward problem, I think." Then he turned to the desk to prepare a prescription. "Please," he said distractedly "you can get dressed now." Fern found his shirt and pulled it on and then returned to his chair by making an arc through the room around Dr. Callan. "Glad you came to see me about this. Let me tell you about a case I know of, a case of infection I read about in Ottawa. Terrible thing, really. Gonorrhea, untreated. Left to its own design, an infection can kill a man, just as it did in that case." He paused and scribbled. "There you are," Callan said, handing Fern a sheet with the prescription on it. "Three times daily, until finished." Pulling on his jacket, Fern found his way to the door and left. St. John Always Callan sighed. *Still. Not the weirdest patient I've had*, he thought.

Half an hour later the doctor emerged from his office to discuss an issue with the staff and to evaluate how many more patients were left. But when he rounded the corner to the waiting area, he found it to be quite empty except for one person. Fern was still there, cautiously and methodically moving up and down the rows of chairs, feeling the seats with his hands and sweeping a foot underneath each one. Looking for something. St. John Callan watched in amusement.

The doctor looked at the receptionist, motioning quizzically to Fern. She just shrugged and went back to her work. After a few minutes more, Dr. Callan finally spoke up.

"Have you lost something?"

"I no longer have the thing I did have, yes," Fern replied. Callan was trying hard not to be charmed by all of this, but it was very difficult.

"Perhaps I can be of some assistance?"

"Mm. Ah. Okay. Yeah. Do you see anything?"

Dr. Callan's right eyebrow went up while his left eye

squinted. "What… sort of thing might I be looking for…?

"Cigarettes. Cigarettes. Just some cigarettes."

"I thought you didn't smoke, Fern. You know, if I'm going to be your doctor it's important that you—" but Fern cut him off.

"A whole pack. Unopened. I need them because they tell me things." Startled, Callan decided he should proceed carefully.

"Do they… tell you things… with their little voices…?" Fern stopped and look roughly in the doctor's direction. He was giving him a 'what are you, stupid?' kind of look. Then he sighed, continued scanning the waiting room, and gave Dr. Callan a terse explanation.

"With careful study and explanation, they can be used to learn a lot of things about people." Gone was the jittery enthusiasm Fern used to have in talking about the subject; maybe he was worn down, or maybe he wasn't that invested in convincing the doctor of his insight. But then he straightened, even brightened, and said, "Even the ones on the street can give you an understanding of who was there, what kind of a place it is, or even who will be there in the future."

Callan was starting to be impressed. He always enjoyed ideas that were a little… not 'extraordinary' in the superlative sense. But also, not just 'out of the ordinary'. That's too dull sounding. Weird and maybe dark and what's the opposite of that superlative kind of extraordinary? Subordinary, maybe? Maybe that. And he liked Fern because, like his ideas, he was a bit broken and only semi-functional and somehow 'below' what's ordinary. Subordinary.

"In fact," (Fern was still going), "I could probably piece together where my cigarettes have gone just by looking at some of the evidence along my route here. But do you think you could help me?" Fern was speaking fairly smoothly, although his hands were moving this way and that, sometimes flapping a little, sometimes pressing into his sides. Dirty would have said he was putting it on a bit, knowing how he behaves when he is actually wound up and excited about something.

Not having any more patients to see, Callan couldn't pass up a chance like this. Quickly grabbing his jacket, he went to Fern and offered him an arm so they could make it to the door together. Fern ignored him, bumped his knees on two different chairs and made it to the door himself. Out in the sunshine the pair paused for a moment, and then Fern was off down the sidewalk mumbling something about people not smoking near doctor's offices.

Quick-stepping to catch up, Callan strained to hear precisely what Fern was going on about. After two blocks they stopped. Completely. And they just stood. The doctor wasn't sure what they were doing, but he didn't want to break Fern's concentration. And then Fern spoke.

"Is there… is there a cigarette butt here… no, three are here, maybe. Do you see them anywhere, doctor? I'm finding it quite difficult with my eyes straining against the sunshine…."

Callan looked down and there, right there, were three cigarette butts on the ground between them. "Why yes, Fern! There they are."

"Would you please pick them up for me?" Fern asked. To his credit, Dr, Callan didn't hesitate to help Fern out. And perhaps as a surprise to no one, Always Callan always carried latex gloves in his pocket. Just in case. Picking up the butts and cradling them in his hand he asked Fern,

"What is it that we are looking for?"

"Mm. Are any of the filters chewed?"

"Not that I can see, no," Callan answered.

"And I imagine that one of them has been smushed, like with a shoe, but the other two have not?"

"Indeed, that seems to be the case!" The doctor was slightly more impressed now. But Fern was frowning.

"Damn. These ones are not going to help us." And he walked on.

Several times Dr. Callan had to grab Fern, stopping him from stepping of the curb into traffic or walking right into a street sign. And several more times they stopped to collect specimens. With each analysis Fern grew a little brighter, suggesting to the doctor that they were getting somewhere. And in fact, they were. The somewhere, though, was the front door to Fern's apartment building. Not that Dr. Callan knew that.

"Fern, can I tell you a story about a young woman I once heard about?" Fern was scanning and squinting, and didn't actually give an answer. "Quite an afflicted young lady, I should say. A number of problems, compounded. And yet, she managed to perform a most exquisite and crucial self-excision. Saved her life, I dare say. And she has gone on to rebuild her health and her life in quite an inspiring way. What I am saying, Fern, is that I would very much like you to think about how you might better take of your health. It is not too late."

"Oh, things are neither so late, nor so dire for me as you might think." Fern said. Then he froze. "It's here."

"The cigarettes?" Callan asked.

"Not exactly. But the answer we are looking for. There's…," and here Fern started to sniff the air. "There's something weird here. It's like… no… it's like… a floating cigarette? Does that make sense? Is there something here around my… around shoulder level maybe?"

Callan frowned, not sure what to make of what Fern was

saying. But then, as he scanned the wall of the building just behind Fern, he saw a little yellow filter sticking out of a crevice in the brick mortar. "Remarkable," he said. "Surely this has something to tell us, yes?"

"Indeed, it does" Fern said, motioning for him to put it in Fern's hand. Running his fingers gently over the filter, and then gently over the burnt end, Fern smelled it once, then closed his hand. There was a pause, then he opened his hand again to show Dr. Callan.

"This end" he said, pointing to the filter, "says 'thank you for walking me back to my apartment safely'. But *this* end" and here he pointed to the darkened part, "this end says that it's probably time for you to give me my fucking cigarettes back."

ABOUT THE AUTHOR

Energized by good story-telling, broadly speaking, Rick Duchalski's time is split between writing fiction, screenplays, and children's picture books, as well as performing story-telling school visits. Having lived in Toronto, Ottawa, Vancouver (and growing up in Bolton, Ontario), he now calls Mississauga home. *Something So Sweet* is his first novel.

I would like to express my deep thanks to you for reading this book. And if you would like to help out an independent author, please take a moment and post a review on Amazon. Every review helps. Thank you!

Manufactured by Amazon.ca
Bolton, ON